Celestine:

The House on rue du Maine

by
F.J. Wilson

CHANCES PRESS
www.chancespress.com

Celestine: The House on rue du Maine

Copyright © 2012 by F.J. Wilson

Cover art design by Geronimo Quitoriano. Cover pictures courtesy of RomanceNovelCovers.com and iStockphoto.

ISBN 978-0-9882302-1-7

Acknowledgements

My editor, Vickie S. Johnson, Tatiana Lipson,
Laura Goodwin Wright, Scotty Posey,
Kirk Halstead, Diane Martin, Bethany E. Bultman,
Mary Anderson Pickard and my dear friend and
publisher, Michael H. Perronne who deserves a
case of valium and good champagne
for putting up with me.

dedicated to my niece nancy goodwin mcnair

Old New Orleans Vocabulary

White Creole: Criollo, a Spanish term meaning a person of European descent born in the New World colonies. When the Spanish came to New Orleans, the local French, most from wealthy French families who'd been here for a hundred years were considered to be 'criollo'. Over the years this word became synonymous with the upper echelon, the rich and entitled and aristocratic members of New Orleans society.

Creole of color: Once the white Creole men began to procreate with the African slaves and free people of color, the light skinned Mulattos, Quadroons and Octoroons who took their biological father's names, built a whole new society and are now considered, Creole also. Today, Creoles are a range of social worlds and nationalities, but for this book, we only speak of the two.

Jib Windows: A window with a sill that rests at floor level, sometimes as high as twelve to fourteen feet, that you can open and use as a door. Usually opened to a balcony or courtyard.

Picayune: A Spanish coin worth half a real or 6 1/4 cents.

Gris-gris: Also spelled grigri. A voodoo amulet originating in Africa. Believed to ward off bad luck and bring good luck. Some people made the amulets to do the opposite. Some used them for birth control. Pronounced Gree Gree

Kainstucks : The first Americans to come to New Orleans came down the river from Kentucky on flatboats. Rough and offensive to the delicate senses of the French and Spanish residents of the city, they were called "Kaintucks".

Calas: Small cakes made from cooked rice, sugar, spices and fried. Breakfast treats to be eaten with the Café au Lait of a morning. Usually shaped like a little bee hive. Not to be confused with the beignets of today. Some New Orleans restaurants still offer them with breakfast.

Praline: A delicious sugary candy made with butter, brown sugar and pecans. Pronounced 'prahleen', not prayleen. 'Prayleen' is a pronunciation given the candy by years of outsiders visiting the city from the north. The original pronunciation, like the original candy is exclusive to New Orleans and the pronunciation is not negotiable. To say 'prayleen' places a person as a tourist who hasn't done their homework.

Les Gen de Couleur Libres: Creoles of color with Latin blood and other free blacks made up a group known collectively as *gens de couleur libres.* (free people of color). The men excelled as musicians, artists, teachers, writers, doctors and in all major professions. They were an integral part of New Orleans life and were as rigid in their social world as many whites.

Quadroon: Historically, mulatto meant a biracial person. Quadroon was borrowed from the Spanish *cuarteron*, and meant one fourth African. An octoroon would be one eighth African. While the quadroon men had options and many times were sent to Paris to study; the beautiful quadroon women had no way to support themselves without the assistance of white gentlemen who took them as mistresses. Not unlike the Venetian Courtesans of history. Some women found the love of their lives, some found misery, either one was out of their control. Only a few found careers outside this institution.

Patois: A language spoken by slaves to speak to each other; not always understood by the 'master'. Mixture of French, Spanish and a bit of African tribal.

Piroque: The slim canoes of the Acadians made from hollowed out logs. Easy to maneuver in the shallow Bayous and swamps of South Louisiana. Pronunciation, pee-roge

Tignon: The beautiful headdress worn by the Creoles of color (Quadroons) instead of the feathered bonnets and hats of the White Creoles. These were long strips of beautiful material wrapped around the head, turban style with wonderful points standing like bird wings. The laws forbade Quadroon women from dressing as fine as the white women, so they took matters into their own hands and produced these gorgeous head dresses. A beautiful woman is NOT going to be undermined when dressing to enhance her beauty. Pronunciation: Ti-yon

Rigolets: French for trench or ditch, the narrow strips of land connecting Lake Ponchartrain, Lake Bourne and Lake Catherine to the flat lands of the Gulf Coast. For many years the two lane road, High Way 90 was the only road between New Orleans the Gulf Coast, Florida and the East Coast. Pronounced, Rig-uh-leez.

Streets: Between 1800 and 1865

Orleans = rue d'Orleans
Decatur = rue du Quai
Chartres = rue de Chartres
Royal   = rue Royale
Bourbon = rue Royalle-Bourbon
Dauphine = rue Dauphine
Burgundy = rue de Bourgogne
Rampart   = rue des Ramparts
St. Louis = rue Saint-Louis
St. Peter, St. Anne and St. Phillip
Rue Saint-Pierre, rue Saint-Anne, rue Saint Philippe
Dumaine = rue du Maine
Ursulines = rue Saint-Ursule
Gov. Nichols = rue de l'Hopital
Esplanade = the Esplanade

Captain Maurice Dubois pronounced *'Du bwah'*
Jean Lafitte the pirate pronounced *'Jawhn Lafeet'* or *John Lafeet*.
M. Bubonnet pronounced *'Du bon nay'*

Chapter One

1795

'Tine waited outside for the stinking customer to get off her mama and button his breeches. When he was done she could go inside and get warm; clean her mama and make sure she wasn't sick on the bed. If the man was generous, there'd be enough money for supper. If not, she'd go hungry again and count the noises in her stomach 'til she fell asleep.

She sat on the carriage block crying into her papa's old neckcloth. She carried it everywhere hoping he'd come to rescue them. He'd bring nice things to eat and maybe a new dress for her and her mama; she prayed on it, wished on it and tried to count on it. He'd been gone the thirteen years of her young life, but he could still come back; he could.

'Tine hated men. She hated how they smelled of rum and sour living. She hated their dirty smelly clothes and their big boots full of mud and horse crap on her mama's worn out rugs. She hated when they grabbed her mama, demanded, grunted and hit her for not being the woman they thought they deserved. But mostly, she hated her mama for allowing the horrible men to destroy and age her far beyond her thirty years.

The man was coming down the little steps buttoning his last button and spitting a mouthful of slimy brown tobacco juice into the street. He stopped to look at her.

"What? You want some too? Your mama said you might be ready. I'm spent; next time, baby tits." He was looking her all over making her sick.

He grabbed the neckcloth from her hand and wiped the tobacco juice off his mouth and stuffed it down the front of her dress. Feeling around inside her bodice, he chuckled as he took his hand out and turned to walk away.

"I promise." He said and let out a breath from a nasty place under his breeches. His horrible laugh and foul breath filled her nose and ears as he swaggered down the street.

She knew this was coming. Her mama yelled at her for a week; she was thirteen and time for her to take customers and help pay her keep. 'Tine grabbed the dirty neckcloth out of her dress and threw it in the gutter. No one was coming to save her; she'd have to do it herself. God didn't answer prayers from the daughters of sinful women who lay with lust crazed men. She'd be damned if she was going to wait for the man to come back. She'd kill him first.

She walked back into the dirty little room and packed her few belongings while her mama slept off the effects of the man and the rum. She went to the side of the bed and looked at the single picayune the man left. She thought of taking it; but decided she wanted nothing from the man, especially the tiny bit of money paid for rutting with her mama.

She walked back out and looked down at the neckcloth soaking up rainwater and horse pee. She picked it up, wrung it out and stuffed it way down in her ragged apron pocket and walked toward the Ursulines Convent.

The city of New Orleans was once filled with joie de vivre but since the big fires and hurricanes, it held only stink and sadness. The smell of sour ashes and the defeat of burned out hopes filled the air with misery and fatigue. The city was a good wife to some and a dock whore to others, and 'Tine was certainly its daughter and the streets were her schoolroom.

She watched it burn to the ground from her hiding perch on the roof of the Ursulines Convent. The screams of burning men and women running out of houses toward the river still haunted her dreams. Mostly, they fell like pieces of charred wood from a neglected fire place; falling and rolling out of the burning buildings; their clothes smoking after their voices were finally silenced.

She watched from the roof of the French Market as the winds and waters of two hurricanes swept the city into chaos and death. The water took people and livestock, alike; some, still alive tried to swim through the big water. Others, their dead faces peaceful floated in the filth that'd been their world. She'd saved herself by quick wits and cunning.

She fought as well as any boy her age and cut many men with the knife she kept in her stocking as they tried to grab her, but she'd never cheated and she'd never lied. She was proud of that.

'Tine knew everything about everything and everyone and what she didn't know, she found out. She knew which white Creole gentleman kept a Quadroon mistress; how often he visited and how many children he had by both his wife and mistress. She visited the Vou-dou ceremonies to make gris-gris bags of black magic to use on her enemies, but rarely used it as it could backfire on a little girl who used it unwisely. She danced with the slaves on Congo Square and knew their patois and how to interpret their chants and messages to each other. She followed the food vendor's home and picked up cake and fruit that fell from a basket worn on a tired head. But it wasn't enough, her world was too small and she wanted more.

Kaintucks, the big rough American men coming down the river from Kentucky, taught her how to ride horses and jump the vendors to scare them to death. This was a favorite of the dock workers, but not the vendors. All the knowledge; where'd it gotten her? A few misplaced spells with ill-advised gris gris, knowledge of a language she'd never use, the names of the big policemen that patrolled the levee and small rice cakes called 'calas' or piece of rotten fruit fished out of the mud and muck of the street. She wanted more.

Going to the Ursulines nuns and their orphanage was a fear her mama instilled and used to scare her when she didn't behave. For as long as she could remember, she ran to the other side of the street when passing the big convent for fear they'd come out and snatch her.

The nasty man's horrible promise changed her whole future. One sentence, one thought, of his coming back with his diseased pecker and sour breath and she was done with her mama and that life. Now she just wanted a hot bowl of something to eat and a safe place to sleep. She'd decide what to do once her stomach wasn't so loud and she could think without crying.

The good nuns were on her mind lately. Watching them go about their daily lives had taken away much of her fear and hearing their prayers to Notre Dame de Bon Secours, from the morning of the big fire, until the morning after had given her much to think about. They prayed without stopping and the convent had been spared. 'Tine saw this as some powerful gris-gris and she needed that kind of power in her life.

Friends in the big market told her they had their hands full with the orphanage, the school and the King's Hospital. They could use help and she needed help. It could benefit both parties.

'Tine couldn't help with the hospital or teaching, but she knew she could keep children from running in the streets and make sure they ate their food.

Anybody could raise children. How hard could it be? Young women in her mama's profession were always having babies; some even lived and they knew how to keep them from dying... sometimes.

She intended to pledge her services and see if she could receive decent schooling from the sisters in return. She wanted to read and write the French she spoke and also learn Spanish and English. She'd heard the little sisters were from good homes and well educated. They read and understood Latin, whatever that was and could chant and recite the prayers and help with the Mass. All 'Tine knew was she wanted to be very-well-educated like the little sisters and get out of the sewage filled gutters that was her life.

She wanted to learn good manners; how to drink coffee from a saucer; how to tell a fork from a spoon and eat from a plate instead of a bowl. She wanted a real privy instead of the river side of the levee and a pair of shoes; she'd never owned a pair of shoes. She wanted to learn how to cook with the herbs and vegetables the little sisters grew in their famous gardens. Oh, to know what it was like to be clean, a wish of a lifetime. She wanted to learn how to sew and make herself a dress that fit; but mostly, unknowingly she wanted to feel safe and needed.

One thing for sure, she'd never lie under a filthy man and have him poke, grunt and knock her teeth out. She'd become a nun first. Neither option was to her liking, but being a nun won hands down over being a whore on the half burned docks of the Mississippi River.

She walked over to rue Sainte-Ursule and looked in the gate. It was clean, peaceful and beautiful; certainly a step up from the whore's crib she called home. She rang the bell and waited for one of the little sisters to come and open it. She could hear her own heart beating and wondered if that was supposed to be.

Ste. Mary Theresa heard the bell and looked out to see her prayer's realized. She'd prayed for years this little hungry girl running the streets outside the big convent in her filthy clothes would seek their refuge and get away from her horrid life. She ran to find Mother Superior and tell her the miracle at their front gate.

"Reverend Mother, look out at the gate, quickly." She ran to the window.

"Quick my child, let her in before she changes her mind. God in his mercy and wisdom has answered our prayers." She made the sign of the cross.

"Shouldn't you go with me?"

"No, my child it'd frighten her. Go gently and welcome her. Quickly, before she changes her mind."

The good sisters had no idea that once 'Tine made up her mind nothing could stop her or change her mind. Celestine Haussey was stepping into her future and she wouldn't turn back.

'Tine had never seen such a clean world, from the shining floors to the beautiful curving cypress staircase; she was amazed at how these women lived. She'd been told they lived in poverty and said penance each day. If this was poverty, she wondered what she'd been living all of her life. She was ushered in to Mother Superior's office and took a chair.

"What may we do for you my child?" The Reverend Mother was treading lightly; this miracle was too delicate. She must watch what she said to this little waif.

"I'm here to help with the children." She set her jaw and didn't care if she was coming across fresh and brazen. Just being behind these walls was robbing her bravery and treading on the determination felt only minutes before.

"I see. Your name is Celestine Haussey is it not, my child?"

"Yes, but people call me 'Tine. If you must know about me, my mother is a whor...prostitute, and I don't wish to follow that life. I like children, and I know I could be of service in this place."

Mother Superior and Ste. Mary Theresa both gave the sign of the cross and looked heavenward in thanks.

"How'd you like to live here and not be obliged to work with the children, my dear?"

Mother Superior's heart was breaking at the bravery of this young girl offering services she had no idea how to give.

"I can work for my keep. I wanna be educated and learn to read and write and... I can learn the lives of the Saints." 'Tine could care less about the Saints or their lives, but she knew how to kiss-ass as well as the best con artists in the city.

"Oh, my dear child, The Blessed Mother has answered your prayers. We know who you are. Let's get you cleaned up and we can talk after you've eaten. Are you hungry?" Mother Superior heard the child's stomach growling like a frog in the pulpit.

"I guess I could eat a little something if you have something left over." 'Tine would eat whatever fell on the kitchen floor, she wasn't proud, and she certainly didn't expect these sisters to share their food with the likes of her. Maybe a small bowl of rice or grits would make her stomach stop clawing at her backbone.

Ste. Mary Clarisse came in with a piece of bread and cheese and escorted her down the hall to the waiting bath the sisters had anticipated her needing when they saw her at the gate.

"Thank you." 'Tine thought this was a grand supper and ate the bread in three bites; hardly waiting to chew before she swallowed. She put the cheese in her apron pocket for later. If nothing else, she'd have food for another day if it didn't work out with the Sisters.

Ste. Mary Clarisse reached into 'Tine's pocket and pulled out the dirty neck cloth and the piece of cheese and wiped it on a serviette.

"Eat it, dear until we can give you supper." She took the neckcloth and left the bathing to Ste. Catherine and Ste. Bernadette.

'Tine couldn't believe her ears, 'til supper? There was more food being offered? She wanted to follow the little nun and get her father's neckcloth back, but she was being undressed and helped into a steaming bath smelling of clean soap and cloves. She could always fish the clothe out of the garbage once she was out of this... this... wonderful smelling hot water.

'Tine awakened in a small cell of a room in a fresh nightgown. Her hair was clean and tangle free and she was surprised to see blonde curls falling around her face. She'd never noticed her hair or its color and certainly never knew she had soft curls. She moved her hand across her head and realized the sisters had cut away the matted dirty hair. She smelled like clean cotton and fresh cloves and she'd never felt so comfortable in her life. She was hungry and the smell of bacon and fresh bread was making her dizzy with desire for the good food. If only she hadn't eaten the bit of cheese before her bath; it'd be wonderful right now.

She'd lived her whole life walking the stalls of the French Market breathing the intoxicating incense of the gumbos and boiled seafood and never knew how good they could be when eaten clean and free of gutter filth. Once when she was still young and cute, a nice gentleman with a kind smile had offered her a fresh peach and she'd eaten half and kept the rest for her mama. It'd bruised and turned brown before her mama could eat it and she'd thrown it at 'Tine's head. It landed in her mama's dirty shoe, but 'Tine ate it anyway.

"Oh good, you're awake. I've brought you some breakfast."

The orphan girl looked to be a little older than 'Tine and wore the stylish clothing 'Tine had seen on young girls walking to the big church in the square going to Mass. It was a simple pink and yellow cotton dress, with fitted waist and ankle length skirt. She wore a white apron that covered the skirt and went up the bodice and across her small bosom. It fit under the big white collar that framed the neck and spread to the shoulders. 'Tine thought it was the most beautiful dress she'd ever seen. Her own dress was one of her mama's old ones held together by an old filthy belt and most likely made by God's grandmother. The tray of food was making her head swim. 'Tine couldn't believe what she was seeing. There was fresh bacon and a small piece of ham. There were eggs cooked with sweet smelling herbs and a nice piece of bread with strawberry jam and fresh butter. She'd eat for a week on this feast.

"I'm supposed to sit until you've finished. Ste. Mary Clarisse says you are to eat it all and not hide any.." Colette laughed, remembering her first day at the big orphanage. She also tried to hide food for herself. Colette knew now how silly it was to hide food when the kitchen had so much to offer.

"There's so much here, won't someone else need some?" 'Tine really didn't care if there was enough for anyone else, but she'd love to squirrel some away for herself.

She looked to see where her clothes had got and saw they were nowhere in the little bare room. Her little bag of pitiful belongings was on the floor under the window and her father's neck cloth was lying clean and ironed on top of the bag. 'Tine jumped out of bed and ransacked her little bag.

"My knife's gone. Somebody stole my knife." She was getting angry and looking at Colette to see if her accusation registered. Guilty people always looked guilty; even the good liars.

"Ste. Mary Clarisse took your knife. Weapons of any kind aren't allowed here. That's a big rule and is never broken by any of us. If you stay here the nuns won't allow you to keep your knife. But you won't need one either." Colette saw 'Tine reluctantly begin to relax.

"I agree there's too much food, but I was asked to wait. If you can't finish it all, I'll take some back to the kitchen and they can save it for you there."

'Tine decided she'd deal with the missing knife later after she'd found the kitchen so she could retrieve this food if she decided to leave.

"My name's Colette. Your name is beautiful; it's the name of a princess. Celestine Haussey, I should think you wouldn't shorten that wonderful name to 'Tine. My mama called me Letty, but I like Colette."

"I never thought about my name before. It's always been 'Tine. Maybe I like Celestine. Now that I'm changing my life, I should change my name also. It's much more grown up, isn't it?"

"We'll be fast friends, Celestine. The sisters prayed for you to come here. I think they prayed for me, too. I lived in Natchez. I was kidnapped by flatboatmen and left on their doorstep. My mama knew the men... in a Biblical sense, if you know what I mean?"

"No, I don't." 'Tine had never heard that term.

"Does it mean she was in the Bible? She'd have to be awful old. I think you're lying. I don't like liars."

"No, silly; it means sexual congress, prostitution, being a sinful... whore. She robbed one of her customers, and he stole me to get even with her. I was only ten." She said shamelessly.

"How terrible; did he know you in a Bible way?"

"Biblical way. No he just wanted to punish my mama. It backfired on him. She was glad to get rid of me, and I was sure glad to get away. I love living here."

"Do you work so you can be 'well educated'?" Celestine asked.

Colette looked at her.

"I help in the kitchen so I can learn to cook for my husband and family one day."

"You don't have to work with the orphans?"

"We're all orphans, and we all help out. We're a big family here, Celestine, and we do what's needed. You'll love your little sisters and brothers and find you want to love and protect them too. It isn't work; it's just living... as a family so to speak."

"I want to be 'well educated'." 'Tine was sure about this. She couldn't respond to the family idea, it was much too foreign to her. To be part of a family would mean she'd died and gone to heaven, and she knew she hadn't died.

"We have classes every day. We're being trained to be good wives and mothers and maybe teaching sisters. There're many men here who need good Christian wives."

"I'm not here to find a man, Colette. I want to be able to take care of myself." 'Tine had been talking and eating at the same time, stuffing the food in her mouth before someone came and took it away.

"Excuse me, Celestine, but it's not polite to talk while you have food in your mouth."

'Tine had never heard such a thing. If you're eating, how were you supposed to talk without food in your mouth?

Colette saw her dilemma; she'd wondered the same thing when she first came to the convent.

"You eat some food and then swallow; then talk; then eat some more and swallow and then talk. You'll get used to it."

"Thank you. Colette? I have to learn manners. Will you help me?"

"Of course, silly, what are sisters for? We're going to be the best of sisters. Now I'll tell you about the others and you'll know what to expect around here. Never speak during Prayer hours. That's very important. Never ever tell Ste. Margaret Mary that her breath smells bad. I learned that the hard way. And try not to fart during Mass. People get very, very upset over that. Again, I found out the hard way."

Both girls laughed, enjoying each other's company. These were the first of many happy golden hours of many years, living, learning, loving and feeling safe and needed. The Ursulines Sisters took away the lonely, 'I' and gave both little girls the lovely 'we' and 'us'.

Chapter Two

1800

Celestine turned nineteen and heard so much talk of the world coming to an end with the turning of the century; she was tired of it. If God wanted the world to end, he wouldn't wait for such organized timing. It'd happen on a weekday in a non-descript year, and it'd be sudden and terrible. All the great disasters happened in the blink of a bird's eye. Pompeii hadn't happened when people expected. The people of Atlantis weren't warned to take swimming lessons. God warned Moses and he warned Noah and a few others of bad things he had in mind, but to her on-going, soon-to-be well-educated mind, he hadn't come down and warned New Orleans that the turn of the century would bring about death and pestilence. The city itself provided that on a yearly basis without God's interference.

She was on the way to Colette's house on rue du Maine with the dress she'd altered to accommodate Colette's big belly. Colette couldn't venture out; she was expecting her first child, and Celestine was keeping her company while her husband was away.

Colette was very excited about choosing a husband. She was allowed to choose from the many suitors looking for young, innocent girls to wed. All had been scrutinized by the Reverend Mother and Colette had chosen well. He was a young Sea Captain, hero handsome from a wealthy family out of Natchez, and he adored his new bride. He acquired a large piece of land up river and was clearing the land to build a home for his new family. Colette regaled Celestine with Pierre's courtship and gentle romantic lovemaking. Each night during the courtship, Colette would weave the beautiful moments she and Pierre spent together into a fairytale of sensual romance to entertain Celestine.

Celestine had never known a man being gentle with a woman and she wasn't sure her friend was being honest. Once she met Pierre David she saw he was different from the men she knew, but he was still a man. He was kind to his wife's friend and complimentary of her needlework and cooking, but Celestine was always waiting for the backhand or insult that'd surely follow the compliments; so far, she'd felt neither. She finally relaxed enough in his company to blush and giggle when he awarded her one of his sweet compliments.

She didn't believe Colette about her wedding night though. She'd seen too many men in sexual congress and there was certainly nothing for the woman to enjoy unless of course one enjoyed a necklace of bruises and bite marks for garters. She asked Ste. Mary Clarisse and embarrassed both when she remembered too late that the young woman knew less than Celestine about the act, and was mortified at being asked.

Colette had been begging Celestine to meet a friend of Pierre's for months; she knew Celestine would love him. He was an older, handsome successful merchant Sea Captain who'd mentored Pierre. He was outfitting a brand new ship and had overseen the building from first board to last. He was happily anxious to have her Christened for her maiden voyage. According to Colette, he was a wonderful man and would be good for Celestine. He could provide her with a good living and a nice house and many babies. Colette assured Celestine that if she'd seen Capt. Dubois before Pierre, she would've been hard pressed to pick her darling Pierre. Celestine wanted no part of it, but wondered what it'd be like to have the security of a real husband. Someone to take care of her and give her jewelry and pretty dresses like Pierre gave Colette. The city was building back nicely since the big fires, but there was still only a modicum of businesses in which a young woman could find work.

She turned on to rue du Maine and walked the short blocks to Colette's. She loved the big house behind the iron gates. The carriageway went directly into the courtyard and was framed on three sides by the main house. The second story went across the top of the carriage way and joined the three sides surrounding the big courtyard. It belonged to Pierre's parents, and was rebuilt a year after the last fire. The courtyard was a paradise of exotic plants and in the corner of the staircase going to the second floor was a Magnolia tree that'd been there forever. The old trunk was charred, but it still gave good shade and beautiful creamy blossoms. The big center fountain was a tropical rainfall and the ancient lamp sconces on the courtyard walls contrasted nicely with the newly painted plaster; old and new living peacefully together.

Colette was waiting for her at a little iron table under a huge banana tree. She was drinking a cup of nice strong coffee with heavy cream and was pouring a cup for Celestine.

"Oh, how nice, I'd love a cup."

She noticed another cup and saucer on the table and before she could ask, a gentleman walked through the carriageway coming from the stable. He was in his late thirties; very handsome in his Captain's uniform; his big, three cornered captain's hat that tucked neatly under his arm. His face was browned from too much sun on the open sea and his rolling gait from a life on water, made him every bit the sailor of her nightmares. Celestine wanted to run away. She'd seen men like him. She knew how they rutted and she knew how they drank rum. She also knew how the backs of their hands felt on a young girl's face if she tried to help her mama. She'd given up her knife and hadn't needed it before today. She swallowed   a   bit   of   vomit   in   the   back   of   her   throat.

He was smiling with clean white teeth; not the rotten pellets that should've been in a face such as his. His breath smelled of fresh mint as he reached and took her hand and kissed it softly.

"Celestine, may I present Captain Maurice Dubois. Maurice, this is my best friend, Celestine. Now, you two have met and you'll be fast friends."

"I'd like that." His voice was tender, and he was looking into her eyes and questioning her terrible fear.

"It's a pleasure to meet you, Captain." Celestine said in spite of her terror. What could Colette be thinking? This man is my most hated fear. Celestine got up so fast she almost upset her coffee.

"I can't stay, I have to get back. The children are waiting for me to read to them before their nap. I'm sorry, but I have to go." The tears were being held back by sheer will power.

"Mlle. Celestine? I've offended you. Please accept my deepest apologies. Please, let me offer my apology." He was searching the face of this divine creature. She was more beautiful than any woman he'd seen in all of his travels. The little blond tendrils coming out of her bonnet were making his seasoned heart beat like a race horse and he wouldn't let her go until he'd made amends. Celestine was standing and looking down at Colette for help. Colette was looking back with angry eyes.

"Celestine, it's an hour before nap time and I still need to try on my dress. Please sit down and drink your coffee. Capt. DuBois has most generously brought some beautiful material for both of us from Paris, and I think the least we can do is not insult him, dear." Colette spat the word and Celestine knew she'd offended both her good friend and this strange but oddly familiar man.

"Oh, I didn't realize how early it was. I'm sorry. I can stay for my coffee, I'm sure the children will wait for me." She'd most certainly take this up with Colette later. This introduction without her knowledge or consent would demand a conversation with her old friend.

Colette was helped up and ushered into the house by Petal, the young girl Pierre hired to care for her personal needs the day they were married.

The silence was horrible to Celestine after Colette left for her fitting. Why doesn't he speak? Her terror was growing and being alone with him was bringing up every bad memory in her young head.

"Colette tells me you didn't fear the coming of the new century? I have to admit, neither did I. I looked on it as just another day, but with a new number." He was obviously grasping for things to say that wouldn't offend her again.

Celestine raised her face to look at the man. She'd never seen such kind eyes except in the little sisters and her friends Colette and Pierre. She could walk into those blue eyes and never return.

The Captain's darkly handsome face was alive with his smile. The same smile she remembered from years before in the big market.

"You gave me a peach once, monsieur. In the Fruit Market; a beautiful velvet peach. I remember it." She remembered that face looking down into hers but mainly she remembered the taste of that intoxicating peach, even after it'd been thrown at her head. The sweet nectar and this kind face were melded into the same memory and she hadn't recognized it until his smile.

"I beg your pardon? I can assure you Mlle.; had I given you a peach, I'd have remembered with pure joy. You must be thinking of another, luckier man than myself." He was in trouble here.

He wanted to be the man who gave her the peach. He wanted those lovely eyes with recognition and wonder replacing the fear, to gaze on him and no one else. He had women in his life; he was even considered a rogue and a lady's man. He'd wanted some he couldn't have but he'd never wanted one this badly and he'd have her.

No, she was too divine; he'd marry her. It was time he settled down. He'd watched Pierre and Colette and for the first time, saw how coming home to a wife and family after months at sea could be a good thing, not the jail he'd always imagined.

He hoped Colette wouldn't come back until he'd rid himself of the embarrassment that filled the front of his breeches and threatened to pop some buttons. He wouldn't be able to stand, and that'd be entirely too rude. He hadn't had this spontaneous reaction to a female in a very long time. A new ship, a new wife, it made good sense.

"You didn't give me a peach monsieur, it was years ago and you gave a little waif a peach." Suddenly she didn't want him to remember her as the little dirty girl in the big market. She was sorry she mentioned it

He still didn't remember; he was always giving the little street waifs fruit from the market stalls. It was just something he did. It must've made a difference in her life for her to remember it this many years later. He'd try to remember it, now; he could use it in his courtship.

God was always on his side and he took this as a sign that God favored his new idea about taking her as a wife. He knew Colette's history and assumed Celestine's had been similar. They both lived and studied with the Ursulines Sisters. He didn't care about their past lives, his was probably worse but he wouldn't reveal it to anyone. If they came from the little sisters they were also virginal and educated in religion, history and languages. He heard these young women made excellent wives. They kept the husbands in their place and out of the woods chasing anything with a womanly quiver.

Celestine finally found her voice.

"I didn't believe God would end the world in so orderly a fashion. I believe the end of the world will come on any Monday or Thursday while men are in their fields and women are at the washing with children playing in the forest away from the safety of home. I believe it'll be a devastating climax to lives well lived and lives lived in sin." She had to fill the vacant space and get his mind and memory off the little dirty waif stuffing a peach in her mouth without so much as a 'thank you' to the kind gentleman.

"I haven't thought of it that way, Mlle. but I do believe you're correct. If God wanted to end this project of his, he wouldn't give the wicked time to take cover." His laugh could be heard all over the house and Celestine found herself laughing with him.

"So you think God's world is a work in progress, Capt. Dubois?" She hadn't laughed since she and Colette and Pierre had their last dinner together.

"Well, it's not over til it's over. The men are in the fields and the wicked are unprepared. So, yes, I guess we're all a work in progress; a sea not sailed." He laughed and flashed her that beautiful smile again.

Colette returned with her altered dress fitting loosely over her round belly. Maurice was able to stand without injury to his privates and help her into her chair. Colette handed a package to Celestine. Celestine almost didn't accept it, she wanted no gifts from this man, but it'd be rude and she was taught by the little sisters that "rudeness to a kindness given" is a sin. Her blush was humiliating her and there was no hole in which to crawl.

Capt. Maurice Dubois felt a modicum of embarrassment; he also wished Colette had waited until later before giving her the beautiful silks from Paris. Seeing Celestine's eyes he knew the sea blue silks would compliment her beauty and he only hoped he'd one day see her wearing it... for him.

Chapter Three

Maurice Dubois visited Colette many times before his ship was ready for its maiden voyage. This would be a quick trip; to Cuba and back, a few months only. He wanted to get used to the feel of his new ship. He visited with Pierre and Colette hoping to catch Celestine in another visit, but had missed her each time.

Colette knew better than to arrange a meeting before Celestine gave permission. They had a terrible row after the first meeting and Colette promised never to invade Celestine's life again. Not that Colette intended to keep the promise; she just hadn't come up with a plan as yet. Her friend and Maurice were meant to be together, it was as plain as the nose on Colette's face. The age difference was a plus for Celestine and also Maurice. Celestine needed a wise man who'd be patient with her past and Maurice needed a fresh, innocent love to smooth some of his rough edges and keep him gentle.

Maurice asked so many questions about her friend that Colette finally inspired him one afternoon with Celestine's life story. She felt he needed to know how untrusting she was of men and why. She told of her coming to the convent of her own will to get away from her mama's life and how untrained she'd been, but how willing to work and help and learn she is still. With each fact, Colette searched the man's face for any hint of disdain or disapproval, but had found the opposite. He was understanding and appreciative of the road Celestine had traveled. Finally Colette tried very delicately to broach the subject of intimacy with the man. She told of how Celestine never wanted to marry because of it and how traumatizing the thought was to her since she was very small.

"So, you see Maurice, if this isn't something you can handle, I'd ask that you seek a wife elsewhere and leave my friend in peace." Please let him see the gravity of this situation.

Maurice saw and understood the gravity of it. He understood it only too well. He'd been a young boy on a prison ship off the coast of Carolina when he was first violated by the older man and nearly died. He'd learned to use a knife and to lie still until the very last possible minute; then his blade came from nowhere and killed the man. He'd saved his friends Andy and John from the same fate and the three escaped the same night. He understood, by damn. He understood and knew if anyone could take her fear and replace it with love, he could. No man would ever hurt her again. He knew what his sweet Anna had done for him when he was Celestine's age. Anna replaced his self-hatred and his total disgust of the sexual act with pleasure and love. He still sought her company when he was in Port-au-Prince. He'd do that for this love, he'd give her the best of his gentle knowledge pleasuring women and he'd teach her how to open herself to his body and his love as his Anna had done for him. But first he had to meet her again. He needed a courtship before a marriage.

Celestine heard the bell on the front gate of the convent and went to open it. The front gate always held interesting challenges; people looking for directions, or people who'd lost their way and were looking for solace or vendors trying to sell things the sisters didn't want or need. Sometimes it was a child like herself, looking for a safe and loving harbor. Those were the best gifts, giving hope to a small child; taking the little hand in hers and walking it into its safe destiny. She knew these children so well. She knew when to look for weapons and which ones were here only to grab food and run; but they were all looking for the same thing: safety, love and a purpose in life.

She saw the big baskets; there must have been half a dozen; all filled to the brim with summer peaches brought down the river from places she'd never been. She could smell them before she reached the gate. The aroma was making her mouth water as the deliveryman handed her a note.

"I meant to give you these a few years ago but alas, they were not ripe.
Your friend and ever humble servant,
Captain Maurice Dubois"

Her heart raced. She couldn't breathe. What did this mean? She ushered the deliveryman around the convent and into the big kitchen in the back. The sisters making lunch were thrilled at the bounty and Ste. Mary Clarisse began to wash and put one at each plate on the long tables.

"Ohh, 'Tine such magnificent peaches. These are such a treat. Look there're plenty left to make cobblers for supper and peach preserves for next winter. Ooh, God's bounty is beautiful." The scent of fresh peach was filling the kitchen and reaching the outside. Celestine tucked the note into her pocket and walked back to her little cell.

'I meant to give you these a few years ago but alas, they were not ripe.'

His signature was bold and masculine, just like his face. She could see his kind eyes and still smell the peaches on her hands and around her mouth from eating one of the delectable delicacies. She loved that the note was funny and not romantic, and he hadn't signed anything about love.

He spent a lot of his time on shore at Colette's and Pierre's and was the reason Celestine never made spontaneous visits. She was beginning to resent his time spent with her friends; she missed their dinners and evenings together.

"You must take some peaches to Colette and Pierre." Ste. Mary Clarisse walked gently into her cell carrying a small basket of the delicious fruit.

"Visiting with the man won't hurt you, 'Tine. Mother had him thoroughly scrutinized and he's a fine man, my dear, he'll not force you into anything. Why can't you just be his friend? If he wants a wife, just say 'no thank you'. You're under no obligation to marry anyone."

Celestine had not thought. What if he did show an interest; it didn't mean anything. It was his problem if he wanted something he couldn't have. She wasn't her mama depending on the coins of ugly men to make a living. Besides, the gift of the peaches was wonderful and she truly thought it was a sweet gesture to the whole convent. She'd walk around to Colette's and give her the peaches. If he happened to be there, then she'd deal with it. She'd write a thank you note first in case she ran into him. She went to her small armoire and took out the dress she'd made from the blue silk he'd brought from Paris. She only wore it for Mass and a Christening; the blue made her eyes shimmer like the sea in the sun. It was a bold gesture, but Ste. Mary Clarisse was right. She didn't have to marry the man, but she'd gotten pleasure from the gift and she'd like him to see the beautiful dress. The weather had been dry and the streets were actually dry enough to walk without boots if she dodged the puddles of sewage and dead animals. Celestine took her note and the peaches and walked through the carriage way into the courtyard.

He was walking across the courtyard to get his horse from the little stable when he saw her coming through the carriageway in the dress. The bodice was cut so low over her full creamy breast he could swear he almost saw a nipple; the skirt of the gown started under her breast and flowed like a shimmering waterfall to the tip of her slippered toe.

She looked up to see him standing frozen, his blue eyes staring with appreciation and to her horror, lust. She lowered her head under her bonnet with a fake smile and walked quickly past him and up the stairs and into Colette's bedroom before he could see her face darken with fear. Colette was in bed where she'd been for the last week, propped on pillows reading and waiting for her baby to be born. She was thrilled with the peaches and reached for one but grabbed her stomach and grimaced instead.

"Oh, Celestine that hurt." She grabbed the covers her knuckles turning white with pain. "Celestine it wants to come out. It wants to come out now! I can feel it pressing to get out." She was writhing and throwing her body around to try to get away from the pain.

"Don't be silly, Colette; you know these things take time. We've witnessed this before, just hold on and I'll send for the doctor."

"My back's been hurting all morning. I just thought it was a back ache."

"Colette, you should've said something." Celestine was beside herself. This wasn't supposed to happen yet.

"No, Celestine, I'm telling you it's on its way out." She was crying and trying to keep her legs together but her body was pushing and she couldn't stop it. Celestine threw back the covers and opened her friend's legs. The baby's head was crowning.

"Oh my God, Colette, you're having the baby right this minute!"

"I told you, damn it, help me." She was crying louder and grabbed the pillow to press down on her stomach. Celestine brought her friend's knees up to her hips and put pillows under her head. She went to the door and screamed for Petal to get the doctor. She could hear boots on the stairs. Maurice came into the bedroom so quickly he startled both women. He was taking off his jacket and rolling up his sleeves. He ordered Celestine to bring the birthing supplies he knew would be in the kitchen for a woman this far along.

"Let's have this baby, if that's all right with you, Colette?" He was smiling and calming her and taking away her fear. He called again for Petal to go for the doctor and if she couldn't find the doctor, tell the sisters to come. Celestine ran to the kitchen and brought back a kettle of boiling water and put it on the commode stand.

"Relax, Colette, push when I say." His gentle voice was soothing even to Celestine.

She ran back to look for the satchel of supplies that indeed were kept ready, but were nowhere in sight. Celestine finally found the satchel under some freshly folded linen and came back across the courtyard and up the stairs into the bedroom. Maurice was standing; holding the newborn baby in his arms wrapped in a pillow case. His hands and white linen shirt were covered with blood and Colette was sleeping peacefully on her bloody sheets. Celestine couldn't take her eyes off of his face. He was looking tenderly at the baby and then flashed her one of his soul reaching smiles.

"It's a girl. Come, hold her; she's beautiful. I'm going to collect her papa. Will you be all right until help comes?"

"How'd you know what to do?" Celestine whispered in total awe.

He reached for the bathing towel to cover Celestine's dress. With one hand he laid the baby gently in her arms and waited until she was holding her securely. He went to the washbowl, washed his hands and arms in the hot water from the kettle and got his jacket.

"I'm a Sea Captain, my dear. This isn't my first time as 'midwife'." He laughed and walked over to her and spoke so softly she almost didn't hear.

"You are magnificent, thank you for wearing that dress. I'd like to give you many more." He reached down and kissed her on the mouth so gently she almost responded. She pulled back instinctively, holding the baby closer to her.

He was on his horse and gone before Celestine could thank him for the peaches or the material or the baby. She surprised herself that she didn't wipe his kiss off her mouth.

Maurice was impressed with Celestine and how quickly she followed orders in crises. She could actually be seaworthy he thought to himself. Yes, he'd take her as his wife. I wonder if she liked the peaches. The baby had come just in time; seeing her in that dress could've cost him the whole courtship. He'd intended to kiss her cheek, but his mouth wanted to feel her lips and smell her skin and his mind had no control over it. He'd think of that later. He had a papa to collect and Pierre was going to be very happy. He'd confided in Maurice he wanted a little girl just like his Colette.

Celestine was still holding the baby when Petal came in with Ste. Mary Clarisse and a young novice training to be a nurse. They began their work right away so Celestine was able to go back to the convent to wash up and change her pretty dress. She had so much to think about. She'd seen her friend spit out the baby like a shelling a field pea on a summer afternoon. She'd never known a baby to be born so fast. Maybe she could manage it after all if she could have babies that fast. Her fear came from the hours of pain she'd witnessed in the cribs as women suffered and died trying to deliver babies born backwards or babies too large to fit the birth canal. She'd witnessed young women trying to pull out babies by their legs and dying in the attempt.

This was different and her friend had a serious 'midwife' that knew what to do and how to do it without worry or stress. He was impressive with his commands to Celestine and Petal and his gentle orders for Colette. He'd generously thought to go for Pierre and was on his way at this moment. She didn't know what to think about this man, this Sea Captain, this handsome giver of peaches. She knew what he had in his pants though; she saw it this afternoon in his appreciation of her new dress and she knew what he'd do with it. Maybe some men were different, maybe some men didn't like to hurt women and grunt when they lay on top of them. Colette assured her Pierre was different. Pierre smelled of clean air and hay and loved to wash himself in Colette's spice filled soaps. She liked that in a man. If she ever did take a man, he'd have to smell good and he'd be just like Maurice Dubois. Celestine crossed her own line. Maybe it was possible for her to like this handsome Captain who could fill the big convent with the aroma of peaches; birth a baby and kiss her gently on the mouth all in one afternoon.

Chapter Four

Pierre saw Maurice riding up the long drive from the river road. He wondered what brought him out here; he was due to sail for Cuba soon. He stepped out onto the half finished gallery and noticed the red on his shirt before he dismounted. It was blood; something bad had happened at home. He grabbed his sword belt and ran for his gun screaming for Jake to saddle his horse. Maurice caught him on his way back out the door.

"Hey, stop, where's the fire?" Maurice didn't know his shirt was full of blood. He'd washed his hands and come to find Pierre. He saw Pierre's face staring at his shirt.

"Oh, damn, Pierre, sorry, I didn't realize. I should've changed my shirt, but I didn't have time… Papa." He watched for a reaction.

"Papa? What's going on?" Pierre was thrown for a loop with this weird visit. Maurice took him by the shoulders, "You have a baby girl, and she's beautiful."

Jake brought his horse around and the two of them started back toward the city. Maurice let Pierre go ahead as his horse could use a rest before catching up. The new father should see his wife and daughter alone before guests crowded in to congratulate.

Pierre couldn't believe it; he hadn't asked Maurice if Colette was all right. Of course Maurice would've told him if she wasn't and he looked happy about the baby. He was a papa; he had a little girl. Next, he wanted a little boy, but right now, he wanted his little princess. Why did Maurice have blood on his shirt? Oh God, he couldn't get home fast enough.

Maurice got back to the city and went to his house and changed his clothes and asked for a bath and shave. Josef had his clothes ready for him on the bed and Marguerite was cooking pumpkin soup out in the little kitchen in the back. The smell was filling his head with thoughts of happy homes and nice things cooking on the big fireplaces all over the world. He was happy for his friends; they were truly blessed to have each other and that beautiful little girl. For the first time in his life, he wanted the same thing. He had his adopted children, Josef and Marguerite, but it wasn't enough. He wanted to see Celestine leaning back on a boatload of soft pillows in a beautiful nightgown feeding their baby at her beautiful breasts. He could see her; looking like the Madonna she was meant to be. He still hadn't heard how the peaches were received. If he knew women at all, he knew they were well received and his name was being praised for sending them. Next, he'd call on Mother Superior. He needed to know if he'd pass muster as a husband before he went any further with this courtship; if he had to bypass the convent and court her without permission, he needed to know that too. One would be easier, but the other wasn't impossible. He walked out of his rooms, a new man. He was bathed and fresh and on his way to ask a woman for his woman's hand in marriage. He was up to the task; he was ready, willing, and able and scared to death.

He rang the bell and was pleased to see a young novice come to the gate instead of Celestine. He was hoping not to run into her as she may suspect the reason for his visit. He was ushered into the Mother Superior's office and offered a seat.

"I'll come right to the point, Reverend Mother. I wish to call on and propose marriage to Celestine Haussey. If she'll have me, I wish to marry her. I can provide handsomely for her and will most assuredly take good care of her." He hoped she hadn't heard the fear seeping through his voice.

Mother Superior was wondering when he'd get around to this visit. She could tell he was nervous and she thought it sweet. She'd indeed checked him out and found him to be quite suitable for any of her girls.

She felt any of her charges would be fortunate to have such a husband, but Celestine was a different matter. Most of the nuns in the order had remarked for years on the nightmares and outburst against men and their brutal carnal relations that awakened Celestine from her sleep many nights. It was a delicate matter and she had no idea how to approach it with this man of the world. She sat back in her chair and closed her eyes. His age would've bothered her, but Celestine needed an older man who'd be tolerant and have the kind wisdom to treat her like the lady she was. It may be a very long time after the wedding before this girl would allow him in their marriage bed.

Maurice didn't like the Reverend Mother hesitating. He didn't like it at all. Why was she? He remembered his first confession after his rapes when he was ten years old and the Priest blamed him for being sinful and wanting the attention. The Priest asked him if he'd flirted with the men on the ship, gone so long from their wives. Had he bartered his body for gifts from the exploited men? What had he done to bring this about? Maurice left the church and not gone back for years. He never mentioned it to another priest and never would. He knew in his mind he'd done nothing to bring on the assaults, but had he without knowing it? He was grown and the Captain of his own ship when he witnessed it happening to one of his cabin boys. The men were flogged and put off at the first port and the young boy was never touched again. Pierre David was forever grateful and worshiped him from then until this very day. It was only then that Maurice knew he'd done nothing to bring on the rapes, but there are men who take advantage.

"My son... There are things in 'Tine's past that may disturb you. She is... she has night mares about her life before this convent and she has nightmares about... her mother's profession..."

"Let me stop you, Reverend Mother, I know about her past and I know about her fear of marriage. I intend to and shall alter that fear."

He didn't wish to discuss Celestine's secrets with anyone, not even this woman who rescued her years ago.

"I see. Then you know my reticence in saying I approve, Capt. Dubois?"

"No, I don't. I've told you, I'm able to kill these dragons and I intend to. I'm in love with your 'Tine and if you really knew me, you'd understand that she needs me and what I can offer her; unless, she's made a decision to follow the order of this convent and become a nun. In that case, I'll not stand in her way, if that's what she truly wants." His heart was beating so fast he knew she could see it through his shirt and jacket. *Dear God, you wouldn't send her to me; then keep her for yourself?*

Mother Superior looked at this handsome, rugged man and suspected he had secrets of his own. Maybe he was the one to save little 'Tine from her past and make her whole again. They'd done all they could and the girl had no intentions of becoming a member of their order.

"I give my permission for you to court her, but it's her choice and hers alone if she wishes to marry you." She said and sighed the sigh of a woman wearing the mantle of judgment.

"Thank you, Reverend Mother. I'll not disappoint you or, God forbid, Celestine." He was trying to stay distinguished and poised, but it was damned hard.

"We all enjoyed the peaches, Capt. Dubois. They were wonderful. Thank you."

"You're quite welcome, I hoped they'd please." He finally got a thank you for the damned peaches.

"You're going to Havana soon, Captain? A few of the sisters' have letters to family they'd like delivered to the post there. Would you be so kind as to take them with you?"

He left her office, carrying a packet of letters, a happy man.

Celestine knew he was there, she'd seen him at the gate. She sent Anne to let him in. She waited for him to leave and see if he was happy or sad. His happiness made her very nervous. On one hand she was hoping the Reverend Mother would've said 'no' and it'd be out of her hands. On the other hand, she was pleased that he'd asked the Reverend Mother first before he approached her.

He was so distinguished walking back out of the gate and down the street. She could do a lot worse than this handsome Captain. Yes, she could do a hell of a lot worse. She once more wondered if Colette told her the truth about Pierre and his gentleness. She'd never believe that Colette enjoyed it though, that was just one of Colette's little lies. She knew it.

There was one last thing Maurice had to do before he sailed to Cuba. He'd win her heart by sheer surprise and grandeur if nothing else. By the time he got back, she'd be throwing herself at him. He knew it; he felt it and he sure as hell hoped he was right. He'd invite her to the Christening of his ship. Pierre and Colette did everything in their power to get Celestine to attend the event, but she had so many excuses they decided she lay awake night inventing them. Finally Maurice arranged with Pierre to have her on the levee the morning he was to sail. Pierre was not allowed to tell her why. It'd take all of Pierre's intelligence and detective work to make this happen, but he knew Pierre would do it, or he'd have Colette to answer to. It was a marvelous idea and when he ran it past Colette, she said she'd hogtie Celestine and have her there if necessary. She was tired of this foolishness.

He decided to try to see her one last time before he sailed. He'd always wanted the joy of saying goodbye to a woman who'd be waiting when he got back. He'd watched husbands do it and boyfriends do it and he knew a woman in every port welcomed him, but this was different. He wanted someone who cared enough to count the days and worry about storms and missing ships. Once they were married he'd build a widow's walk for her and outfit it with a telescope of the first measure and she could wait and watch for his ship and his returning love. He was a very romantic man and he'd make her appreciate him for it. Most husbands didn't remember their own anniversary. He knew this from the many married women who'd offered themselves to him over the years.

Celestine had been wondering about Pierre for two days. He had her up every morning early, helping him get things for Colette and the baby. She was beginning to get tired of it. They had servants, why couldn't they get the first shrimp off the boats or the best fruit from the market? This morning was the last favor for a while. She had work to do in the kitchen and in the gardens each morning; she didn't have time to do his bidding each day. She purposefully stayed away from the big docks where the Christening was taking place, but Pierre was so sweet and promised if she'd do this last favor, he'd not ask again. She was walking on the levee looking for the chicory that Colette loved when Pierre was suddenly standing beside her.

"Good morning, Celestine. I see you've come to see the Captain off to Cuba and points south?" Celestine looked at him like he was daft.

"I'm here, Pierre to get Colette's chicory; like you asked. Why would I come to see Capt. Dubois' ship leave the harbor?"

What was this about? She knew it; he and Colette hadn't given up as promised.

"Well, look, there she goes. Pretty isn't she?" Celestine looked toward the river and saw the beautiful ship hoisting sail as she headed down the river. At the bow of the ship was freshly painted: 'Le Celestine' and the figure head was a beautiful wooden woman with blonde hair wearing a sea blue dress painted to look like her own.

She didn't hide her tears from Pierre. It was the dearest thing anyone had ever done for her. A gift so fine, she didn't know what to think; or how to repay her future husband. If her mama could put up with a stranger's grunt then maybe she could put up with Capt. Dubois' love making no matter how terrible. Celestine stood on the levee until the ship had turned and gone past the crescent and out of site down the river. She ran back to the convent and prayed for his safety; the first of many lonesome, worried hours for her man's safe return from the sea; mixed with the fear of his safe return and what that would mean.

Chapter Five

Pierre and Colette were spending more and more time at the new house with the baby. Colette was getting ideas for decorating and fabrics. She and Pierre made a huge list for Maurice to bring back from his next long trip abroad. Celestine wondered when that'd be. He hadn't returned from Cuba and the West Indies. She'd finished the gift she'd made him a month before. She was lonesome without her friends and little Letty. It'd been three months and Pierre said it'd take less than two. She hadn't heard anything from or about Capt. Dubois. Maybe he'd changed his mind. Maybe there was a beautiful senorita in Cuba that'd captured his heart. After all, he wasn't the marrying kind or so Pierre told Colette in the beginning. Maybe he had a fling with the idea of Celestine and then run away in the light of day and the open Gulf. She'd give him his shirt anyway. It'd be her thank you for the peaches and his helping Colette bring little Letty into the world. She decided to give up and think about a life on her own. She'd miss thinking about him; she realized in trying to give him up, she liked him very much and it hurt to think that he didn't care anymore. She thought of him much more than she wanted and she kept very busy or thoughts of him would'd haunt her. His image came to her in dreams and woke her from sleep; desiring his gentle mouth on hers. This last was something so foreign she prayed for hours to get it out of her mind. She didn't like thinking of that smile charming another woman; it made her feel an unfamiliar anger.

She went to Colette's to feed the cat. There were no servants. The only two they kept were with them in the country. Pierre thought the cat would eat mice and get by, but Celestine and Colette both knew the cat loved milk and left-over bits of fish from the market. The poor little creature never left their courtyard and so Celestine went every other day and left nice treats for the cat to eat.

This particular day, she took Capt. Dubois' wrapped gift to Colette's. She intended to leave it on the main table in the music room. She'd leave it and when and if he ever came back, Colette could give it to him, but she changed her mind; maybe she wouldn't give it to him at all. It was Celestine's finest needlework and when she first began, she was anxious to see how handsome he'd be wearing it. It was of the finest linen; so light you could see through it for those hot summer days in the tropical city. The full sleeves caught the slightest breeze. There was a delicate linen neckcloth with his initials (MDE) embroidered in gold thread. It pleased Pierre that she made the shirt for his friend. Celestine hoped Pierre wouldn't be too disappointed in Maurice for turning her away. She wrote a note with the package:

'Capt. Dubois,
For kindnesses rendered.
I meant to give this to you before you left, but alas,
I hadn't thought to create it.'
Sincerely, Celestine Haussey

She changed her mind, picked up the package and the note and went down to *rue de Quai*. She loved standing on the levee watching the big sailing ships load and unload, going and coming on the big river to the open Gulf with their goods. There was always energy and people laughing and talking on their journeys to somewhere exciting. She didn't want to go back to the convent and answer questions about her tears. The sun was going down and the smells of the food in the market were making her hungry. As she turned to go home she saw a ship leaving and as another ship shifted, she saw, *Le Celestine*. The gangplank was lowered. How long had it been in port? She couldn't move. *She'd just watch for a few minutes to see if maybe, maybe... this was silliness; she had to let him go.* She thought she saw her Captain at the bow. The wind was in his hair and her heart was in her throat. She wondered if he was sorry he'd named his ship after her. She should leave; he'd think her forward to be standing waiting for his ship. What if he ignored her? What if he felt uncomfortable and stayed on the ship? She turned to walk away; she didn't want him to think she was a silly girl, waiting for his ship… and him. She was half way down the levee when she heard him call. He was walking toward her, closer than she expected and then he had her in his arms. She raised her face to his and he kissed her. He took off her bonnet and the curly blonde hair blew around her face. She felt strange all over and things were awakening that she didn't know existed. The pit of her stomach was on fire and fear mixed with desire was about to strangle her.

"Oh, my little dove, you're here to meet me. Oh God, Celestine I've dreamed of this."

He kissed her again, gently with his big strong arms holding her close and she felt something hard in his breeches through the silks of her dress. She tried to back away, but he held her close and kissed her again. She melted into him and wanted to feel it again, his manhood. It was his desire; his love for her and she thought she'd lost it. He picked her up in his arms and walked back to the ship and across the deck into his cabin and shut and locked the door. He laid her on the bed and stood back to look at her.

"Will you marry me, Celestine?" She looked up at him through half closed eyes and nodded 'yes'.

"Oh, my little dove; I love you. I've missed you so much; the two of us in this cabin. We could sail around the world if you like, or you can stay here; I'll buy you a house and come to you from the sea."

He was totally crazed at this moment. He'd imagined having to coax her out of the convent or renew his courtship, but she was on the levee waiting for him as he'd seen so many women waiting in so many ports for their men to come home. He could die a happy man, but not before he'd married this wonderful creature.

"I thought you weren't coming back to me." She was looking at him with big sad eyes reproaching him for something he hadn't done. He had to get that look out of her eyes, it was breaking his heart.

"Why'd you ever think that, my dove? Is that why you were walking away? Please, don't ever think that again, Celestine. I promise; I'll always come back to you." He took her face in his hands and whispered into his kiss. "Celestine, I'll always come back to you."

She received him and responded to his kiss as he began to remove her dress and unlace the few strings on the short stays that covered her breast. Before he knew it his hand was on her breast feeling the silky skin and the nipple; he stopped.

"Oh my God, Celestine, I'm so sorry. I can't believe this, I'm a cad." He was trying to pull her stays back together and get the strings laced again. He was beside himself with worry for what he'd almost done to this delicate creature that needed time and patience.

From the moment he kissed her on the levee she knew what she'd known as intimacy was disgusting men rutting with a whore. His kiss, what she felt, and what Colette told her over and over again was right. It could be sensual and loving. She reached up and pulled his face down to hers. She kissed him and let him run his tongue inside her mouth and whispered.

"I love you, Maurice. I know you'd never hurt me." She kissed him again and got up. She stood in front of him; took off her dress, petticoats, and corset and walked in her chemise back to the bed. She picked up the package and gave it to him.

Maurice was dumb struck. Where'd she come from? Who was she? This was not the girl he was warned about. Had she taken another man while he was gone? Had she taken a lover? His head was spinning with questions. Celestine looked at his face and in his eyes. There was confusion and anger all boiling around in those great blue eyes.

"What... what...um what about your past and... your fears...? Was that a lie, Celestine?"

She stood shocked and confused. Why did she have to explain? Why was he angry?

"No, but when you kissed me, I wanted more." She didn't know how to tell him how she felt. She didn't know why, or what she'd done, but he was angry with her. *Oh, so that's it? I knew it was too good to be true.*

"You're just like all the rest; judge, blame, yell, grunt... hit." She was crying and trying to talk. *She'd tell him what she thought of him before she left and he could go lay an egg.*

"Nothing has changed in my world; but this time, I felt it, not my mama. You've never had anything bad happen to you; so you don't understand what it's like when something shifts and changes... and all of a sudden the fear's gone... and desire is strong... pulling you into a place you never knew. You just don't understand. Now I've made a fool of myself. I'm standing in your room with my chemise on with my clothes at my feet and I could die; you'll not grunt over me you oaf, but you can be proud of yourself, you managed to make me want you before you struck... and that will never happen again." She was crying and sobbing and grabbing for her clothes. She'd die from humiliation and hate before she could get off this ship.

"Yes." He couldn't believe how stupid he'd just been.

"What?" *Yes to what, what was he saying yes to?* She'd managed to get her petticoat on and was stepping in to her dress. She'd have to hold her corset under her dress so no one could see it.

He walked over and took her in his arms and she fought until he whispered. "Yes, I do know what it's like. I do know. I'm so sorry." He kissed her and fell into her love and wrapped them both in his love and his strength. He held her until she was calmed.

"Celestine, I love you. I want to marry you. Let me make love to you."

He gently took her dress off; removed her petticoat and sat her on his lap in his reading chair. She was still crying but holding on to his arms. He held her to his heart and hated himself for being so damned clumsy. She put her arms around his neck and kissed his cheek.

I'm a big stud man of the world for God's sake; a big ladies man; and I've bumbled the most important moment of my life with the love of my life. He knew exactly how she'd felt a moment ago. He'd felt the same thing with Anna in Haiti years earlier and she'd made no accusations and asked no questions.

"Tell me you're sure you want to do this, Celestine. Tell me you're not afraid. Tell me to wait until we're married and I'll wait. I love you." He was trying desperately to regain his footing and start again.

She had to think. She was confused, but he said he loved her; maybe she'd been wrong again. She wanted to stay in his arms and let him make everything bad go away. His safe arms were the first she'd ever felt, and the most familiar thing she'd ever known.

"If we wait until our wedding night; I may change my mind. I invent dragons while waiting, as I did with your return. If this is as pleasant as Colette says, I'll marry you. If it's what I fear, I may not. But, if I wait, I'll surely be too afraid to marry you."

She didn't know where this bravery was coming from; maybe from his strong arms, but it was the truth. She reached her face up to his and opened her lips for his kiss.

Maurice had never had such pressure on his love making or ability to perform. It was his fault for misjudging her desire earlier. No, damn it, he knew in his heart she was to be his. He met her mouth and pulled her close to him. If she was ever to relax and make love to a man, it was now. She was right, if she waited, it'd get worse, just as it had with him.

He could do this; he could love her as gently as the great lover he was known to be. He reached under her chemise and opened her legs as he whispered for her to relax and let him take care of her.

"We'll go at your pace, my dove." He reached into her center and found the blockage that he was hoping was there. He picked her up and sat her on the chair and began to undress himself, slowly keeping his eyes on hers and thinking gentle thoughts. He kept his eyes free of lust and filled them with the love he felt for her at this very moment. Once he had taken off his shirt, he heard her gasp and he knelt down to reassure her she was still safe. Maurice had no idea that once Celestine makes up her mind she doesn't waiver, but steadies her course as she did walking in to the Ursulines convent years ago. Seeing him without his shirt sent strange shivers from her groin up to her breast and into her head. He was beautiful. There was no hint of the horrible flabby dirty men she'd seen with her mama. His chest was a wash board of muscles and brown chest hair making a beautiful design around his nipples and down into his breeches. There was a jagged scar on his side and she wondered if it was from a pirate's sword. She wanted to see more. She wanted to feel him. He smelled like the sea and fresh rope and her head was getting dizzy from her own lust awakening in her.

Maurice sensed something had changed in this young beauty. He didn't see or feel the fear she'd carried so bravely minutes before. Her breasts were beautiful, full and heavy. She was taking shallow breaths and staring at his manhood under his breeches. Her lips were open and wanting. He began to unbutton himself and slowly let his pants down to show her the full him. He was so nervous he began to wonder which the virgin, and who the mature lover?

Celestine sat in the chair watching him and fighting the last bit of fear in hopes he wouldn't see it and stop his advances. She didn't want to be treated like the little virginal victim. She wanted him to take her as his love, as Colette said her Pierre had done. She wanted Maurice to do the same. He came back to the chair, and sat with her on his naked lap without entering her. He kissed her breasts and was amazed at the silk of her skin. The little, pink rosebud of a nipple was velvet and warm in his mouth and caused her breathing to deepen. The little moans came from deep in her throat and made him crazy with desire. She couldn't stop her hands going through his hair and holding his head to her breast. He reached between her legs and felt for the little center that brought such pleasure to a woman when it was massaged, and began to give her pleasure.

He didn't want his erection to hurt her; he'd wait until she was in her ecstasy to enter her. He kept the steady rhythm with his massage, listening to her moans getting deeper and closer together until he heard her catch her breath and hold it. She opened her mouth to scream and he covered it gently with a big hand. He felt every muscle in her body tense and stiffen and he knew she was about to release. He lifted his knee and put one strong arm under her to move her hips over his erection. As she began to shudder and clutch his head to her heart, he sat her down hard on his member and felt the resistance give with a little 'pop'. She was moving herself in her release up and down his erection. He was delighted and surprised that she could fit him inside of her and sheathe him in her warm, wet center. He shifted to let her adjust herself to him and he pulled her hips up and down to her own rhythm until he could stand it no more. He spent his seed into his love; three months at sea desiring her and three months in port before that. She was still riding him to give him pleasure. He was enjoying a woman down into his soul for the first time in his life. He doubted if she could spend again as it was her first time and he didn't want to disappoint her, by making her sore.

He let his erection dissipate and pull itself out of her. He looked into her face. She began covering his face with kisses and taking his mouth in hers again and breathing calmer and settling herself into his chest.

Within seconds he heard her breathing turn to sleep and tears were filling his eyes. He'd never let her leave his arms.

When Celestine woke, she was sitting on Maurice's naked lap and he was asleep. She wondered how long they'd been asleep and if she had dreamt the wonderful afternoon, or was it real. She gently moved his arm from around her waist and started to get up, but it came back down strong and immovable and held her in place.

"You'll never get away from me that easily, my dove. Where do you think you're going, my pretty wench?" He was kissing her neck and she could feel his manhood waking up against her bottom.

He was kissing her breast again and suckling the tender nipples and she felt herself awakening again and felt the now familiar rush of erotic juices flowing in her center. She was awakened from her groin up into her stomach and chest. Her womanhood felt tender and a little sore, but she was willing to overlook that to feel the pleasure she felt a while ago. He picked her up and walked with her to the big bed. She saw the moon through the porthole; they'd slept for some time.

She wondered if Ste. Mary Clarisse was worried about her and would she cover for her until she could get home? Celestine looked over at the chair and saw blood on the cushion.

"Maurice, there's blood on the chair. Should there be? Am I all right?" She never dreamed she'd ask a man such an incredibly personal question as this, but it felt right to ask, it felt normal to ask this man who'd be her husband. He laid her on the bed and got in next to her.

"Shh, it's natural my, little dove. That was your old life leaving and your new one beginning. You're a woman now, my dove and you've given me your gift. You'll release when I enter you in the future, my love, until then you'll spend from other means. You are magnificent, my lady love." Maurice decided not to make love to her again. She'd be sore and he'd never hurt her. It'd worried him to press so hard in taking her the first time; he didn't think she felt pain, only the joy of her release and a bit of pressure. But he wasn't going to chance it again too soon.

Besides, if he kept her here longer, he'd want to spend the night with her and never let her leave his arms and that'd never do. Maurice got up and went behind the screen and found a dressing gown.

"I'll go on deck, my dove while you dress yourself. You'll find the washing bowl behind the screen." He kissed her more passionately than he intended. "If you need help with the bathing, call me, I'll gladly lend a hand." He smiled like the letch he felt himself to be and walked out onto the deck.

Celestine got up from the bed and went behind the screen. The soap was a manly soap not fit for her delicate parts, so she washed with the cool water and got dressed. She was nervous about going out on deck, what if someone from the convent saw her?

Once she was dressed, she opened the door and saw Maurice talking to a man on the deck. He walked back into the room and went behind the screen to wash himself. He came around the screen with his breeches and boots on and his suspenders hanging around his knees. He walked to his chest to get a shirt and when he turned she was holding the one she made. He was stunned. His life just kept getting better by the moment. He pulled the shirt over his head and felt the soft linen on his skin. It fit perfectly; how had she ever gotten it to fit so nicely?

She took the neckcloth and wrapped it around his neck and tied it so the initials could be seen clearly. She walked him to the shaving mirror and showed him the results. He was the happiest man alive. He pulled her up to him and held her off the floor with his big arms as he kissed her. Celestine watched as he put on his big jacket with the gold piping up the sleeves and took a sailor's whistle out of his breeches pocket and went to the door and opened it a crack and blew a series of short toots. She could hear boots running and doors slamming and then quiet. He opened the door and ushered her out onto the deck.

"What was that, Maurice?"

"My men making themselves disappear, my dove. Your ladyship?" He was offering her his arm to walk down the gangplank.

She couldn't move. She was shaking with anger. She wanted her knife; she wanted to cut his cock off, or at least an ear or two. This had been a tryst like how many others? His men knew the drill very well. It hadn't taken them two minutes to "make themselves disappear" for their stud Captain. The Captain who had a woman in every port; she must be his New Orleans's whore. Funny, she hadn't seen any money for her services. She was fighting back the tears. To think she'd been fooled into loving him.

"Ahhh," her gasp was audible. She'd just given this man her virginity and he hadn't even tried very hard for it. She presented it like passing the salt at table. She was waiting on the levee for him like a dock whore and he'd seen her as such.

Maurice reacted to her gasp. He looked down into the angriest face he'd ever seen on a woman and he'd seen many. Her beautiful blue eyes had turned the color of brackish lake water and before he could take a breath to speak, he felt the sting of his knife blade under his chin. She could cut his throat or leave a nasty scar; he was prepared for neither. He'd never seen such power and cunning in so frail a woman.

"You're not worth it." She returned his knife to the sheath inside his jacket.

"You may come back to your work, men. The Captain's harlot is leaving." She was down the gangplank and running away from this man who'd used her and degraded her for his own pleasure; just like all men.

Maurice's head was spinning. *She could've killed me and damned near did. What had I done? Harlot? Captain's harlot?* He wiped the blood from under his chin and saw the red soaking into his new shirtsleeve. What the hell just happened?

He was afraid it was too good to be true when he saw her waiting on the levee for him. *God give me strength to deal with this woman, it's going to take me and you working together. I'm not giving up; I'll have her. Just show me her demons, Lord, and I'll destroy them, or die in the trying; most likely the latter.*

Chapter Six

Celestine didn't stop running until she was back in her little cell in the convent. Ste. Mary Clarisse and Mother Superior followed her into her cell.

"What's happened, my girl? Has someone harmed you? Speak to me my child." The Reverend Mother knew a broken heart when she heard one. Was she wrong about Capt. Dubois? She'd been told his ship arrived earlier in the day.

Celestine was indeed heart-broken. This man had taken her heart and thrown it to the wind and watched as birds of prey attacked and devoured it. But he'd summoned the birds of prey and now he'd probably have her arrested. A girl didn't threaten to kill a mighty Sea Captain on his own ship full of his own crew; it was rude and probably illegal.

"Sister Mary Clarisse lock the big gates. We'll not be receiving Capt. Dubois again." The Reverend Mother's voice was controlled and stern and she'd not be taking back her decision anytime soon.

Celestine buried her face in the Reverend Mother's bosom and cried.

She didn't leave the convent for a week. Maurice was turned away several times. The Reverend Mother had to admit, he'd seemed confused and contrite but neither he, nor Celestine would tell her anything. Colette came to visit but couldn't get Celestine to talk. All Celestine said was she'd made a mistake about Capt. Dubois and she wished him well.

Celestine looked for three days before she found her knife in the back of the linen closet under some old bandages. She began to wear it again in her stocking. She thought about it; but changed her mind about killing him; he deserved at least to lose an ear, or maybe a finger. She knew she'd see him sooner or later and then it'd be a blow against everyman who'd ever taken advantage of every woman in her life. First would be for her mama and the next would be for the men who kidnapped her friend Colette, even if it had turned out for the best. Finally the last would be for her self-preservation. Her anger and hate were filling her with poison. She wasn't good for anything but planning the mutilation of the man who'd made her body betray her and come alive to his touch.

Maurice couldn't fight Mother Superior and the whole convent and they'd made a fortress against him that was damned powerful. If he ever became a wanted criminal, he knew where to hide. He was leaving on his next voyage soon and he wanted this settled before he left. If she'd just tell him what he'd done, he could deal with it, but he didn't know if it was something he'd done or something from her past that appeared as a result of their love making.

The love making he wouldn't think about. The sweetness of the love and the horror of her grabbing his knife and running away from him were too strange to relive. He knew too well the feeling of love and hatred in the same moment. He didn't have his Anna to advise him in this. Had Celestine been raped by the men who took her mother? No, she was a virgin. The answer seemed to lie in Maurice's own actions.

He'd begged Pierre and Colette to find out for him, but they'd been able to get nothing; only that she'd made a mistake. *Damn, women could be irritating. God forbid they ever went to war; the generals would just throw down their arms and beg for mercy.*

On the third week he wondered if maybe he'd made a mistake. Maybe she was too complicated and broken for him to fix. He wasn't a healer like Anna and didn't want to be. Maybe she was too far from his expertise and her demons were too big and too ensconced in her being, for him to conquer. He thought God would help, but so far no miracles had come, and he was leaving in a day for a very long voyage. By the time he returned she could've taken her vows or married some little boy she could mold and control. She certainly didn't have any problems in the bedroom. He'd like to take credit for that, but he couldn't be sure anymore.

Colette was determined to get to the bottom of what was happening to her friend. If Maurice had purposely hurt her she'd cut his heart out. Knowing someone in the parlor doesn't mean you know them in the bedroom and men could cover up their bad behavior without blinking an eye. Pierre was no help, he just kept saying he knew the Captain loved her and would never hurt her. It took Colette nagging constantly three days before he finally gave in and told her the truth about Maurice and Anna. He'd sworn her to secrecy, but he really didn't know his wife. She had no secrets from Celestine and she was bound and determined that Celestine would have no more secrets from her.

Celestine had finally ventured out to Colette's and Pierre's for dinner. She needed the good fun company and to feel alive again. She carried her knife and she knew she'd get her chance. It may take time, but she'd know when and where.

"Darling, you look wonderful." Pierre took her arm and ushered her into the drawing room through the courtyard. The night was beautiful and the soft breeze was sweeping the curtains into the big room across the big worn cypress floors. The candles in the chandeliers flickering in the breeze; made wonderful shadows on the high ceilings and threatened to go out in spite of their crystal shades. Celestine loved this house; she'd always felt at home here and hoped she'd always be welcomed.

"Celestine, how beautiful you look." Colette was walking down the big staircase and entering in a new dress that fit her perfectly.

Celestine was wearing the blue dress she loved; she'd decided not to burn it. It wasn't the material's fault an ass had bought it. They'd be having dinner in the courtyard and the table was lovely and inviting.

"Celestine, we want to talk to you." Pierre was not expecting this. He hoped the women would wait until he'd gone to bed before Colette started her inquisition.

"I have nothing to say, Colette. Please, let's have our dinner. Pierre, tell us some funny stories from the workmen up river."

Pierre scratched his head and rang for dinner to be served. He wanted to eat before this got out of hand. Colette had two glasses of wine before dinner and was saddling up for some high hurdles. She was always too involved with Celestine and her love life and it made him nervous.

"All right, Celestine, since we're only acquaintances and aren't good friends, I'll not ask why you've broken the heart of my friend. Who loves you... and is heart sick over your treatment of him." Colette was getting angry just thinking about Maurice's face when he begged them to find out what he'd done.

Celestine knew this moment was inevitable; besides, it was their fault for introducing her and pushing her to the man. It may as well be now.

"Colette, it's embarrassing, but if you must know. Your friend took advantage of me on his ship and when I was leaving he blew a whistle to warn his men to hide so his 'harlot' could leave unrecognized. I was on the deck of a strange ship just having given myself to a man I thought loved me and he showed his true colors as the womanizing, whoremongor he is."

Colette was up and holding her friend to her.

"Oh, my darling, how awful." She looked at her husband as if to say, your friend is a cad, but Pierre was laughing and shaking his head.

"That's it? That's the horrible thing he did?" He couldn't believe the ignorance of these two women.

"You women are such idiots. That's a Captain's privilege when a lady is aboard ship, so the men don't think her of ill repute? Or, in your words, a harlot? Why do women never ask before jumping into a bayou full of alligators? Would one of you answer me?" He was calming down enough to eat his dinner and shake his head again at the foolishness of women in love.

"Celestine, take that damned knife out of your stocking and give it to me. I owe the Captain too much to watch you gut him like a fish. I saw the scar you gifted him." Pierre reached out his hand and took the knife from Celestine.

"So, the old man got your virginity before the wedding, eh? He makes me proud to be a man." It was hard to chew his food and laugh at the same time.

"Oooh." Celestine couldn't believe she'd just confessed to what she was doing on board the ship, and she'd announced very loudly to Maurice's crew that she was, indeed a harlot. She'd die of embarrassment.

Celestine started crying and Colette knew it was going to be a long one. There was so much to cry about. One, she may have chased away the love of her life. Two, she'd given up her virginity and confessed it to her friends over dinner. Three, she'd have to find a way to tell the Convent it was all right for Capt. Dubois to call if he ever wanted to see her again. Four, she'd lost her knife to Pierre and Colette knew he'd never give it back.

Colette took Celestine upstairs to a guest bedroom; got her undressed and put her to bed. Celestine wouldn't be good for anything until this news had settled and she could figure out what to do and how to make amends. Colette sent Pierre to find Maurice. She knew her husband would be back soon; he hadn't had his dessert. Pierre found Maurice in a bar a few whiskeys away from sober. He helped him get his coat. Maurice paid the bartender and took the young lady off his lap and sat her on her stool at the bar and steadied her. Pierre buckled the sword belt around his old friend and told him if he hurried, he could share his dessert. Maurice walked unsteadily out of the saloon with Pierre, having no idea where he was going or why.

When he walked into the courtyard, Colette sighed and asked Petal for some hot water. She helped Pierre clean him up and gave him mint leaves to chew and escorted him into the dark bedroom and into bed next to Celestine. Neither Colette nor Pierre knew why they did this; it just seemed like a good idea at the time. They backed out of the French doors and went to have dessert.

"I guess if we hear a scream it didn't go well." Colette put to Pierre.

"If I know my Captain, there'll be no scream." Pierre admired his boss and his way with women. He'd been an inspiration when Pierre was courting Colette.

The storm clouds were rolling in and the wind came up the river from the Gulf and attacked the trees in the courtyard. The rain soon followed and Pierre and Colette ran to close the big double doors and windows. Thunder and lightning made for a safe night at home.

Maurice thought what good friends Colette and Pierre were. God only knows where he'd have ended tonight if Pierre hadn't come and gotten him. He was confused about his sex life. He didn't know if God wanted him celibate and waiting for Celestine, or if he could spread his seed in every port and walk away. He was tired and he wanted to sleep off the bad whiskey. He'd think about things in the morning.

Celestine cried herself to sleep. God sent her a beautiful husband and her jumping to conclusions and depending on her shady past to guide her destroyed her chances of being happy. Of course what Pierre said made sense. A whore wouldn't care if other men saw her leaving the Captain's quarters; she'd probably consider it good advertisement. The Captain certainly wouldn't care that his men saw a harlot leaving his quarters. What was wrong with her that she couldn't figure these simple things out before she ran off like a ninny with a knife in her stocking?

Maurice awakened first before dawn. His first thought was whether he'd paid the whore in his bed or should he get up and find his coat and get his money ready. He might like a little slap and tickle this morning, but he wanted to see her first. He'd awakened in strange ports with really strange women in his life and he knew not to start something he may not want to finish when sober. He rolled over and smelled a hint of cloves and saw the blonde curls spread on the pillow. *This was not your ordinary whore, he thought. Is this what Pierre had in mind for me last night and did I enjoy her? Oh my God, it's Celestine. His heart was racing like the storm outside.*

She rolled over and he was looking into her eyes, his hand began brushing the hair out of her face and she was crying and begging him to forgive her. She reached up and traced the little scar under his chin and started crying again. He held her and thanked God for her. It was as if they'd been sleeping in the same bed forever. It was warm, familiar and safe. God was good to give him back his woman.

He kissed her and she cried and kissed him at the same time.

"Do you still want me?" She sounded so small and helpless. He took her bottom in his hands and pulled her closer and she felt how much he forgave her and how much he wanted her. She didn't care about the men in her mama's past; she wanted to lie under him and have him enter her and make her his woman. God was good to give her back her man.

"Open to me, my dove and let me pleasure you." She gently pulled his arm over her to let him know she wanted him to enter her. He made love to her until the aroma of good strong coffee forced them to deal with the day and the storm.

"I want to wake up every day making love to you."

"Yes." She smiled and wished it true.

Chapter Seven

They were married one week later in the Cathedral of St. Louis. It had been easy explaining to the Reverend Mother that his proposal had sent her into a downward spiral. God, Pierre and Colette convinced her he was a good man and she'd learn to love him and be patient as his wife. The Reverend Mother was very relieved, she thought she knew people and to make such a mistake about the man had disturbed her greatly.

Maurice carried her through the muddy streets to the Cathedral to protect her shoes and dress. The wedding was sweet. Celestine wore her blue silk. Maurice wore his new linen shirt once Ste. Mary Clarisse got the blood out of the sleeve and his big blue coat with the gold piping.

Celestine visited the new perfume shop on *rue Royale* and M. Chenier created a scent for her. He'd sniffed around her hair and her shoulders and had decided on a light scent of soft Jasmine. She and Maurice were both pleased with the fragrance.

Ste. Mary Clarisse was making a shirt for Maurice. Celestine had almost finished another one by the time he was due to leave. He wouldn't know until he was out to sea that Celestine embroidered her name running through a tiny heart on the front of both shirts along the tail. Her name would be worn next to his manhood and none would be the wiser. It'd please him to know she was so close.

She filled his sea chest with clove soaps, mint leaves, and wild doe tongue leaves, to keep his clothes fresh on the long voyage. She filled his personal chest with peach preserves, strawberry jams, pickles, candied orange slices, Colette's alligator jerky, pickled quail eggs and wonderful things he'd want from home. Under his pillow she placed one of her handkerchiefs filled with her Jasmine scent.

The weather was too bad to leave that week, so he stayed on another week. In the two weeks before he left he'd accomplished a great deal. He'd married his sweetheart, bought her the house on *rue du Maine* from Pierre and Colette; put everything he owned in her name including *le Celestine* and helped Pierre and Colette move up river and... He was pretty sure he'd impregnated his wife. If not, it wasn't for the lack of trying. He'd be gone for almost a year but he hadn't had time to build the widow's walk before he left. That'd be his first project once he returned. He left with a list of furniture from Pierre and Colette for their new house and a smaller list from Celestine for their newly acquired dream house. He left thinking there was something important he forgot to tell her, but he was too busy being happy to remember anything but his charts and clothes she packed for him. Josef and Marguerite were closing up the little house on *rue des Chartres* and would be moving into *rue du Maine* with his new wife. Life was good.

Celestine was beside herself, she had the house of her dreams, but she was losing her man to the sea. She wouldn't be able to bear it; she knew it. She wouldn't be able to sleep without his arms around her and that big hairy chest under her head; maybe she should keep the cat as a pillow. The house was too big for just one person.

He hadn't been gone four days when the bell on the gate of the carriage way was ringing incessantly. She walked out to open the gate to see a young African girl she guessed to be around fifteen and a young man a couple of years older standing at the gate; both with satchels and baskets of their belongings.

"We're here, Misses." The young man had taken off his hat and was holding it clutched to his chest.

"Who are you and what do you want?" She figured they had the wrong house.

"Captain sent us misses; we're here for you." He looked confused, why did this woman not know or expect them.

"My name's Josef and this is Marguerite." Celestine had no intention of having slaves in her home.

"To whom do you belong?" She asked with her heart in her throat, she'd never had the discussion with Maurice, but she knew many of the ships were slave ships and she wouldn't condone that.

"We belong to you, misses. Captain bought us."

"Ahh," her gasp was audible. "Come in, please, get off the street."

What to do with this dilemma?

"When did my husband make this... purchase?" She was finding it hard to breathe.

"We've been with Captain for a long time." Josef was more confused, how much should he tell her? Would she turn them out before the Captain came back to rescue them? He put an arm around his sister. She was trying not to cry.

"Please go around to the kitchen and have some milk and a cookie. I have to think." She was incredulous. She'd love some help to keep her company; clean the house and take care of the horse and carriage, but she wouldn't own another human being. She'd seen too many slave auctions in the parade ground outside the Cathedral. Miserable children dragged from their mother's arms, young women holding onto husbands they'd never see again in this lifetime. She'd never be a part of that.

She walked into Maurice's new study and opened the drawer to the big desk. She grabbed the papers he'd put in her name. She was shuffling through the deed to the house and the ship and then in the very last of the papers was an old bill of sale for two slaves, one Marguerite Dubois and Josef Dubois. Born in Port-au-Prince, Haiti and sold to one Maurice Dubois in 1795.

These two people must have been children when he bought them. What did that say about her husband that he would buy children? He hadn't signed these papers over to Celestine. She found a legal document giving her power of attorney. *Praise God from whom all blessing's flow. She made the sign of the cross and went back out to the kitchen.*

"Josef, Marguerite? It seems my husband has made it possible for me to give you your freedom."

"Please, misses you don't understand. We don't want freedom."

"I don't believe God intended us to own each other and I'm religiously, morally and emotionally against owning another being. Therefore, I have to speak to my husband's lawyer and find out how I go about releasing you. Until that time you may stay in the rooms off the kitchen as my guests." She knew the guest part was totally taboo, but she had to think this through and decide what could be done.

She was ushered into Mother Superior's office and took a seat. She had the bill of sale in her hand and told the Reverend Mother everything.

"I agree with you, my dear. I think it's a good idea to go to his lawyers. It's important that this is a legal agreement so they can't be put back on that horrible slave block." She didn't want Celestine to see her face. The Convent had owned slaves, but not children. Why would this man buy children? Celestine walked around to *rue Royale* and spoke to M. Dubonnet. He wasn't in total agreement with her wish to give these people their freedom, but under the law, she was entitled to this action. He'd draw up the necessary papers and bring them around to her in a couple of days. He'd also send a letter with his next packet to let Capt. Dubois know of his wife's actions. This business of signing your things over to your wife was a bad citizen and he was against it from the beginning. What if she decided to sell *le Celestine* out from under the Captain? He'd then see his folly. If he were here, it didn't matter if her name was on a paper or not, a husband owned his wife's property, but with him gone for so long, she could sell anything and be gone before he returned.

Celestine went home and explained to the couple what she'd done. There wasn't the rejoicing she expected.   There was terror from

Marguerite and confusion and fear from Josef. She explained that they could stay in the house while she was gone up river to visit friends and when she returned, the papers should be completed.

She needed to speak to Pierre. She knew he didn't believe in owning slaves either and was a big reason he'd left his parents' plantation in Natchez. She needed to know what he thought about this whole business. She wondered if he knew about these two.

Chapter Eight

Maurice was gone four days before he realized he'd forgotten to tell Celestine about Marguerite and Josef. It didn't bother him much; he'd given Josef a letter of introduction and instructions for their safety. He'd write to her and tell her more and include it in the packet he'd be sending back from Haiti when he picked up a packet from his lawyer, M. Dubonnet. It'd only take a couple of weeks before she received it. He also decided to include some nice spices for Colette with his love letters to his wife and maybe a few souvenirs for Letty.

He found the shirts and couldn't wear them too often; he walked around with a huge erection knowing her name was resting on his groin. Maybe she could embroider his pillow cases instead. He laughed each time he thought of it. He slept next to her handkerchief each night and dreamed of her constantly. He never knew love could rob your time and energy and cloud your mind. He'd known sailors to moon over their wives while at sea, but he never understood until now.

So far the weather had been good and except for the choppy, square waves of the Gulf waters making the big ship feel like broken wheels on a rocky road, he made better time than expected. None of his men mentioned the incident with Celestine and her announcement on the levee; he appreciated it more than they knew.

Josef and Marguerite watching over Celestine and the house made him feel safe, but guilty that he hadn't introduced them as his wards. He worried about her being alone. With Pierre and Colette so far away she only had the little sister's to look after her. He wondered what Josef and Marguerite thought of his new wife. It'd take time for them to clear out the little house he kept in New Orleans before the new owners moved in. They were such a part of his life he couldn't imagine any acquaintances of his not knowing about them. He couldn't risk their being seen at the wedding; it was too dangerous but Marguerite would've loved it. She loved the ceremony and the pageantry of the church. He'd make sure the packet contained gifts for Marguerite and Josef from Anna. His life was working out better than expected. He didn't know his life was empty until he met Celestine. He should've told her about the two kids. The letter explained as much as he could write, the rest should be spoken and not written. Pierre could clear up any questions she may have, or she could ask the kids directly.

Maurice was a day out of Port-au-Prince when the weather began to turn ugly. He left the crew to weather the storm and went to his cabin to finish his letter to Celestine. The choppy boat was comforting and familiar. There were times when these storms frightened him and made him worry for his crew and cargo; but over the years he learned to read the sea and the wind. He knew when to worry and when to let it happen. This was one of those storms that could rock you to sleep or out of bed, but keeps you close to God. He'd always been a religious man; he'd weathered many storms with the old man's help and mercy. He found him in times of trouble and fear and he trusted him now to see his ship and crew into calm waters and the safety of Port-au-Prince.

Anna would know he was coming before he sailed into port. She'd have the little house clean and spruced up just for him and he was looking forward to seeing her and telling her about Celestine and his new life. He wanted to tell her how Marguerite was growing into a beauty and Josef was getting stronger by the day. She was so proud of them. One day he'd talk her into coming to live in New Orleans and give up her voudou. If she insisted, she could practice her religion in New Orleans. He was not her judge, if God needed her to change; he'd deal with it. Maurice would love for her to know Celestine but he didn't know how to handle his long time mistress and wife under the same roof. It could get a bit messy with one carrying a knife and the other carrying strong gris-gris. He could end up dead... or worse.

He could never give up Celestine, and he didn't want to give up Anna. She'd been his safe harbor since he first saw her. She turned him into a lover and taught him not to be afraid of his own sexuality. It wasn't an easy task, he'd been combative, mean and he fought like the devil not to feel anything but disgust for the whole business.

She'd won and her gentle ways and love for him had given him a normal life. He'd never wanted men, but for a while after the rapes, he didn't know what he wanted and he was afraid the men saw something in him he didn't know was there. He didn't want a man, but he didn't want a woman either. He listened as his friends bragged about the women they'd conquered and how mighty and manly they were in bed but it just made him want to hurt someone.

Killing the man trying to rape him on the British prison ship hadn't helped him feel good about himself. He was only eleven when he ran away from home to fight in the revolution of 1775. Before he was twelve he was captured and sent to the prison ships out of Charleston Harbor with other boys who'd done the same. He'd watched in horror as the other boys were exploited and hurt. He waited for his turn, he knew it was coming and he was prepared. He'd prepared a weapon from his spoon and used it right as the man was trying to enter him. Watching the man bleed to death with his pants down and pecker going limp, still haunted him. But the man's death allowed him the opportunity to escape and take a few of his friends with him. Once he was free, no one, not even the British, suspected a little boy had done such a brutal murder, but he knew he was capable of it and that terrified him. He went to sea as a cabin boy and never went home again.

Anna dealt with the memories of his past and killed the demons the memories created. He first saw her in the market of Port-au-Prince reading palms and telling fortunes. She was a black haired beauty, full breasted; her peasant blouse showing more than half of her dark-brown, silky breasts. An old leather belt held up her skirts and encircled her tiny waist twice. The end of the too-long belt hung over her groin like a long, limp penis. Her thin ankles and parts of her long legs could be seen when she propped one sandaled foot onto the carriage block. Her raw sexual beauty stirred something in his groin for the first time and he was intrigued to find this creature giving him an erection. He'd just turned nineteen and was celibate for so long, he'd given up the whole idea. Most times when he thought about the act, bad memories flooded in and erased any pleasure he was feeling.

He thought her a fake when she read his palm and told him he was a great lover. He liked her holding his hand though. He liked feeling her skin and looking into her black eyes. Her long curly lashes seemed to blink slower than most and he thought she was becoming aroused just speaking to him. She was intoxicating and he fell under some spell to follow her; listen to her laughter and watch her eyes looking deep into his soul. He followed her around the old square watching her take on more customers; hearing her laughter and watching as she drew them into her web. When she walked it was like dancing and when the music started in the square, she was dancing and she'd dance for the sailors and they'd throw money to her. He watched as hardcore sailors offered her their full pay to go with them. She laughed and stuffed their money down their breeches and felt around before she withdrew her hand and sent them on their way. Teasing them with: "Oh Monsieur, you are too large." Or "Oh Monsieur, I'd lose my heart to you and that monster in your breeches."

She was enchanting to an awkward, backward nineteen-year-old virgin and he thought he'd found the fountain of erotic lust. He followed her home later that night hiding in the shadows. She stopped and turned to him at her door and spoke into the shadows.

"You are a pitiful puppy." She moved to him, reached up and kissed him on the mouth. She smelled of spices and rich heady flowers and his head began to spin.

"Do you want to come in? I've seen you following me all night. Have you no girlfriend?" He shook his head 'no'.

"Why is that? You're a handsome young man and you have the smell of the sea in your hair. Did you not leave a girlfriend behind in America?" She knew exactly what his problem was; she'd seen it in his palm and she'd read it in his eyes and in his heart. He was an abused little boy who knew nothing of love nor pleasure or forgiveness. He was very angry and wanted to hurt someone. He was a dangerous young man and the challenge to heal him aroused her and pulled her into the danger.

She walked inside and held the door for him to come in. She poured him a drink of fine rum and showed him to a chair. He saw children's toys and clothes hanging on furniture to dry.

"You have children?" Maurice asked dumbfounded that this woman would have a normal life outside the market.

"I have a little girl, but she's with my mother the nights I work."

"Do I pay you?" He was so naive, but it'd be nice, he wouldn't have to think or feel.

"No, my bebe, I'm not a prostitute. I'm a fortune-teller. I don't want your money; I'll help you."

"Help me? I don't need help!? Who do you think you're talking to? I just came in here to buy sex. If that's not what you do, then I'll leave." He knew he was trying to swim in mud. He had no idea why he'd followed her in. But she embarrassed him in his ignorance.

She took his coat, put it across a chair and offered him the big chair. She gave him some more rum and sat gently in his lap.

"I allowed you to follow me home, mon ami. I'm lonely and I need a man; I need a kind lover and I believe that's you. The stars sent you to me."

Her voice was barely a whisper and so kind he wanted to cry on her shoulder and tell her about his life. He looked into those black eyes and wanted to please her and make her feel safe and take away her loneliness. He knew about loneliness. He could write books on loneliness. He was kissing her hard on the mouth and he thought he might break her lips. He was inhaling the delightful, heady scent of tropical flowers and humid nights and his erection was uncomfortable.

She reached up and pulled away from his mouth. She put two fingers on his lips.

"Shhh not so hard, *mon ami*; go gently into your kiss."

She took his mouth and kissed him gently and opened his lips with her tongue. He responded for a second and enjoyed her soft wet tongue on his. His mood changed and everything about her made him angry. How dare this whore tell him how to kiss a woman? He felt the need to punish her for the very erection he was glad to have. He was carrying her to the bed; taking off her clothes. She was undressing him and he caught her hands and threw them off. He threw her on the bed and spread her legs. He was too rough and he didn't care if she was lonely or needed a gentle man. He was driving toward a release he'd never had and he wanted her to suffer for choosing him and wanting him when he wasn't worthy. She needed to be punished for her choice of lovers. He spent and fell onto her and the rum and her scent and his release sent him into a fitful sleep.

He didn't wake until morning when he felt her mouth on him. He was about to explode; she was going down on him with her warm, wet mouth. He was seeing colors and wanting to spend and she tried to move her head and he wouldn't let her. He grabbed her head and held it down hard and before he could think, he was spending in her mouth. She was gagging and couldn't breathe and he was spending more and thought it'd never stop. He knew what he'd done wasn't right, but he didn't care. He'd pay her if she wanted. He didn't know how to please her so he'd offer her money. He could have no respect for a woman who would allow him to follow her home and spend in her mouth. What did she want from him anyway? She had a child for God's sake, what kind of mother was she? He made some stupid excuse and grabbed his clothes and left. He left money in a little box on the mantle as he crossed the little sitting room.

By the time he got back to his ship, he was angry. He was mad at himself for wanting her, but terrified; he hated that part of himself that'd tried to hurt her. He was confused that she'd aroused something in him that made him want more. The sea was his mistress, not women or men. He'd go back to his first love, the sea and the sea would soothe him and let him bury the feelings Anna had awakened in him.

There was a knock on Maurice's cabin door. The knock woke him from his memory and thrust him into present day.

"Will you be wanting dinner, Capt.?" Robert didn't like disturbing the Captain but knew if he didn't order dinner, he'd be hungry later and wonder why it hadn't been offered.

"No, Robert, thank you. I have some bread and mutton left from lunch."

He went back to his letter writing and tried to get the memories of Anna out of his head.

Chapter Nine

Celestine came out onto the courtyard, she'd have to hitch the buggy, a job she could do, but didn't like. It could get messy and dirt was always coming from somewhere to find a home on her skirts. She stepped through the carriageway into the stable and Josef was waiting with her Phaeton and her beautiful bay. An early birthday gift from Maurice; the bay was prancing and ready to go.

"Josef, thank you. You don't have to wait on me. I can fend for myself." She didn't even know how to treat these people who'd only known bondage. She was glad he was there though. Josef helped her into the rear seat of the little sports buggy.

"Josef, I don't think I can manage the reins from back here."

"No, Mme. Dubois, I'll drive. Captain says I'll drive." He'd never understand why Papa Maurice chose this silly woman.

Celestine had to do something soon. She was in ignorance here. She'd allow him to drive her this one time. Maybe she could hire them as servants; after all if they were to be les gen de couleur libres, they'd need work. She liked not having to deal with anything in the stables and her cooking was lacking in many areas. Colette was the cook, Celestine was the seamstress.

She told Josef where they were going and he headed toward River Road. They reached the new house sitting back from the river and were amazed at how beautiful it was. She felt like she was coming home. Josef drove up to the stairs of the big gallery and Pierre was coming down to greet them.

"Josef, so glad you found us, little brother." He grabbed Josef and gave him a big bear hug. He helped Celestine from the carriage and pointed Josef around to the back and the stables. Celestine waited for the Phaeton to go around the house before she turned to Pierre.

"You knew about him and Marguerite?" She was finding out a lot about this man and his Captain.

"Of course, didn't Maurice tell you about his two favorite "slaves"?

Celestine was incredulous. She was running up the stairs calling for Colette before Pierre could stop her.

"What's going on down here?" Colette was gliding down the grand staircase holding Letty in her arms.

"Did you know Maurice owned slaves? Children, Colette? He bought children in Haiti and now they are in New Orleans and I'm to deal with them and God only knows how many others he may own."

Pierre had run up the stairs trying to stop her from running away with her crazy ideas.

"Calm down, darling. It's not as it seems. He bought them from the hangman's noose and brought them here to save their lives."

"What?" She was more confused, "If he saved their lives, why're they still slaves, five years gone?"

"Pierre, explain to our dear, Celestine. She's worried that she's now a slave owner. They aren't slaves, dear?"

Pierre was not comfortable with this. Maurice should've told her before he left. He didn't like getting between a man and his wife with intimate details of their lives. To tell his Colette was one thing; a man often confided things in his wife, but to tell another man's wife things about her husband's past was just not done.

"It's not my affair to tell, Colette. Just suffice it to say Celestine, they are not now nor will they ever be slaves."

"But, I've seen the bill of sale. I gave it to our lawyer."

"WHAT, YOU DID WHAT? Woman, when are you going to learn to trust your husband and not go off on your own before you know the facts?"

Pierre was running out and around the back calling for Jake to saddle his horse. He yelled to Josef to hide until he came back and not to show himself to anyone. He told the women not to betray Josef no matter who asked for him. Celestine and Colette were left holding on to each other and wondering what the hell she'd done that was so wrong. They watched as Pierre pushed his horse to its limits down the drive and onto River Road.

Chapter Ten

Young Maurice had not wanted to go back to Anna, but once he was in port again, he couldn't stay away. He'd mellowed toward her over the last few months at sea and he thought of her often. He was still afraid to touch any of the women or wharf whores his friends found so amusing. He knew himself and he knew he'd hurt them or not be aroused by them and be labeled a woman in man's breeches. He walked into the market in the big square and she was there, sitting under a Pomegranate tree as if waiting for him. She smiled with her arms open when she saw him. She held him tightly and wouldn't let him go until he finally put his arms around her. She could feel how glad part of him was to see her. She walked with him back to her little house and as he hoped; the house was waiting for him with something cooking on the little fire in the back. It made the lonely and homeless Maurice feel welcomed. She gave him a drink of her fine rum; he sat in the big chair and she took his boots off. She pulled his shirt over his head and sat in front of him massaging his feet and cooing her happiness at his return. He was happy for a few seconds and then the old anger crept in and he looked down at this woman who knew nothing about him or his disgusting soul. How horrible and dirty she must be to find him loveable. Anna looked at his angry face. He was frightening her with his hatred. Maybe she'd mistaken this young man for a savable soul. She'd been wrong before. She couldn't believe she was wrong about Maurice; he had such sweet eyes and she'd seen good things in his palm. She'd weather the storm and see where it went. She reached over and took his hands in hers and brought them up to her lips and kissed his palms.

"Oh darling, you've been hurt in your life. Let me love you."

"How much?" He was staring at her; his jaw muscles about to break his teeth. He wanted to leave, needed to leave or he'd hurt her; but he wanted to finish what he'd started.

"I told you, I'm not for sale. I just want to hold you."

"You want to hold me? I don't want to be held, by you or anyone else. What kind of game is this? Where's your daughter? Huh? She with your mama while you're… 'working'? Tell me, Anna, why shouldn't I pay you? I paid you last time. You took the money, right? You took the money?" He was getting to the point of no return when the evil takes over and he has no choice but to follow; he'd felt it before and like the dope fiends in the brothels, he'd do anything to have his 'fix' and release the anger. She walked over to the mantle and pulled the coins out of the little box where he left them. She opened her palm and let them fall to his feet. How dare she, she was asking for it. He picked her up by her shoulders and threw her onto the bed. She was a dirty whore and he'd have her as a dirty whore and if she had any self-respect, she'd fight him off and throw him out. He'd gone too far, he knew he was about to rape this woman and hurt her but he couldn't stop. The knowledge of what he was doing made him angrier still and hate himself to the core; but still he couldn't stop. She raked his face with her nails and he backhanded her onto the bed and grabbed her blouse and ripped it open. He had a knee between her legs and was opening them in spite of her and he hit her again. He felt his fist in the flesh of her face and hit her again. He was struggling with his breeches… then he felt the blade in his side and felt the warm blood collecting in his clothes. She stabbed him. He fell back onto the floor holding his side and watching the blood seep through his fingers. He saw his breeches were down and his flaccid penis was lying across his groin. He'd reached hell and crossed a line into evil and turned into the very man who'd raped him years before. He hoped and prayed to die.

Maurice awakened in a filthy jail in Port-au-Prince. His side hurt and he had dried blood on a dirty bandage wrapped around his waist. If this was death he was in hell where he belonged. He groggily realized he'd become his own worst enemy. The man he hated for so long had taken his soul. A kind Priest was standing next to his bed with a bowl of warm soapy water.

"Lie quietly, my son. This will hurt, but we have to clean your wound, again."

"I don't deserve to be cleaned, Father." He began to cry like the broken child he was.

"We all deserve to be clean, my son. Anna has come to take you home. Will you go with her and behave, or should she keep the knife by her side?" Maurice had to take this in. She was coming to take him "home". Surely the Priest wouldn't let him go back to the place where he tried to rape a woman; to her very house? She deserved to kill him.

"No, Father I'll go to my ship." *Ah the safety of the sea, he thought. The mistress who could kill without pain, just a few strong intakes of her salty elixir and you could rest in her arms for eternity; peaceful, with no anger or fear.*

"Your ship has sailed, M. Dubois. You've been here for three days. You need to heal, you almost died. You still need to be tended."

He had to go back to her; he had no other place to go. Besides, he deserved her knife for what he'd done. His money was with his things on the sailing ship and his clothes were full of dried blood.

Anna was holding the door when Father Jerome walked him in and helped him into bed. Her little girl peeked around the corner of the little kitchen to see the man her mama stabbed. The neighbor children told Anna Marie about the night the constable had come and taken the young man to prison. Maurice had so much he wanted to say to her. He wanted to beg her forgiveness and tell her about his past and how he hated himself for what he'd become. He just didn't know where to start. He knew what he'd been through could either destroy a man slowly; or it could make a dangerous warrior to be feared and honored as with his little friend Andy Jackson from the prison ship. He realized he'd never be a warrior general and it was up to God to keep him from destroying himself and others.

Anna walked over to the bed and began to undress him and take his dirty clothes. She had a bowl of hot water with good smelling soap. He smelled sandalwood as she began to bathe his tired bruised body. Her face had a huge bruise where his fist caught her under the eye and another one on her beautiful cheek. He wanted to die from shame. He saw bruises under her arms and around her neck and he knew he wouldn't be able to bear the disgust he was feeling for himself.

"Why don't you throw me to the gutter, Anna? You and I both know that's where I should live." He was not looking for sympathy. He'd never been more honest or serious in his life.

She put the wet, bloody cloth back in the bowl and picked up his hand. She opened his palm and followed the lines with her fingers.

"This tells me who you are. You're not the man who hurt you; you're only a product of that hurt. You're good and you want to be kind, you just don't know how. You think he touched you because you weren't worth anything. The kindness you showed to your friends in killing the man and helping them will come back to you in the future and will change history.

"My friends?"

"Yes, little Andy and John and the other boys you saved. You have a happy life ahead of you, *mon ami*." She looked deep into his eyes. How did she know his past, maybe she could read his damned hand? *How did she know about Andy and John? No one could have told her these things about him. As far as living a happy life, she was clearly mistaken.*

"That man is now dead in you; I killed him with my knife, just as you did." She reached over and kissed him sweetly on the lips and he wanted to hold her, but his side hurt and he couldn't stand being that close to the bruises he'd caused on her face. She took his face in her hands and stared into his eyes and soul and whispered.

"It wasn't your fault what that man did to you." She waited for his reaction. But he had none to give; no one had ever said that to him, not even himself.

"It wasn't your fault. It wasn't your fault." Her whispers were balm to his soul. "It wasn't your fault. It wasn't your fault."

Maurice began to feel his muscles relax and his soul was moving and stirring and relief began to flood over him and he could see the sun coming in the window and a breeze catching the little curtain.

"It wasn't your fault..." She was still whispering the mantra in his ear and around his head and into his heart.

"Say it, my darling."

"It wasn't my fault. It wasn't my fault, it wasn't my fault." Tears were coming out of his eyes and wetting his cheeks and his nose was beginning to run and the muscles in his legs were relaxing and his mind was uncoiling and he saw black anger rising from his being like dark smoke from an evil fire. Some ugliness burst in his head and the poison was being drained from the terrible infection in his memory. He was breathing deeper than he had in years and he was seeing the bruises on her face as talismans for her martyrdom for the safety of all women from this boy who was broken by a horrible man. She was his savior and he'd cherish her and protect her for the rest of his life. He knew it, down where he was too young to know, he knew it.

He reached up and gently touched her bruised face.

"These are my fault though, Anna and I'm so sorry." She kissed his hand and continued his bath. She'd gotten through to him and she could relax. No woman would ever need a knife around him again. He let her finish his bath and then he cried himself to sleep. Maurice was learning to live with the newly found freedom from the fear and anger that'd been his jailors. He was up and about within a few days. His love for Anna was sweet and grateful and he'd miss her on the long nights at sea, but he'd be back. He hired on with a merchant ship leaving port going back to New Orleans. He'd be glad to be at sea again. He wanted to breathe the salt air and wind and take it into his clean soul and sail into his new life.

Maurice was awakened from his memory by a jolt from a bad wave; said a prayer of thanks for Anna and his past and continued his love letter to Celestine.

Pierre went straight to the lawyer's office.

"I'm sorry M. David, it had to be done. The girl is wanted for a brutal murder. I couldn't leave her to roam the streets of New Orleans and murder another innocent man, now could I? Capt. Dubois will understand when he knows what they did in Haiti. Her brother will be picked up soon."

"You don't understand, M. Dubonnet. It was all a misunderstanding. The children are not murderers. Besides, they belong to your client, why would you turn them in?"

"They belong to Mme. Dubois. She has asked for their freedom and I've honored that request. You must take it up with her, Capt. David."

"Where is Marguerite right now?"

"To my knowledge she is resting more comfortably than she deserves in the belly of the Cabildo. Good day, Capt. David."

Pierre turned back to the lawyer.

"I wouldn't want to be in your shoes, M. Dubonnet when Capt. Dubois knows what you've done with his children."

"What are you saying? These are Capt. Dubois own children? But they are murderers, cut throats?"

"No, M. Dubonnet; they are wrongly accused children of Capt. Dubois and I wouldn't give a piss of Gulf water for your life once he knows what you've wrought."

"Sit down, Capt. David and tell me everything and we'll see if I can reverse this action.

The lawyer knew of men who kept their own bi-racial offspring in bondage; he didn't' understand it, but these were strange times.

Pierre told the lawyer of Maurice and Anna and their long "friendship". He wouldn't mention Maurice's past, that was for no man to know. He told of Anna and how she'd healed a knife wound from an 'assailant' on the young Maurice and saved his life. He told of her little girl, Anna Marie dying in a yellow fever epidemic when she was very small. How Maurice tried to console her for years until she found and married a wonderful man, M. Moreau, who had given her two children; Josef and Marguerite. He told of the tragic death of this fine man and Maurice taking over the financial responsibility of the two children and their mother.

Once Pierre had M. Dubonnet's full attention he told of how Anna was attacked by a young English Sea Captain and the young children, ten and twelve killed the man to protect their mother. The man's friends pressed horrible charges against the children and they were in prison waiting for the hangman's noose. Captain Maurice Dubois sailed into port and "bought" them from the jailor and hid them aboard his ship and sailed out the same day. They'd been raised on board his ship until they were of an age to stay in port alone. He carried their papers for their own protection against the law. Pierre had seen the wanted posters himself in the ports of call around the Atlantic seaports. Maurice was hoping they would be forgotten eventually but they weren't as yet. For the last five years there were still sightings of the murderous children and their black evil hearts; strangely never growing any older in the rumors. Once they became of age, both children had pledged themselves to their "step father" and were his trusted companions and if you will,' servants'.

M. Dubonnet was astonished at this horrible news and what his actions may have caused. He'd never heard such a story and he had no idea how to rectify what he and Mme. Dubois had done. He and Pierre went to the magistrate's office and attempted to get Marguerite released as a case of mistaken identity, but the coup of capturing and jailing this young girl was too good for the magistrate to allow her freedom. He fully intended to get her brother and hang them both in the Place d'Armes so no other little black bastards would ever think of killing a white man over a whore.

Celestine couldn't calm down. What had she done that was so terrible? Why was she always in trouble for trying to do the right thing? She sent for Josef but was told he was nowhere to be found. That was ridiculous, why was he hiding from her? She sent word to the barn that he'd not be in trouble if he'd just come and speak to her. Petal found him and coaxed him back to talk to Mme. Dubois. Celestine was sitting on a little settee in the main drawing room when Josef entered the room looking around to make sure it was safe.

"Josef, please take a seat." The young man took a seat nearest a window in case he needed to make a quick exit. He was holding a wrinkled piece of paper. He held it out to her. She took it and continued.

"I'm a kind woman. I don't believe in slavery. I didn't know my husband had the inclination to own other human beings or he and I would've come to an understanding before he left. Please be so kind as to tell me why you reject my offer of freedom. If you feel strongly about working for Captain Dubois, I can pay wages and you and Marguerite can stay on as free people of color."

"My sister and I aren't slaves, Mme. Dubois." Celestine was surprised to hear he spoke as well as any gentleman in any parlor. He must have seen her surprise.

"I found this in my basket, it was under my books." He pointed to the paper she was holding.

Celestine opened the crumpled letter:

My Wife,

May I present my wards, or in my heart, my children? The lovely Marguerite , and the handsome Josef. They are as fine as I have told you and are looking forward to meeting you. Please let them help you in any way. They are more than happy to care for you while I'm away. They must not venture far from rue du Maine. Pierre will explain. I'll not write here, but will allow Pierre to embellish. I hope you will love them as I do. Their mother has been a great friend to me and I owe her my life.

Your loving and devoted husband, M.

"He didn't tell me. He told me nothing. Tell me now Josef, what was Pierre to tell me?"

"Papa Maurice is a friend of our mother's and he rescued us from being hanged in Port-au-Prince for a crime not of our planning when we were still children. The slave papers are a reuse for our protection from unjust laws." He was staring at her to see how his news was being received.

"Capt. David has gone to save Marguerite from the same fate if he isn't too late. We're still wanted criminals on the Atlantic Sea Coast, Mme. Dubois."

"Josef, why didn't you tell me? Why did you wait until now?"

"We've never told anyone. Our lives have depended on our secret for five years. I thought papa Maurice would've told you about us. His letter says he did." Josef was afraid he was saying too much.

Celestine was horrified at what she may have done to Maurice's ward-child. Why hadn't he warned her? He must have meant to or he wouldn't have put it in the letter. She would've loved to know she had people to care for while he was away. People he loved and trusted; part of him and his past; young people of color who called him, "Papa Maurice".

"I must make this right, Josef. Please saddle a horse for me. I'll not take the Phaeton and you'd better stay out here." She found Colette and told her as much as she knew and asked for a pair of Pierre's breeches and a shirt. She could not ride properly in a dress and corset. She was not cut out for the lady's riding habits and the sidesaddle was just silly and a man's invention. She was taught how to ride bareback as a wharf orphan, but she preferred a saddle. She hadn't forgotten how; she enjoyed the feel of the big horse between her little legs and the power they gave her.

On the way down the front stairs she turned to Colette.

"Give me the knife, Sister." Colette shook her head, Pierre would be mad as hell at what Celestine was doing, if she gave her the knife, he'd never forgive her.

"Give me 'MY' knife, Sister. Don't challenge me on this, Colette. I have a wrong to right and if I'm too late it'll come down bad on my husband and I won't have that. Give me my knife." Colette reached into her apron pocket and handed her the knife.

"Please be careful, my darling. God go with you." Colette always knew Celestine was much braver than she.

Colette didn't know this Celestine, however. Her voice was lower and her eyes were dark and she seemed much older than her years. Colette realized she was talking to the streetwise, wharf rat who bettered her life and soul but not her self-preservation and fighting spirit. She felt sorry for anyone trying to stop her at this point.

Celestine road down the river road not knowing what she'd find but feeling she needed to get Marguerite back up to Colette's or to the convent and keep her out of trouble. She had to get things straightened out with M. Dubonnet. She turned onto *rue du Maine* and saw the constable standing in her carriageway. She rode calmly and quietly into her courtyard.

"Bonjour, Monsieur may I help you?" She wouldn't speak until she knew what the hell was going on; maybe she was finally learning to think before acting.

"Bonjour, Madame Dubois. We're looking for a slave named Josef. We believe you may know of him?"

"No, I don't. I gave him his freedom. If that offends you, I'm sorry, but I don't believe one of God's children should own another." She was so calm she made herself nervous.

"If you'll excuse me, I've been riding and I need to freshen and start dinner. *Salut, Monsieur.*" She walked her horse into the little stable and loosely tied it to the post and walked calmly into her house.

The constable left. She seemed to be telling the truth. He didn't understand people who could afford slaves not having any. He thought it was the greatest system in the world. He'd love to have a couple.

Pierre was sitting calmly in the kitchen waiting for her when she came out of the stable.

"Marguerite is in jail in the Cabildo. I have to get her out. You have to help me by staying here and keeping the facade of innocent wife waiting for husband to come sailing in. This is important, Celestine."

"I know it is, Pierre. I'll not be blamed for this, damn it. If you or my husband cannot share with me the most important things in his life, how am I to know? Huh? Answer me, Pierre? How the bloody hell am I to know." She pulled her knife out of her waist and saw a spot directly over his head and threw it so fast he ducked. He heard the rat before he turned to see its blood dripping down the old kitchen wall. Pierre's head reeled. He'd never met street wise Celestine. *He wondered if his friend had seen this side of his sweet little dove. He was sure glad she was on his side.* She walked over and grabbed the knife and the rat and threw the rat out to the cat, wiped the knife with the shirtsleeve she was wearing of Pierre's and put it back in her waistband.

"I'm going to see Mother Superior. You'll stay here and play the calm guest waiting for me to return from the market. For once in your manly life, do as you're told, even if it is by a woman."

He was still gulping air from the knife coming so close to his skull. She didn't mean to speak so angrily to Pierre, it was meant for her dunce of a husband, but he wasn't here to take her anger. She was back out onto the streets and into the convent. She went into the back and ran to Mother Superior's office. What was she to say? She'd been brave up until now, but this was different. This was a place of gentle living, prayer and refuge, she was once more out of her league and approaching a woman who knew more about life than she ever would. She was thirteen again and the clean floors and gentle movements of the long black skirts were soothing and scaring the crap out of her. She couldn't imagine what Marguerite must be fearing at this moment. She knew she'd come to the right place. She knew it. She bent down and kissed Reverend Mother's hem and looked up at the kind eyes.

"I've done a terrible thing, Reverend Mother. I've put my husband's ward in terrible jeopardy and she'll surely go to the gallows if I don't save her."

Mother Superior had already heard of the young girl's plight. The city was still a small village full of gossips. The knowledge of his two wards had come up while checking out Captain Dubois and his past. Not that they were wanted for murder, but that they traveled with him. She should've told this young wife, but she had no idea he wouldn't have told her himself. She'd have to help Celestine. She wouldn't let an innocent child die knowing she could've helped.

Mother Superior and Ste. Agnes went to the prison to visit the young girl. They were taking her a basket of bread and cheese and some oranges. Mother Superior raised her sun veil to speak to the jailor. She knew him as a good man who wouldn't give them trouble. They were ushered in to see the young girl. She was nervous and clung to Ste. Agnes for support. They were only in with her a short time before they left the way they'd entered and walked quietly back to the convent.

The jailor was puzzled at the weird veils the nuns wore, but he'd seen the Reverend Mother himself. Still, something wasn't quite right. He went back in to see for himself. Mother Superior was sitting in the cell eating an orange and offered him some bread and cheese.

"Reverend Mother!! Do you know what you've done?" He was incredulous.

"Yes, my son, I've offered you a piece of my good cheese. Tell me, Gerrard. Where is the young girl that was in this cell a moment ago?"

"You helped her escape." He started to run to call for help.

"I wouldn't do that, Gerrard. You're going against God's law, my son. The young girl in your jail was a novice of mine and was put here by mistake." God would forgive her this lie and she'd confess the sin of it this very night.

"How did you get her out of the cell and you get in?"

"The lord works in mysterious ways, doesn't he, my son?"

He was going to be in such trouble.

"Now if you'd be so kind, as to unlock this cell, I'll help you out of your jam." He walked over and unlocked the cell door.

"HELP HELP, SHE PUSHED ME DOWN AND RAN AWAY, HELP HELP." The Reverend Mother winked at Gerrard and fell to the floor.

"Now quickly, run and tell your superior I was ambushed and the young girl escaped."

After answering questions from the main jailor, she walked slowly and calmly back to the convent. She enjoyed this wicked adventure, maybe too much. She'd have much penance for her enjoyment alone, not to mention the act itself.

Chapter Eleven

Celestine did not stop until she was riding into the long drive up the River Road. Mother Superior sent Ste. Mary Clarisse to tell Pierre to go home right away he was needed. She stayed and closed up the house on *rue du Maine*. Pierre was only ten minutes behind Celestine and wondered what the hell had transpired for him to go home so fast. Was he going to have to hide Celestine also? He saw her horse turning into his drive. She was not alone; she had a nun with her. He caught up to them as she dismounted and was reaching up for Marguerite. The young girl was crying and Josef came rushing down the ladder from his hiding place on top of the water cistern. He grabbed his sister and held her close to him. Pierre marveled at this woman who'd been his Captain's shy, sweet wife only a few hours before. She was getting out of a nun's habit and taking her horse around to the stables. What the hell had turned the world around? When had women started playing Robin Hood and nun's started wielding knives? Pierre caught up with her at the stables.

"Do I dare ask?" He was looking for the horns that surely protruded from her soft curls.

"Easy as stealing eggs from a hen's nest; rush in; grab Marguerite; rush out. What; you thought it'd be hard? Men." She was laughing and fell into Pierre's arms shaking all over. She let the tears release the fear she'd been hiding. She was holding on for dear life to this friend with the strong arms and gentle nature. *Why couldn't all men be like her Maurice and Pierre?*

"You're safe now, my darling. Shhh. You were very brave and now you're safe. Pierre is never going to let you do that again. Understand? Do you understand, Celestine?" He was looking into her face with his stern eyes telling her how dangerous her mission was and how foolish she was to have done it alone.

"Do you have any idea what Maurice would do to me if anything happened to you?" She had to admit, she hadn't thought of that.

"I couldn't help it, Pierre. I couldn't take a chance on his going to jail or losing his little girl." She knew she'd have to do it again if it kept her husband out of trouble. And she might if they couldn't hide Marguerite and Josef.

"Oh, Celestine, my darling, are you all right?" It was Colette running into the stable and upsetting the horses.

"Marguerite told me what you and Mother Superior did for her." She grabbed her friend from Pierre and was walking with her back to the house.

Pierre felt like a stud horse too soon out to pasture. *Women using men, love us up then leave us out to pasture.*

Celestine knew what she had to do. She'd dress and drive back into town as if nothing had taken place. She had to make this right. With the whole Parish looking for them, they'd surely be found. The whole country was brilliant at catching run-a-ways, it was an art form, there were people who made their living doing it, hired on for large sums of money and usually got the terrified people they sought. She had no good place to hide these two. This was one mistake Maurice was going to have to rectify before she took anymore of the blame. Once more she forgot she had Pierre on her side. The same day, he sent his wife and child and two young "slaves"; gifts for his parents to his parent's home in Natchez on the Mississippi. Letty was almost a year old and hadn't spent much time with her grandparents and her visit was a wonderful gift for her and his parents. Colette would be too worried about him and Celestine to do anything but sit on the long porch and shred handkerchiefs.

Celestine went back to the city, opened the house and waited five days before going back to see M. Dubonnet. She found him sitting at his desk in a nervous fit watching her glide into his office as if nothing had happened.

"What are you doing here, Mme. Dubois?" He bent to whisper in her direction.

"I'm here to inform you of the death of two of my slaves. They were found in the bayou down in Barataria. I've had them buried down there and I'd like two death certificates drawn up if you wouldn't mind, Monsieur."

"This will never work, Madame. There are too many people looking for them. They've been at the convent every day since the girl escaped."

"Then they should've looked elsewhere and found them before they drowned in the swamp like animals, Monsieur."

She was holding steady and not about to change course.

"I don't wish to charge anyone with their deaths. I'd like it to be quietly recorded in the court and I wish to hear no more of it. Once my husband returns he can go to the proper authorities. This is a man's business and I'm just an uneducated woman trying to do the right thing." She looked up at Dubonnet with cold steel blue eyes that threatened to cut his throat if her request was not granted.

"I'll draw up the papers, Mme. Dubois. I must warn you, there'll be officers wanting to examine these graves." He looked to see a reaction but got only a lovely smile instead.

"Of course, M. Dubonnet. I'll be glad to escort them myself."

She left his office and walked back home. What the hell would she do if asked to present graves and bodies? She hadn't been home two hours when she heard the cries on the street that the young murdering slaves had been found dead in the swamps of Barataria. Another hour brought the constable to her gate. He had an entourage and wanted to see for himself the graves and bodies. Celestine went upstairs and dressed in her traveling clothes and met them back in the courtyard. She'd said prayers and rosaries and given it over to God. The children were in His hands at this point and should be safely in Natchez. She had done all she knew how. She knew the trip to the non-existent graves would take two days on a small boat and she had to pack and pray.

She was sitting in the front of the little boat using every brain cell she could muster to invent her next lie. She was actually surprised they believed her thus far.

Pierre was told of her excursion when he went to the house to check on her. Neighbors on either side were anxious to tell him of the deaths and her trip to show the men where to find the bones.

Oh damn. What had he and Colette done by getting Maurice involved with this crazy woman?

He paid a visit to M. Dubonnet and found the gossip was true and he should set off at once. He hired a boat and started down the bayou. Pierre knew he could go faster than the boat full of men, but they had a half day's head start. Celestine was becoming more worried by the hour. What would they do to her? Would she be jailed? That'd be a nice homecoming for her husband. Would they hang her? No, Pierre and M. Dubonnet would never let that happen. Would they? Both men were exasperated over her mistake and this latest lie wouldn't make them happier.

They were in the morning of their second day when another boat approached from the south. There were three men in the boat looking like the men she'd grown to know and hate mounting her mama in the little crib back on the *rue du Quai*. Maybe she'd come full circle. If they meant to do mischief the men in her boat could do some damage also.

Chapter Twelve

Jean Laffite had been told about the little blonde haired woman; the wife of a Sea Captain who rescued a young slave from the gallows almost single handedly. He was new to this territory, were there more women like her, ready to cut a man's throat for pleasure? He looked into this boat and saw the most beautiful young woman he'd ever seen. An angel with a halo of blonde curls escaping her hood; with skin that'd be warm milk to any Tomcat. Surely this was not the very one who'd ridden into town in men's clothes and attacked the twenty jailors at the Cabildo? What a treasure! He wasn't usually envious of another man, but this was a woman to be reckoned with. *What the hell was she doing on his bayou and how could he keep her here?*

The men pulled up alongside the boat holding Celestine.

"*Bonjour, Monsieur.* What brings you down my way?" Celestine looked over at the dangerously handsome man dressed in black. He was not at all like his men. He was classically handsome, with a large black mustache and bright hazel eyes. He had broad shoulders and muscular legs with the air of the open sea about him. He'd be at home on a ship or in a fine drawing room. This was a man to be noticed.

"We're looking for the graves of two young slaves Mme. Dubois says are around here. She says they were drowned and buried in these swamps and she's here to show us where."

"No need, Monsieur. I buried them myself, but alas, I'm sorry to say Mme. Dubois, the graves you chose were too shallow and the gators ate both bodies." He looked at his men who both shook their heads sadly and removed their dirty hats in respect of the dead.

"How could you let that happen? Monsieur... " She didn't know a name so she left it at that, she'd heard lately of a pirate moving into the area, but had no idea this would be he.

"Monsieur what, Mme. Dubois?" It was the guard asking her the question and looking at her face.

"Don't be ridiculous, Monsieur, Jean Laffite and Captain Dubois go way back. Don't we, my pet?" He was bowing and giving her a darkly handsome and very sensual smile. She caught her breath at the beauty of his hazel eyes with the long black lashes.

"Of course... Jean. I'm sorry I accused you. You're right; I chose the graves myself. I should've known they weren't suitable."

She smiled at the man and relaxed into the smile he gave back.

"You must stay for the night, Madame. My men will take you back in the morning. We have so much to talk about. How is your dear husband?"

"He's fine... Jean. He's in Haiti at present." Why had she not said he would be sailing into port any moment? Now this pirate knew her husband was not going to be home anytime soon.

"Give me your hand, my pet; we don't want the gators to see you as dinner." She had no choice; he could give her over to her lie at any second if he so chose. She reached out her hand and felt to see if her knife was still hidden in the little sheath sewn to the bone in her corset under her arm. It was snuggly safe and waiting.

"I'm taking your word for this, Laffite. If you say the slaves are dead, then I believe you. You have no reason to lie about this."

"Of course not, Monsieur. What do I care if the gators eat a couple of lost souls?" He looked at Celestine's eyes turning dark and angry.

"Sorry, my pet; just having a laugh with the officer."

Pierre had seen the exchange from a distance and wondered what the hell had transpired. He'd catch up to them soon; he may not be able to save her, but he could die trying. If he knew this waif, Celestine she still had her knife and the pirates had better fend for themselves.

Maurice received Dubonnet's packet and headed back to New Orleans the same day. It was his fault; he knew his wife didn't believe in keeping slaves. It'd never crossed his mind she'd try to free them before he returned. He'd been headed back for five days. He was making better time coming back than he expected. Anna had asked him to leave the day he arrived; she'd begged him. She knew her children were in danger, but he couldn't turn the ship around on her premonition alone. If anything happened to the children he'd never forgive himself for not telling Celestine to protect them. He thought he had. Had Josef not given her his letter? Why had Pierre not stopped her? He'd reached the mouth of the Mississippi when he stopped a fishing boat to inquire of news of New Orleans. If the worst had happened he'd be a sitting duck sailing into the harbor to be arrested and then he couldn't help anyone. All the fishermen could tell him was that the two young slaves had been killed in the swamp and eaten by the alligators. Jean Laffite had buried them himself.

There must be some horrible mistake, why would Josef and Marguerite be down this far in the first place. He couldn't let it rest. He had to see for himself. He put *le Celestine* at anchor and took the dingy into the bayous. He knew there was a mistake, there had to be a mistake. Anna would never forgive him and he couldn't stand her losing another child; especially since it was his fault and his alone. He didn't want to think about losing them either. They'd been with him five years on sea voyages and land and before that they were the only family he knew. Marguerite was only a baby when her father died, and Josef was a toddler. He'd taught them to read and write and the sailors taught them how to read the stars and use a sextant and other instruments of the sea. They worked as his "servants" because they wanted to pull their weight and there was no other reason for a white Sea Captain to travel with two young people of color around the Atlantic. They kept in touch with their mother and sent her gifts from far away ports. Maurice made it possible for her to spend time with them on the safety of his ship when they were in port. It'd worked out as well as could be expected. He left them in New Orleans this time so they could help Celestine and she could watch out for them. His stupidity may have caused their deaths and he'd not rest until he knew for sure.

Celestine was in way over her head. She may be a street rat, but she was in the company of a pirate for God's sake; and not just any pirate, Pierre told her he was known as the Terror of the Gulf and you don't get a nickname like that by being a friendly uncle... And, she owed the dangerous man a huge favor. He was smitten with her. She knew it. He was the perfect host to Pierre and herself and kept them in his compound for two days. Pierre was trying to stay brave, and she knew if push came to shove, he'd die protecting her and she sure didn't want to leave Colette a widow to raise Letty alone. Celestine looked over at Pierre's bravery and thought he seemed more like a brave mouse in an owl's nest than the seasoned sailor he was. Whatever happened she'd tell Colette of his bravery under pressure. She'd gotten them both in this mess, and she needed to get them out. The children would be safe until she could get back and have their names officially changed and new papers drawn up, but they'd not be slave papers; they'd be official adoption papers.

She needed this man's protection. His dark good looks and beautiful eyes would turn her head if she weren't so in love with her husband. This was a man to be reckoned with in any situation.

Celestine was discovering that a dangerous man with beautiful eyes and gentle manners was a sweet challenge to any woman's affections... and lust. Asking for protection for Marguerite and Josef until her husband came home would be another big favor, but she needed it.

After dinner the men all disappeared except for Pierre and Jean. She knew Pierre wouldn't leave her alone with this man. She hoped he wouldn't; but not for the reason Pierre suspected. She was on dangerous ground here with her newly awakened power over men and wasn't as comfortable as she should be in this particular situation. She thought of playing the damsel in distress to the pirate, but he'd regaled his men at dinner both nights with her exploits at saving the girl single handedly from the gallows.

"Come, my pet, walk with me in the moonlight." Your friend can watch you from the gallery. He wouldn't be much help if I intended you harm, nez pa?"

"Don't underestimate him, sir. He's very brave and owes my husband many favors." Surely that didn't sound as simpleminded to him as it did to her.

"You're the brave one, my pet. Tell me, why'd you come into my world if you thought you'd be in danger? Does danger amuse you?"

"Of course Capt. Laffite; why else would I be walking in the moonlight with such a handsome, dangerous man as yourself?" *Woe, she was alluring now. Yes sir; She'd have him eating out of her hand in no time at all.*

The big pirate turned to her; put an arm around her waist and pulled her so close she could feel his response to her flirting. He kissed her deeply and found her tongue a willing partner before she could take a breath.

"Do not toy with me, Madame. I can be a generous lover or a very dangerous adversary. Or, I can be your friend. Which would you prefer?" He released her and stood back. His look told her he was deadly serious.

I'm in such trouble here, oh damn; what have I done? She turned to see if Pierre had seen the kiss, but he was looking at something coming up the bayou.

"Capt. Laffite?" *She had another idea.*

"You were calling me Jean at dinner, why am I now Capt. Laffite?" He was enjoying this much more than she.

"Jean... I'm only a simple woman in a man's world and I need someone intelligent and powerful like yourself..." He was laughing before she could finish her sentence.

"Take the knife out of that... oh, so beautiful bosom, and we can discuss your frailty, my pet." He whispered a bit too close to her face. His desire was growing and making her nervous as hell; she was realizing too late she was just a few sweet words away from being seduced by a master of the art. She had no idea he could see the knife, obviously he'd been looking closer than she cared. *Oh my God, he felt it when he kissed me.*

He ran his hand over her breast and felt the silky soft skin and felt her shutter as he reached into her dress around the short stays and pulled out the knife. His eyes were still laughing at her when they both heard the dark voice coming from the Bayou.

"Is there something in my wife's dress that interests you, Captain Laffite?" Maurice was standing; hand on sword waiting to draw, his blue eyes dark with anger. The two men on either side of him were prepared to die defending their Captain and his wife.

Pierre came down from the gallery.

"Hold back, Maurice, Laffite is displaying bad manners, not a threat. He's the hero here. He helped us lie to the authorities and rescue Marguerite and Josef from certain death."

"Are they safe?"

"Yes, they're safe at my place in Natchez." Putting your hand down a woman's bosom in front of her husband was far more than bad manners, but Pierre knew how many men were in and around these palmettos waiting to spring at Laffite's command.

Maurice read Pierre's intentions and stepped back.

"Pierre get my wife's cloak, we're leaving." Pierre ran back to the gallery to get the cloak and satchel she left on the gallery.

Maurice walked over, picked up his wife and put her over his shoulder. As he was carrying her off, she put out her hand, frowned and snapped her fingers twice and Laffite threw her knife which she caught in mid-air.

It was amazing how brave she could be on top of her husband's big shoulder. She gave Laffite her best smiling 'thank you'. She wouldn't forget the part about 'dangerous adversary' and she didn't know if she'd need his kindness again. They could hear his laughter all the way back to the dingy. Maurice got to the dingy and sat her down and gave the order to go back to the ship.

"Maurice, I..."

"Don't speak, wife." He was murderously angry and the pirate's laugh made him want to kill.

"Maurice, may I just say..." Maurice turned to Pierre and the young man hadn't seen his Captain this angry since he had the man flogged for raping Pierre years ago.

"But, husband..." Pierre was motioning for Celestine to be quiet.

"One more word, wife and I'll throw you overboard and the alligators can have their way with you." That was rude. She wouldn't tolerate rudeness.

"How dare you, sir?" She'd had enough. She stood up...

With one flick of his big hand and arm he tilted the dingy fast and hard and she flew over the side of the boat into the bayou. Pierre went in after her.

"Maurice, help me! Get me out of here." She was holding on to Pierre and trying to reach the boat before an alligator could come and get her.

"Keep talking wife; it's a long swim to New Orleans, but you already know that, don't you? You've made the trip before." He turned back to the bow and kept his eyes straight ahead.

Pierre and the men fished her out of the water and covered her with her cloak. She wasn't even going to say 'thank you' to the men. She had her swamp bath for the evening. She saw the masts of the le Celestine and knew he'd be wishing he could change the name now, for sure. They came along side and Maurice went to the back of the dingy and put her over his shoulder again and climbed the ladder back onto the deck of the great ship.

She was crying now. She didn't like being treated like a bad child. She didn't like her handsome husband mad at her and she certainly didn't like being humiliated in front of the whole crew.

"Robert, prepare my wife a cool bath, please." He took her into his cabin and threw her on the rug.

"Don't move. I don't want my cabin smelling like the swamp. It's bad enough that I have swamp on my clean coat."

He poured himself a brandy and sat down in his big chair behind his desk.

"It's not my fault. I didn't know about the children and you should've told me."

"You think that's why I'm so angry?" His eyes were dangerous but finding dark humor in what she was saying. She was becoming frightened. She felt for her knife.

"Isn't it?"

"You allowed that man to put his hand down your dress."

"I couldn't stop him. What was I to do, fight him off in the middle of a swamp and have his men kill me and Pierre both? If that's why you're angry, then you'd better direct the anger toward him and not me."

Maurice looked over at her and was deadly quiet for a moment.

"I saw your eyes, Celestine."

"What?"

He looked back over at her and surprised himself at his anger and the
depth of his fear. He hadn't felt such fear since his days with Anna when
he was young and stupid with hate.

"You enjoyed it. You enjoyed the man's hand on your breast." His
voice cracked just enough to make him want to leave the cabin. He
finished his brandy, threw the glass against the wall, and walked out onto
the deck.

She wanted to scream obscenities at him and scratch his face and cut
him with her knife, but she couldn't. She'd indeed enjoyed it and to her
unbearable sorrow; her husband, the love of her life, the reason for her
happiness was witness to it and was hurt by it. *Thank God he hadn't seen the
kiss.*

Her bath was set up in the cabin and she went into it sore from being
pulled from the swamp; stinking like the swamp and wondered what the
hell happened to her in the swamp. She let the clove soap melt her
tension and ease her sore muscles. She dried herself, put on one of his
nightshirts and got into bed. She rolled over and sobbed herself to sleep.

Maurice found Pierre and sat down with him. He wanted to know
what happened with the children and legally where they stood. Pierre
told him everything. He told how Celestine was angry about finding he
owned "slaves" and how she'd come to him for advice, but only after she
had gone to Dubonnet. Then he told of her getting Marguerite out of jail
and riding with her all the way up river. He told of her calmly going back
to New Orleans and waiting a decent time before notifying Dubonnet of
the "death" of both "slaves". Finally; he told of her going alone into the
bayous with the authorities and how Jean Laffite had lied to save her and
both the children. He also told him about the rat and how dangerous his
wife could be with a knife. Finally that cut through to Maurice and he
laughed in spite of his anger.

"My little wife scare you, did she?" The look on Pierre's face said it
all. Maurice could believe his little wife in men's clothing wielding a knife

dangerously. He still had the scar from the knife under his chin. His desire for her was growing in spite of the fear of what he'd just seen in the bayou.

"Tell me honestly, Maurice. If a beautiful woman, not your wife, put her hand down your breeches, would you not enjoy the moment? Honestly, *mon ami*. Would it make you think less of your wife or desire her less?"

Maurice stood smoking his cigar by the railing looking out at the river. Pierre knew he'd hit a nerve with his friend. He'd wondered how Maurice dealt with Anna when he sailed into Port-au-Prince.

Maurice remembered his thoughts of Anna and how his love for her couldn't compare with what he felt for his wife. He could even make love to the woman and still desire and think of Celestine while he was at it.

"Yes, I'd enjoy it and no, I'd not desire Celestine any less."

Maurice walked over and clapped a hand on Pierre's shoulder.

"Thanks, my friend. I owe you for protecting my wife and family. I'll do my best to keep her from getting you killed in the future." Both men laughed at how true the statement could be.

He walked back in to his cabin. His wife was asleep with red eyelids and puffy cheeks from crying. She was gently hiccoughing in her sleep. *Could a man love a woman anymore? She looks so tiny in that big nightshirt cuddled into the pillows. God, I'll give up Anna, just don't make me have to compete with that bloody pirate.*

He got undressed and got in bed. He put his arm under her neck and she snuggled close to him and buried her face in his chest. She woke up and looked at his face. She was still hiccoughing a little.

"You get one of those in a lifetime, wife. Don't let it happen again; and certainly not with that damned pirate." He took her in his arms and kissed her and she opened her mouth and hiccoughed into his kiss.

"I love you, husband. Let me pleasure you."

"Will it get Laffite out of your head?"

"Who?" She pulled him down and took his mouth in hers.

"Pleasure me, wife." He lay back and thanked God for this woman, once again. She sat up; got on top of him and opened her legs. She let him in slowly until she could feel him touch her core. She cinched him in and nestled herself around him and decided she liked having sex with this man. He tried not to spend too soon, but she felt so wonderful and the idea that she preferred him over the handsome pirate, made him crazy with lust and desire and he couldn't hold it any longer. They slept for what seemed like days.

They sailed into New Orleans and he went to the house to get her some clothes to wear. They walked together along the market and bought food to have in the kitchen and she bought some peaches. They picked the best shrimp and oysters; fresh onions, garlic, peppers and sausage to make a wonderful gumbo. He picked his favorite hot breads and she picked her favorite sweet cakes and went back to the house. The two of them made a feast fit for lovers and ate and talked half the night. He told her about the children and how he'd been the only father they'd ever known. He finally told her about his past and saving his friends, Andy and John from the prison ship. Then he told how Anna saved his life and his sanity and he told her about his life in the little house in Port-au-Prince. This gave her the courage to open up and tell him about her life and her mama. Her awful guilt for not going to her as she was dying and asking for her, and how it'd haunted her for the last four years. They held each other and felt the bond only a husband and wife can feel once they've cleared the air of old secrets. They slept until the sun came in through the big French doors. Maurice wakened first and whispered in her ear.

"Open to me, wife and let me pleasure you." A morning request that Celestine wanted to hear for the rest of her days. She rolled onto her back and welcomed him between her legs and thanked God the memory of her past life was dead. He was her husband and would be welcomed in her center forever. Suddenly, she pushed him off and jumped out of bed and went behind the screen.

"Ah, morning calls." He said to the air.

Maurice knew he had to make decisions before going back out to sea. He couldn't leave her and the children after what they'd just been through. He made the decision to take them with him on the long voyage. He wouldn't tell her yet, but he'd talk her into it. If not, he'd have to kidnap her, like the sailor he was; sling her over his shoulder; up the gangplank; hoist the sails and down the river to see the world, kidnapping. It'd be fun. He was smiling to himself and picturing the whole event as he heard her retching behind the screen. His little dove was sick. If she'd gotten something from the swamp he'd never forgive himself. There were fevers and illness in the brackish water and he'd thrown her in himself. He heard her washing her mouth in the bowl and waited to see how she looked when she came back around.

"I'm hungry. Husband, please bring me some of that cake from last night? Please dear, I'm hungry and I think this baby might have a sweet tooth."

He sat up in bed and sighed. Well, his prayer was answered; he wanted her to be with child, but not so soon. He couldn't take a pregnant wife on such a long voyage, especially a first time pregnancy; and he couldn't take the children, they'd have to stay and help her. He got up and took her in his arms and looked down into her eyes.

"You knew I wanted you on this trip didn't you?"

"Yes," She didn't want to show him her disappointment. She'd planned to ask him to take her and Marguerite and Josef. She couldn't bear his being gone so long. I'm still hungry... and I didn't plant this seed by myself, husband. I believe it was your first entry into a little virgin, on a beautiful ship with a gorgeous name." He laughed and walked out of the bedroom and down the stairs to the kitchen. She felt her stomach to see if there was a mound, but she was flat as ever.

He finished in the kitchen and started back up the stairs.

"You won't be able to walk around the house naked once the baby is here and the children are back. You know that, right, husband?"

"Yes, wife, I know that." He got into bed and held the cake for her to come and take it from him.

"Why are you holding my cake in bed?"

"If you want it, come and get it." He put the plate on his stomach and gave her his best lecherous smile. She reached over for one of the peaches, picked up her knife and peeled it; cut it in half and took out the pit. She shaved the rough edges around the nest where the pit lived until it was smooth and wet.

She was remembering what Pierre told Collette. The head of the cock is like a strangely shaped little fat heart. Caress under the little indention in the heart with the tip of your tongue and then take the head in your mouth and go from there. She got into bed next to him and held it for him to take a small bite; then cupped it around his big erection until it was covered in the sweet juice and bits of fruit. She moved the cake to the side table and went down to suck and lick the peach juice and bits off of him. She started with the tip of the heart and then took the head and took just enough in her mouth to lick the juice and then allowed the flavor to fill her mouth with saliva and she went all the way down until the spongy velvet head was touching the back of her throat and farther down. She gently sucked the sweet juice coming back up and circled the head again and went back down for more juice that collected in the hair around his seed. She could do this all day. He smelled of fresh cloves and peaches and the scent was filling the room and making her dizzy.

He'd had women gift him this pleasure, but this was different, he never felt anything like this, but he was worried where she'd learned it. She kept going for what seemed like forever; the stickiness of the juice and the warmth of her mouth were driving him toward an explosive release. He couldn't move or think and he wanted her to do this forever, but he knew he couldn't wait much longer. He'd moved her head and she'd gotten the peach again and started all over. He tried to move her head away again and she wouldn't. He spent and went farther down her throat than he thought humanly possible and she continued until he pulled her up to his kiss. She tasted of seawater and peaches and he was dying with love for her.

Reality set in and he knew there were questions that had to be answered by this woman carrying his child. Where could she possibly have learned this? She'd been a virgin, he was there, he knew; he'd experienced it first hand, but a woman could be a virgin and still have done this before. The thought of his wife's mouth going down on another man's cock was raging inside of his head and bringing up anger he no longer thought he harbored. She was lying next to him and she looked over to see his eyes changing with his mood.

"I knew it, damn it, I knew it. I told Colette this would happen. Don't look at me like that, husband." She should have told him first, but she wanted it to be a surprise. She turned away from him. She didn't want him to see her cry again.

"Turn to me, wife." She turned back to him. Usually she loved it when he gave this little order, but at the moment, she didn't love anything about him.

"Just tell me what it is you knew, wife?" He was waiting for an answer. He wanted to kiss her again and use the peach on her, but he had to know. She stared defiantly at him and aimed to wound.

"My friend, oh what was his name, something to do with 'feet'. Remember him, the nice man from the bayou?" *There, take that my ass of a husband.*

He was out of the bed and pacing and running his hand through his hair and didn't get the joke until he looked back and saw her smirking at his jealousy.

"Why would you do that to me, Madame, why? Are you out of your mind?"

"It amuses me." She knew it was a terrible thing to do, but if he was jealous of a lover who didn't exist, then he deserved it. What he'd seen in the swamp was hurtful, but hadn't the last two days of making love convinced him of her desire for him and only him? He grabbed his dressing gown and walked angrily out of the room and onto the gallery.

"If you're going to the kitchen, bring me another peach." She got up and found her wrapper and ran down after him.

He was in the kitchen stirring the ashes in the big fire place to get coals to make coffee. She could see he'd never been teased this much and he was trying to be patient, but was more angry and confused than amused. She went up behind him and put her arms around his waist. She spoke as lovingly and softly as she felt at the moment.

"You cannot possibly believe that man does anything for me, husband. Not when I have you. Don't you know the power you have over me? Is that it? You don't know how much I desire you? When you're not here I have to keep from touching myself thinking of you."

He didn't answer her. He was taking in everything she said and wanting to believe it so desperately. Anna never joked like this and his long relationship with her was the only thing he had to compare to his relationship with Celestine. His women in the other ports wouldn't dare try to make him jealous. He didn't know how to handle it.

"And, while we're talking, do you want this baby or not? You haven't even said you're glad?"

"Oh, wife, of course I want this baby." He turned and took her in his arms. "I just didn't think it'd be this soon. I wanted you to go with me and now you can't. I have to leave you here in your confinement and worry about you every damned day."

"Why can't I go? You know how to midwife and the sea air would be good for me. We need to get Marguerite and Josef out of here until things calm down."

"I only know how to midwife in emergencies, Celestine. You need to be under the care of Dr. Pabon and the good sisters. You need to eat right and not live in the stale cabin during bad storms. It's out of the question, so just keep still." She took the cup of coffee he handed her.

"But..."

"Keep still, wife." She knew that tone well enough. She loved when he called her wife, but when he said it in the mood he was in, it reminded her of stinky swamp water and rotting vegetation.

"I'm sorry, my love; I'll do as you say. Maurice, you have to know, I'll always do as you ask, my love."

"Then answer the first question you didn't let me ask in the bedroom?"

She looked up at him and decided she'd better tell him the truth. She sat down at the table, defeated; her one try at mature romance and mystique squelched by her husband's petty jealousy.

"Pierre taught Colette and she showed me on a banana." *She hated telling her secrets, why couldn't he just find her mysterious?*

He stopped to let this sink in. He started laughing. He picked up a banana off the table and handed it to her.

"Wife? Each time you see this, please think of me while I'm gone." He was laughing so hard now he started coughing.

"Or do you need a bigger banana?" He was still laughing.

"No, that one will do just fine... once I bite it in half." She turned and stomped back upstairs. *Why did men make nice things women did for them so hard to appreciate?* She turned and headed back downstairs and walked into the kitchen.

"The next time Colette teaches me something, I may seek out a pirate and try it on him?" He came over and took her in his arms again.

"You think he'll want you now, fat and round with my seed growing in your belly?" He was laughing at her again.

"Ooh, Husband." She pulled away and marched back upstairs.

Maurice picked up a peach and walked back to the bedroom. He liked to eat a peach now and again himself. The smell of peaches wafted through the bedroom for more than a day. She'd been stuffed with fruit and cleaned out like a filled peach tart until her legs stuck together. He'd been licked and sucked and left limp and sticky with fruit juices. They were happy and the only thing they had to fear was a few fruit flies and hungry ants.

Chapter Thirteen

Marguerite had known gut-wrenching fear in Port-au-Prince while she and Josef watched as the little gallows was being built outside their cell. She was so young and wanted her mother, but Josef assured her God was not going to let them die. Josef had powers like her mother, but watching the weapon of your death being built by big men and their hate; made her doubt her brother's promises and bravery. She wanted her mother, but didn't know if she was alive or dead in the little hospital where she was taken after the man stabbed her. She could still see and smell the blood and didn't know a human body held that much. She knew some of it was from the young English Captain but the rest was from her mother. The man took her knife and turned it back on her over and over again.

Josef acted first and hit the man with his mother's big black skillet, but Marguerite had grabbed the knife, slippery with blood and stabbed the man with his pants down. She didn't know if she killed him or not. She only knew that she wanted to. Josef took the knife from her and plunged it into the man's heart.

When the man's friends came to take him back to his ship, they yelled bloody murder and called down the street for help. Now she and her brother were in this stinking cell covered in their mother's dried blood and their own nauseating fear.

Marguerite's mother brought angry men home to 'heal' them. This was part of Marguerite's life. The only life she knew; it wasn't strange to her just different from what other mothers did. Her friends on the street tried to tell her it was not right, but their mother's took men to their beds for money. Marguerite knew that was not right. What her mother did was an act of kindness, Josef told her that. She remembered being very small and seeing a small portrait of her sister, Anna Marie and wondering where she was. Her mother couldn't talk about her without crying.

Papa Maurice sat her on his lap one day while her mother was gone and told her the story of her beautiful sister and her death. He told her how unhappy her mother was until she and Josef came along; the two of them had saved her life. Marguerite's father died before she knew him. Papa Maurice said he was a fine man and he loved her and Josef very much. The only father Marguerite knew was her Papa Maurice. He was a handsome Sea Captain who showed up un-announced three or four times a year and sometimes stayed for weeks. He brought them big hugs and kisses with gifts from faraway places and books with wonderful stories. There were other men in her mother's past, who came to visit, but Papa Maurice was different; he belonged in the small house with the little family. It felt like home when he was at home.

Once, he came and had a terrible row with her mother about taking up with bad men, and he left angry. She and Josef didn't speak to their mother for days for making Papa Maurice leave. When he returned, he was angry with them and gave them stern lectures on how to treat their mother and they never did it again. Sometimes when she or Josef was in trouble they'd go to the harbor and watch for his ship. He'd never let their mother spank them when he was in port. It'd make her mother mad as hell, but he stayed true to his word, as they knew he would.

She started crying all over again thinking about him and how sad he'd be to come home to find his little family dead. She wanted to sit on his big lap and bury her face in the smell of his shirt and hold the match while he lighted his big cigar.

Josef loved to watch him shave and was allowed to fill the shaving brush with the sweet smelling soap his mother made. Those days were gone and Josef told her she'd have to be brave and wait for the miracle he saw coming. She wished with all her being she could feel as calm as

Josef, but she heard his tears at night. She knew most of his bravery was for her.

The hammers stopped. She and Josef ran to the window. It was finished. The smell of new wood was making her sick. She and Josef stood entranced looking out of the window at the two little ropes hanging from the new structure.

Marguerite heard his boots running on the old tile floors of the jail and Josef looked back at the door to the cell. She could smell the cigar in his coat before the door was opened. Papa Maurice ran into the cell and grabbed both. He picked her up in his arms and bent to let Josef climb onto his back and he was out of the old jail and down the street. His men on either side, swords drawn and ready to kill anyone trying to stop them, would follow their Captain to hell if it came to that. He was running toward the harbor. Josef jumped down and ran ahead of him. The dingy was dipping and swaying in the water as if calling them to hurry. They were in the little boat and Marguerite still wouldn't let go of his neck and he didn't expect her to. Josef was sitting so close to his papa they could've been joined at the hip. Papa Maurice still looked stern and she knew they weren't safe yet. She didn't care now, as long as she was buried in his shirt and could hold onto him, nothing bad would ever happen to her again. She wanted desperately to ask about her mother, but was terrified of the answer. Crying gently into his shirt she listened as Maurice bent his head to their ears and said.

"Your mere is safe and getting well. She'll be in hospital for a few days, but she loves you and she'll be fine. The bad man's dead and she's not blamed. She tried to take the blame, but they didn't believe her." He was staring into their upturned faces to make sure they'd understood him. He got to the ship and carried her up the ladder. His men were bringing up their belongings and putting them in the bunks they'd prepared for them. She never knew how he'd known to come and find them, nor how he'd found her mother, but that magic was part of him and his store house of powerful gris-gris. That was her Papa Maurice, and she loved him with everything in her young soul.

Marguerite's fear at being in this jail in New Orleans was far worse than her fear in Haiti. Josef was there then and she had Papa Maurice. She didn't even know where Josef was and Papa Maurice was out to sea for months. She'd seen more sorrow and fear in her fifteen years than most people see in forever. She'd wanted to go with him on this trip and see her mother, but he'd asked that they stay and look after his young wife. Of course they'd agreed. She still hoped her mother would give up healing young men and move to New Orleans and they could all be a family again, but now that he'd married Celestine that'd never happen.

He wanted them to love her and they'd try. They'd certainly try. They'd do anything for him. He was her father and if he wanted her to mend his socks and wash his under clothes, she'd do it. It's what daughters in her world did for their papas. But he wasn't here and he wasn't coming and the God he'd taught them to love must have a reason for calling her home to heaven. She'd seen the Ursulines in their gardens and she wondered what it'd be like to be one. She always liked helping people, especially young mothers with their children. She loved children and thought of having many, but first Papa Maurice would have to find her a husband and set them up in a safe place away from the bad laws that kept her and Josef captive. She'd never know about having children now, she'd have to wait and see if God would let her attend to baby angels in heaven. Heaven was a wonderful place; she'd see her sister and her real father and wait for her mother and Josef and Papa Maurice to follow. She discovered this heaven on the big ship during rolling storms that wouldn't stop and nights passing pirate ships on the horizon waiting to attack.

Papa Maurice always out maneuvered the deadly pirates and flew flags of all nations to disguise his ship from the enemies that waited to slit a little girl's throat. He knew each of the dangerous ships and which would attack which flag. He wasn't a Captain to take his cargo lightly and was probably why he was sought by the wealthiest merchants to carry their goods.

She heard the soft fluffing of the heavy material and saw the dusty black hems of two nuns from her bunk as they walked up to the cell door. The guards said something to the two nuns and left them alone. One pulled a knife from her habit and slid it into the lock and after a few twists and turns the big door came open and Celestine was holding her in her arms and putting a hidden habit from her skirts over her head and down around her slim body. The Reverend Mother was fitting a wimple over her head and pinning it under her hair. There was a strange veil coming down and over her face and she was being walked out of the jail and into the sun. She was walked up to the convent and around back. Celestine mounted her horse; reached down for Marguerite and helped her up onto the saddle in front of her.

Celestine   rode   up   rue   du   Quai and traveled along the curving river until she got to River Road, on her way to Colette's. Marguerite didn't even ask about leaving the Reverend Mother behind in the jail cell. They rode until Marguerite was feeling sick at her stomach from the fear of being in jail and the strange escape; plus the rocking of the horse's big muscles. It seemed like forever and it was getting dark. She saw a drive up ahead. There were horse's hooves behind them and Celestine pushed her horse faster and they turned into the drive. Marguerite saw Josef climbing down from a big water tank and running toward them. She was handed down from the horse into Josef's arms as Pierre rode up beside them. He rushed them into the house and up to the third floor and ran back down to Celestine.

The very same day she and Josef were shipped off to a place called Natchez. It'd be safe, but she'd act as Letty's nurse and Josef would work with the horses. She missed her mother and Papa Maurice but was glad to be safe again and she had Josef.

They'd stay until it was safe. Letty was just learning to walk and each day Marguerite took her along the levee and pointed to the different boats and what they were hauling and how fast they could go. Letty loved the big river, but was afraid of the water.

Marguerite was falling in love with Colette. She wanted to be just like her. Colette taught her how to do her hair and make the curls that looked like God himself made them. She didn't like being treated like a slave by Pierre's parents, but she'd rather this than the dank cell in New Orleans. Colette was worried about Celestine and Pierre and wanted to go home, but they had to wait for him to come and get them. If that didn't happen, Marguerite wondered if she'd actually become a slave. She didn't know what would happen to them. They'd already been here too long and she didn't like the way people expected things of her that wasn't fair. She'd had to take care of Letty, and do laundry and kitchen work. She had milked cows and was the last to be allowed to go to bed at night. She was sleeping on a cot in Letty's room and she was up at dawn with the baby and not in bed until late at night. Still, it wasn't jail and there was no hangman's noose waiting for her. She sure wished there was a happy middle ground.

Colette called from the front of the big house and ran down to the levee. Pierre and Papa Maurice were coming down the river. The keelboat was pulling into the pier extending out to the big river and the men were walking onto the pier.

Marguerite screamed for Josef and jumped up and down with Letty. She hadn't been this glad to see him since he rescued them in Port-au-Prince. She knew he'd come, she knew it.

He and Pierre were on the levee and Papa Maurice was walking toward her with the biggest smile she'd ever seen. She and Letty ran up to him and he picked them both up and swung them around until Letty was screamed with joy at seeing her Papa. Josef was running from the stables and calling his name.

"Papa Maurice, you're here." He stood back looking contrite and a little ashamed.

"What's wrong, son what've you done?" Maurice knew when Josef had been into mischief, he could never hide his shame.

"I forgot to give Madame your letter. I forgot you gave it to me." He was about to tear up.

"Don't blame yourself, son, I take the blame here." He reached over; grabbed him to his big chest and gave him a hug so tight Josef thought he was being burped.

Maurice's strange little family was together and safe. He could leave on the long voyage and only worry himself to death over the health of his wife, not the imprisonment of his children. He really should stop calling them children, they were grown and Josef was almost an adult and big as an ox. Marguerite was holding him around the waist and trying to walk and he wouldn't dislodge her for anything in the world.

M. and Mme. David were giving him a strange, disapproving look from the front gallery, but he could give a rat's ass. He liked being a papa.

Chapter Fourteen

Maurice was gone seven months when Celestine had their baby boy, and didn't come home until the baby was three months old. The birth was hard, but un-eventful with Marguerite in attendance. In the last year, Marguerite was being trained as a nurse at the convent but she really wanted to be a midwife and help the African women in the city. They weren't allowed the hospital and too many were trusting in voudou and African folklore to help with difficult births. Marguerite felt there was a nice combination between the scientific medicines of the day and the medical gifts from the forests and each was equally important.

She helped Celestine through a long labor, but her body was so prepared to give birth after the months of plying her with medicines from the woods and feeding her the right foods, that Celestine considered her a genius. She hadn't gained one unwanted pound and her skin was oiled and greased into stretching without leaving marks and if one didn't know, they'd never guess the young woman had gone through child birth. Marguerite taught her how to nurse the baby and keep her nipples from getting too sore and her breast from sagging with the heavy milk. Marguerite enjoyed her work and used Celestine as a grand experiment to see if her lotions and potions worked. So far they'd been outstanding and her Tante 'Tine was a grateful recipient.

Josef was working for a blacksmith. Celestine had gotten him an apprenticeship and he was enjoying learning a trade, but he still took care of Tante 'Tine and was devoted to her.

They both fit nicely in les gens de couleur Libres and Josef was seeing a young woman named Augustine. He thought she'd make an excellent wife and was anxious for papa Maurice to give his blessing. The people of New Orleans accepted them as servants for Captain Dubois but still talked behind closed doors about the murderous children killed in the swamps and buried by Jean Laffite. Some said they were twins and were under ten when they were eaten by the big alligators. Some said, no, they were closer to fourteen or fifteen, but none knew them as the two young people working for the Captain and his wife. Josef knew gossip had a way of destroying itself and turning ridiculous along with the truth it destroyed in the process.

Celestine kept herself busy during her husband's absence. She had her charity work through the convent and part of that work was to visit the cribs and little houses along the levee and make sure the children had food and warm clothing in winter. She knew what that would've meant to her as a child; a nice hot meal once in a while. She saw herself in so many of these lost children and she saw women like her mother still plying their trade; accepting the horror they thought they deserved. Most days Marguerite went with her, but many days she went alone.

Jean saw her going in and out of the little cribs and places a woman expecting a child shouldn't frequent; one of his men watched her at all times for her own protection.

Josef kept him informed of her outings and unbeknownst to her, her safety was in Laffite's control, not hers. Josef was working as an apprentice in Laffite's blacksmith shop run by Jean's brother Pierre, if you could call it an apprentice. He mostly fronted their shop and worked on his own ironworks. He suspected they were running slaves and plunder from the back, but he wouldn't ask and he certainly wasn't going to tell. The brothers were glad to 'help' when they discovered this was the infamous, Josef, the slave 'buried' and eaten by the alligators in the swamp. The whole idea amused them.

The first Jean saw her after his kiss in the swamp was on market day several months after her husband sailed out of New Orleans. She was a little thicker around the waist and he guessed she was with child. He knew he'd never leave her unattended if it were his child she carried. He had many children and his women were always protected during the long months of their confinements, not necessarily by himself, but there was always a man of his choosing watching for trouble. He loved his mistresses as any man, but this little waif was different. She was a fair maiden and she needed a dark, handsome knight and he wanted to be that knight. Of course, this little maiden would cut your throat and feed your heart to the crabs, but that only made her more desirable to his jaded heart.

He'd been accused of being a pirate, but he considered himself a privateer, a corsair, and would shoot any man who said differently. Lately, he wanted to be a dangerous pirate and sail with her around the world by his side; her knife ready to cut or kill, her soft breast and mouth desiring of his touch. He was a hopeless romantic, but he'd kill any man who said it.

She was startled when he approached her in the big market. He thought he captured a bit of embarrassment on her beautiful face; why not, she was a married woman and she'd responded sensually to his kiss and he felt her shudder when he ran his hand along her breast. It'd changed his life and filled him with a desire he hadn't been able to quench with other women. He'd been jealous of her husband for months and now to see Dubois' seed under her dress was almost more than he could take.

"Madame Dubois; how nice to see you." He was the parlor gentleman at his best.

"Captain Laffite. I knew we'd meet again. I'd like to thank you again for the favor you did for my husband's wards. Josef is very happy working with your dear brother." She offered her hand and he turned it over, gently took off her glove and kissed the palm. He held it and breathed in the Jasmine scent a bit longer than she found comfortable, but she was safe with her husband's child in her womb and her head couldn't be turned by his charms. If anything, he caused her to miss her husband; seeing and feeling this handsome virile man kissing her hand. She gently pulled it back and began to put on her glove.

"I believe that belongs to me."

"For now, Madame, but who can read the future, nez pa?" The dark green and gold of his hazel eyes were bringing back the old feelings from the swamp.

"You go too far, sir. You forget, I'm a married woman." He'd angered her with his insult and she needed to leave before she said something she'd be sorry for later. He bowed and allowed her to walk away. He had his answer, she desired him as much as he her. She just didn't trust it yet. Had she not been angered; had she flirted back, he'd have known it as innocent flirting. But she felt something that frightened her. That was a good sign. A very good sign and her idiot Sea Captain left her alone for months, what a fool.

Celestine went on with her life, missing her husband and anticipating the birth of her child. The next she saw of Capt. Lafitte was months later. She was coming out of one of the cribs when she saw a man start to strike a little girl. She rushed to stop the violence. Jean stepped from nowhere and grabbed the man by the collar and threw him away from the little child. She rushed to the child and held her close.

"It's all right, my little lamb. You're safe now?" The little girl was crying. Jean stepped up and took the child in his arms and walked with her to the market and sat her at one of the stalls.

"Oh monsieur, you've saved my little girl. You're a good man. How can I ever repay you?" The woman was over playing her role. He looked at the bad actress and raised an eyebrow and nodded his head for the woman to stop. Celestine missed that bit of theatrics, but she knew the child didn't belong to the woman in the stall selling peppers and onions. She stood back and watched the performance as the big pirate pretended to sooth the child and take his compliments like a hero.

"Berti?" Celestine said. "Isn't your mere waiting for you to help with the milking?" The child looked past Celestine and up to the big pirate and gave a shrug.

"I tried to tell him you knew me, Mme.'Tine. Men don't listen to little girls." She was off and running down the levee to her family's barn.

She stood trying not to laugh; waiting for him to say something.

He was speechless. He'd never been speechless in his life; he could hold a conversation in any drawing room in any mansion, he spoke four languages fluently, but he was totally speechless. He tipped his hat.

"Good day, Madame." He was walking off when her laughter stopped him.

"That's it? That's all you have to say?" She was hurting she laughed so hard but once the laughter stopped, the pain didn't. She was big with this child and suddenly she was standing in a puddle of water and she thought she'd wet herself.

"Ahh, Jean, Help me?" She turned to him first, he had many children; everyone knew he had many children by his beautiful quadroon mistresses. He looked over at his beautiful torment, her eyes were full of fear and she was looking to him for help. She lost the water holding Dubois' child in her womb. She was in trouble and she called on her knight. *That fool of a husband of hers; he doesn't deserve her.*

He picked her up and walked up *rue du Maine.*

"Why are you out alone so close to your time, Madame?" Celestine was surprised at the anger in his voice.

"Where is your husband and why does he allow this?" He opened the big gate calling for Marguerite.

"Hush, Jean. Please don't criticize my husband." The contraction made her grab her stomach with one hand and the lapel of his big black jacket with the other as she buried her face in his jacket. He was met by Marguerite in the courtyard and shown to Celeste's bedroom. Once he put her on the bed, she perked up and thought maybe it was a false alarm, and then another contraction hit and she cried out to Marguerite.

"I'll return with the doctor, Madame, please don't fret."

He was gone and Celestine was left to deal with the pain and her embarrassment of losing her water in front of this man who reproached her husband for making a living. She was angry but was in too much pain to care. She, the doctor and Marguerite worked all afternoon and into the night. When the doctor placed her little boy in her arms and finally left, Jean got up from the little table under the banana tree. He didn't notice the mangled and bent decretive iron scroll on the table he caused each time his damsel cried out in pain. He hadn't moved since he brought Dr. Pabon back to her, nor would he consider it when Josef offered him supper and a carriage home.

He walked upstairs and saw she was sleeping. He bent and kissed her forehead and left his card on the empty pillow next to her. He'd be back. *What a damned fool her husband was.* Jean lost his only wife in child birth; he'd not wish it on any man. *Dubois shouldn't have left her alone to walk the streets big with child so near her time.*

Chapter Fifteen

Maurice was a month longer than expected. She'd spoken of it to Jean during one of his afternoon visits with her and the baby. He showed her on the charts where *le Celestine* had been and for how long. He was told that *le Celestine* was in Port-au-Prince a full month longer than needed. Celestine was devastated to hear this news. She'd envisioned him pacing the decks rushing home to meet his child and take his wife in his arms.

Jean was a good friend and she depended on him to fill long evenings and winter days when the baby was too young for her to venture out. He was kind and gentle with the baby. He made her laugh and remember times before her husband left and took the life out of the big house. Jean hadn't gotten personal since the day on the levee and his behavior endeared him to her even more. She looked forward to his calling card on the little silver tray in the music room off the courtyard. It meant he was waiting for her or he'd gone but would be back. She didn't know how lonely she was until he started visiting. The friendship was a terrible mistake.

When the baby turned two months, he stopped coming around. She missed him and wondered if she'd done or said something to offend. She took Marguerite and Josef and the baby for a fortnight's visit to Colette and Pierre. She was glad to be out of the city and looked forward to lively dinners and seeing little Letty. Colette hadn't seen the baby and wrote that she must come for a long visit. The visit was lovely, but Colette and Pierre were distant. It wasn't until she'd been there for most of the visit when Colette asked her about her 'affair' with Jean Laffite. She was dumbfounded; where'd this accusation come from?

"The city is small, 'Tine and he's infamous. His every move is followed and watched. Don't you love Maurice anymore?"

"Colette, what are you talking about? Of course I love Maurice. There's no affair with Capt. Laffite; he's just been keeping me company, that's all. Why'd you ever think such a thing?" She was trying not to get angry, but these were serious allegations and she could lose her beloved Maurice. She hadn't forgotten how jealous he was of the Pirate.

"Maurice has been told and he's written to Pierre to have the rumors dispelled or verified." Celestine's heart was in her throat.

"Maurice has been told what? There's nothing to tell, Colette."

She was mortified. Why were her actions up for scrutiny in the first place?

"Did Maurice ask Pierre to keep his spies on me; is that what this is, Colette?" She wasn't going to sit and hear any more of the horrible accusation that could ruin her marriage. Pierre walked innocently into the room full of venom flying like poison darts between the two old friends.

"Well, Ladies, a game of cards this evening?" He looked from one to the other and everything in his being was shouting, *'Women angry, run away, fast. Women angry, duck and cover.'*

"Pierre, tell me what you said to my husband regarding Capt. Laffite, please." She sat watching his face turn from happy man to pig at the slaughter.

"Colette, what've you been saying?"

"You may as well tell me everything. I'll not leave you alone until you do." She watched as he showed disgust at his wife's bad manners.

"Maurice was told that you've been entertaining the pirate. He's very angry. He asked if I'd check it out and I did. I discovered that the rumor got to Maurice from one of Laffite's own men, probably at Laffite's request."

"Tell me what my husband was told, Pierre." She was dying inside. She knew Jean was capable, but she hadn't counted on his trying to destroy her marriage in such a vicious manner.

"He was told… where is this taking us, Celestine?"

"Tell me damn it, if I'm to be branded for adultery, I would like to know the charges."

"He was told that Laffite moved in and is living in the house, but leaves before day. He was told that Josef works for Laffite's brother and is the liaison between you two." She was going to be sick.

"Why did my husband stay in Port-au-Prince a month longer than necessary? Does it have to do with this gossip? Is he with Anna?"

"Celestine, this is getting us nowhere, leave it." He'd walked out of the room and up the stairs.

Celestine turned to Colette.

"Is this why you invited me here; to see if I'm a whore like our mothers, or can we assume that Jean Laffite is a lying ass?"

"I had to know, Celestine, I had to see for myself and look into your face." Celestine wondered if she'd have questioned Colette in the same situation. She'd like to think she wouldn't but people get carried away with gossip and tales of romantic interludes; after all she was the wife of a seafaring man and he'd be gone from home over a year. And… she was befriended by a very dangerous, infamous, man.

"And?" Celestine stood back and waited for an answer.

Colette ran and put her arms around Celestine.

"My darling, I've been too long up here with nothing to occupy my silly mind and thinking stupid thoughts about Maurice being gone and you in that lust filled city."

Celestine could see how that would happen, this place was beautiful; but there wasn't much to keep a person away from stray thoughts and horrible gossip.

"You need to take up charity work, Colette. Or, maybe some hobby other than my non-existent love life."

She wanted to know more of why her husband stayed so long in Port-au-Prince. *Was Anna winning him back, after all she was the mother of the two most beloved people in his life and his longtime mistress? Bile rose to the back of her throat.*

Pierre came back into the room. He decided the woman was owed an explanation. If her husband was going to kill a pirate and kick her out of her home, she should know about his peccadilloes also.

"Sit down, 'Tine." He told her everything. He told her about Maurice and Anna, but not about his childhood. He told of Maurice finally finding true love with Celestine and how devastated he was to think that Jean Laffite had been living with his wife in his own home. He stayed a month more than planned with his mistress until Anna finally calmed him down and almost convinced him that the rumors were lies. But, Maurice was Maurice and Pierre wasn't sure if Anna had convinced him or not.

Celestine didn't know how to respond.

"Thank you for being honest with me, Pierre. I know about Anna, but thank you for telling me anyway. I'd like to return to the city tomorrow. I have things I need to do."

"Of course; we understand."

"No, we don't understand. Pierre, she needs to stay right here until this horrible scandal is old news."

"No, Colette, I'll be fine."

Celestine knew what she had to do. First, she'd straighten out one very bad mannered ass of a Pirate and let him know his foolishness hadn't worked. Second, she'd save her marriage and keep her son from being fatherless. Third, Josef would have something to say about the lie told on him and he'd want a chance to explain to his father.

Celestine knew just enough of the bayous from her one trip down to Barataria to hire a small pirogue and a man to row it. She'd used some of Josef's old clothes and put her hair under a rag. She'd take her horse as far as the first bayou, then hire a boat. She'd never be noticed as anything but a small man in a pirogue. She spent the first night wondering why anyone in their right mind would live in the mosquito infested swamp and not go insane from the buzzing and the bites. She hoped she'd left enough milk for the baby, but Marguerite assured her he'd be fine. Marguerite was more worried about Papa Maurice discovering she helped Tanti 'Tine go into the swamps.

The second day they waited outside Laffite's big compound in a palmetto thicket and watched as the grand house was being built and again wondered why he'd choose this desolate place to build a mansion. The boatman explained to her the location being available to unload his cargo and keep his ships safe from the Gulf. He did his best to explain the real beauty of the Cypress swamp and how the water could light up on a sunny day, and glow like fire in a sunset, with the beautiful birds and cranes. She failed to feel his enthusiasm and was glad when dark fell and she could finish what she'd started.

She was strangely calm. She knew Jean would never hurt her, but she didn't know about his men. They were certainly not the sort with whom one would have a romantic walk on a moonlit night along the big bayou. She remembered his kiss that first night. It'd moved her; now the thought made her mad as hell. That started this whole business. She left the boatman and walked calmly into the open and around the new home being built and around to the old house still being used by Laffite.

The men were at a very raucous but beautiful dinner. The silver candleholders were polished and gleaming; the white linen was clean and pressed accentuating the beautiful plates and crystal glasses; too bad his men weren't half as clean as their dinner service. She walked around to the back and looked in the tall windows, she found his room; his big jacket was slung over a chair; he'd been unpacking. Had he been on a voyage? His shaving things were still damp and a big wet bathing towel was drying over his privy screen. *So that's why he hadn't been around, he'd been gone; probably terrorizing the gulf, or another woman's marriage.* The bed was made and the covers already turned down for his night's sleep. She wondered if all pirates were this pampered or just the one trying to destroy her?

She slipped in through the big open jib window easily and placed the note under his pillow. She rubbed her neck with his pillow to be sure to leave her jasmine scent and left as easily as she'd come. She was back in her own bed in New Orleans before the sun came up on the second day.

Celestine was feeding the baby and wondering what Maurice would like to name him when she heard familiar boots coming across the open courtyard. She was nervous and knew being too frightened would show guilt where there was none. She heard him running up the stairs and across the gallery. Maurice looked into his bedroom and saw his wife leaning against a boatload of pillows in a beautiful nightgown feeding their son from an alabaster breast and remembered his wish. He stopped to take it in. He'd planned to accuse her right away, but he walked quietly over to the bed and looked down on his little son nursing on the beautiful breast. He caught himself falling into her trap. She'd have to explain herself before he folded so easily.

"That's mine." He said harsher than he intended, his lips clamped in stifled anger.

"Your son? or my breast?" She asked reaching up for his mouth.

"Both." He almost yelled and turned his mouth away from hers.

He undressed down to his shirt and breeches and got in beside them. He lay on one elbow watching his son. He was still her husband; if he wanted he could move the baby and take her right now.

He was amazed at this little creature he'd created with this woman. He wanted to cuddle them both and meld into the little family he dreamed about for so long. But he wouldn't be made a fool of again. He'd take this wonderful child himself and disappear if she wanted the pirate.

Celestine looked over at his jacket with the beautiful gold braid running up the big sleeves hanging over his chair, the sword and belt hanging from the rack in the corner and the big hat resting on its stand. His boots were standing in front of his armoire; one falling over into the other and it almost made her cry; these were the signs that her man was home from the sea and in residence.

"I wanted to be on the levee when you came home." She turned to him barely keeping the tears from flowing.

"I love watching *le Celestine* sail into safe harbor." She was getting breathless with fright. She'd hoped that seeing her with their son would calm him and help him get some perspective, but it seemed to agitate him even more.

"You're here, Celestine and that's enough for now. What have you named my son?"

"I was waiting for you." She could see he was surprised and pleased with her decision to wait for him. He wasn't expecting that. If she were going to leave him for the pirate, why would she care what he wanted to name his son?

"Philippe."

"Philippe?" She'd never heard him speak of a man named Philippe.

"Yes, Philippe after my father." The baby was through nursing and he took his son and put him over his shoulder and gently burped him.

"You never told me about your father." She purposely left her breast uncovered and wiped a residue of milk off seductively with her fingers; she knew the power the damned things had over him.

"I never knew him. He went down in a storm off the Irish Coast." He was trying not to take her in his arms and cover the breast with his mouth; the same beautiful breast that had so recently given nourishment to his amazing son.

"Oh, then, Philippe it is." When was he ever going to tell her about his life before her? He'd told her all about Anna, but very little of his life before going to sea. He'd never mentioned his parents and she'd never asked. In her world, one didn't ask a person's lineage.

He turned onto his back and put the baby on his big chest. He couldn't touch it enough, this miracle of his wife's doing.

"So, Mme. Dubois, you've built a person. It's a job well done."

He was purposefully not calling her wife or Celestine. Not a good sign. Was he reminding her who she was? Celestine got up and walked to her dressing table. She picked up her brush and began to brush the soft hair from around her face. She wanted him to notice Laffite's calling cards scattered around her dresser. She and Marguerite had gone all over the house looking for the discarded cards to place them in view on her dresser. A wife wouldn't hide cards from an innocent friendship.

"Wi... young Philippe has wet my shirt, come and take him please." He'd almost called her wife; the home life was working as she prayed it would.

She walked over and took the baby and put him in his cradle by the side of her bed and changed his diaper. She went back to the bed and took his shirt and put it in the basket with the laundry. She sat in the big chair by the fireplace or she'd faint from desire. She'd truly forgotten that magnificent chest and what it did to her. She wanted him more than she'd ever wanted anything or anyone in her life. She turned back to him and tried to study his face. She couldn't go through with her plan. She had to make this right.

"You promised me, Maurice. When I first gave myself to you on the ship, when I trusted you enough to open myself to you; you promised that you'd always come home to me, you promised." She was angry that the tears were coming when she wanted so badly to be calm.

"Now you come three months late to meet your son. How could you believe lies about me? How could you? Do you hate me that much; no, do you hate yourself that much that you can't believe I love you and only you and will never love anyone else?" She was moving full steam forward. She was getting angrier at the thought of his not trusting her and writing to Pierre instead of asking her in any of his letters to her. She picked up his boot from the floor and slung it hard and it missed him by inches.

"If that'd been my knife, you'd be a gelding now, sir." She was sobbing and marching out of the door when he caught her and picked her up and brought her back to the bed. He was almost there when he spotted the cards on the dresser. He dropped her on the floor. *Her first plan had just interfered with her second plan and now there was no plan.*

He picked up a few of the cards and looked down at her.

She'd try to re-implement her first plan.

"I'm sorry, I didn't know I wasn't to have friends while you were away, or stop a man saving me in the market from giving birth to your son on the levee. Next time I'll know better." She was picking herself up and pulling her wrapper around her breast.

"Madame, tell me what was going on in my house while I was at sea and mind you tell me the truth." His voice was low and rumbling. She knew what one of his sailors must feel when he'd done something wrong, but damn it, she'd done nothing wrong. She was in labor for fifteen long hours giving him a son, she nursed until her nipples wanted to fall off and now she had to answer to him about some bloody pirate.

She was feeling the effects and consequence of gossip on innocent women down through the ages. No gossip monger has to come up with facts, only the gossiped about. He'd crossed a line. She rang for Marguerite.

"Papa Maurice, you're home." She threw herself into his arms. He stared over at Celestine.

"This isn't over."

"No, it's not, Captain Dubois." He reacted to her using his name and not husband. She noted the effect.

"Rite, darling would you get your brother? Papa wishes to speak to us all together."

"Of course, Tante 'Tine." She left; running downstairs and calling for Josef.

"What are you doing?" He was so confused, she was messing with his head and he couldn't trust what she was doing or why. What the hell was going on in his home while he was out making a living, by damn?

Celestine had walked back down to the courtyard with the baby asleep in her arms. She sat at the big wrought iron dining table and put Philippe in the little bed Josef made, next to her.

Maurice followed putting on his jacket and pulling up his boots. Josef came around from the stable with Marguerite. He waited for Maurice to finish dressing and hugged him.

"Please, sit down." Celestine addressed her strange little family.

They sat at their usual places; Maurice at the head with Josef to his right and Marguerite to his left and his wife at the other end of the beautiful table.

"Your father has questions for all of us. First, I'd like to ask each of you. Josef, did you ever know Capt. Laffite to stay overnight at this house, or was he ever in my bedroom?"

Maurice was up and booming.

"You go too far, Madame." He was truly angry now, why would she subject his children to such personal adult problems?

"NO." Josef was emphatic. "We've heard the rumors Papa Maurice and they bare no truth." He hoped he'd be believed. He knew he was telling the truth, he watched them both. He'd never have allowed it and was ashamed when he finally realized his spying on her was for nothing. He helped the bad Captain in the beginning when Tanti 'Tine would go to the levee and work among the poor in her condition, but he'd never been the liaison for which he'd been accused.

"Marguerite?" Celestine would have it out here and now and he could leave or stay. If he stayed there may not be enough bandages in the house to stop the blood.

"Papa Maurice, when you accuse Tanti 'Tine you accuse me and Josef also. Do you not love us and trust us to do right by you? You're being unfair to her and she deserves better."

She was beginning to cry. This man had slept with her mother for years and hadn't married her. Why would he be so brutal to this little woman who loved him and had been so brave waiting for him to come home? Men were allowed their women, but women weren't allowed one friend in breeches. She was beginning to see the convent as a better life for her if this was marriage. She also liked Capt. Laffite, he'd done many favors for her and brought her the herbs she needed for some of her creations and he'd never treated her like a servant or anything more than Tante 'Tine's ward and friend.

"Marguerite, of course I love you and Josef. Stop this, Celestine."

"My turn, Capt. Dubois. I have a couple of questions for you. First and foremost, why would I leave my lover's calling cards for my husband to see? If you can answer that, then you may have a case."

"Of course I can answer that. You didn't know I was coming home." He stood and looked at his family at the table. He'd not wanted to be right. His heart would break.

"Where is your reasoning, husband? Josef, when did you know your father would be home?"

"Yesterday morning, the man who brings you news of the ships coming into the harbor announced he saw *le Celestine* coming up the river, one day out."

Maurice sat back down. What a fool he was. Anna had told him everything; she'd even seen this fight and her children's loyalty to his wife.

"Children, may I speak to your papa alone, please." They both bent to kiss his cheek and left the two strangely embarrassed people alone.

"You forced me to do it, husband. You'll take full credit for this."

"What was your next question?" He knew he'd been played a fool by the black hearted son-of-a-sea witch, Laffite. He just hoped his trick on the pirate was as humiliating as his had been on him, even worse. The pirate's whole crew would witness Laffite's shame.

"Did you bed Anna? Be careful how you answer. I want the truth, Maurice."

"Of course I didn't bed Anna. You should know by now, I could never touch another woman." If his lie was ever revealed, he'd be a dead man; and it wasn't worth it, Anna was falling in love with a new man. He felt it in her touch and he'd only lain with her in some jealous retribution to his wife and the pirate and Anna could feel that too.

"I'll see you in the morning." She walked upstairs with the baby and locked the doors to her bedroom. Maurice turned and walked back out onto the street. His embarrassment was getting the better of him. How could he be so damned blind? He walked up to *rue des Chartres* and found a saloon. He'd never get used to the muddy sewage bogged streets of this damned city. He walked off his ship, not an hour ago in clean boots and now he had mud up to his arse and hated it. He wanted his clean ship under his feet. A man had to walk steady on dry land and hold fast or rumors and gossip could drag him down like the mud on his boots. He drank a whiskey and left the bar. He'd have to face the music. What he'd done to his little dove was appalling. He was ashamed and embarrassed by his accusations. Most Sea Captains received similar news in their careers and many were false... some were not. After all, the wife of a Captain was not, as a rule, a shrinking violet, they could be lusty women full of the devil and his was no exception. He was lucky to still have his manhood. If she discovered his lie about Anna after his theatrics over Laffite, he'd lose his for sure. Another prayer went to heaven.

She heard the gentle knock as she was putting the baby in his cradle. The glass on the long doors rattled with another knock.

"I'm home from the sea, wife. Did you miss me? I brought pretty trinkets for you and the baby." He was standing and tantalizing her with that all powerful smile she could never resist. She hid her smile.

"You'll have to wait your turn, you've frightened the baby." She reached for her son and walked back to the bed.

"I can wait. I can wait as long as it takes." The smile hadn't left his face and he stood at the door like a repentant school boy waiting for his punishment. She started laughing in spite of herself. She put Philippe back in his bed and opened the door and stood blocking it.

"Do you promise to trust me? Answer me, husband." His smile got bigger.

"Do you promise to stop being a bully and respect my choice of friends? Answer me, husband." He picked her up and took her to the bed and threw her into the soft down of the bed.

"I promise to make you forget how stupid I've been for the last several months. You can punish me later if you wish. How's that?" He was kissing her; taking off her clothes; pulling his legs out of breeches and getting his shirt caught on his arms and couldn't get to her fast enough.

That was the homecoming she expected from a sex deprived Sea Captain after months at sea. She was feeling the pressure in the small of her back and knew it wouldn't take much to rise to her groin and she'd be embarrassingly ready for his entry. If he'd waited with his accusations, he'd have seen how eager she was for his love making. No woman could've been sleeping with a man and been this needy for a male body. She was insatiable and he'd be sore for days.

Celestine thanked God for his safe return. She knew he lied about Anna; but he loved her enough to lie. She couldn't get enough of her husband. She'd been in the pirate's room and it had affected her and she'd been moved by the pirate's scent and the intimacy of his things. It frightened her and if Maurice hadn't come home when he did, she didn't know what she might've done. She'd go with him from now on or he wouldn't take such long trips, it wasn't good for their marriage. She'd be firm on this.

Chapter Sixteen

Laffite hadn't found her note until he was in bed and trying to rearrange his pillow to find where her scent was coming from. He drank too much wine and stayed talking to his men too late. The dinner itself was strained; his men were trying to ignore the recent goose chaise their Captain had taken them on.

They were weeks in the Atlantic before they realized there was no English merchant ship carrying gold bullion into the Carolinas. He passed it off to his men as bad timing, they'd missed the ship and it had passed un-noticed in the fog one night. He knew though. He knew he'd been duped; he just didn't know by whom. The man who told him of the ship was a good man and not up for mischief, so that man had also been lied to. He called the man into his cabin and questioned him. The man was told by a very worthy source in Port-au-Prince. A merchant Captain with an outstanding reputation hadn't realized he was talking to one of Laffite's men. He let the news drop about the gold. He was the Captain of le Celestine. The Captain had sworn the man to secrecy when he realized his mistake in talking out of school.

That son of a bitch; muttered Laffite to himself. Dubois may get the rooster out of his henhouse, but he couldn't get the rooster out of her head that easily. Then insult to injury, he found she was in his very bed and his men hadn't seen or heard her come or go. Her scent was on his pillow; that'd have to be enough for now. He opened the note:

Jean dear,

My husband is home and I find I will be too busy pleasuring him every day and every evening to visit with you.

Our time was nice and you were kind to keep me from boredom, but I need my man now.

Au revoir.

Mme. Captain Maurice Dubois.

She was bloody magnificent. He'd have trouble sleeping for days.

Between the two of them; he should've given up, but it isn't over until someone's dead and he had plenty of time. He wouldn't tweak the captain again, he'd met his match and it could cost him his lively hood and the respect of his crew. The Captain's wife however well… he'd wait; he knew her coming into his world alone and pressing her face to his pillow was not something a woman did out of anger, no matter how much she tried to convince herself. She could tell herself whatever she wanted; he knew her better than she knew herself. He'd loved, angered and placated his fair share of women and she was one of the best.

He was home a week when he ran into Captain Dubois in a saloon on *rue Bourbon*. They were standing at either end of the long bar and hadn't known the other was there until the patrons standing between left.

"Captain Laffite." Maurice acknowledged the man. Several customers witnessed the exchange and rushed from the bar. The whole town knew the rumors of the handsome pirate and Dubois's beautiful wife.

"Captain Dubois." Laffite didn't like awkward moments in his life, he lived an organized existence and planned his every move. It was one of the reasons he'd only seen the inside of a jail cell, once and only once.

"How do you find our weather, sir?" Maurice would play with him a while, the news would get back to his wife before he returned home, so he'd give the messengers time.

"It's a bit too warm for me, Captain. May I buy you a cool drink?" He'd have to be careful here. He never confronted a powerful husband, most of his bedroom adversaries were milksops who couldn't or wouldn't keep tabs on their wives. He had no intentions of getting into hand to hand combat with this man.

"No, thank you, I'm wanted home to... dinner... with my wife. Maybe another time, sir?"

"Of course." Laffite picked up his hat.

"Captain Dubois?"

"Yes." He stopped to turn back to the pirate. It was all he could do not to ram his fist into the man's face.

"Are we even, then?"

"I've no idea what you mean, sir." His smiling blue eyes said he did indeed know what he meant. Maurice certainly wasn't going to admit to the Terror of the Gulf that he'd put the man's ship in harm's way to keep him out of his wife's bed. That was so revealing on so many levels, it was ridiculous.

Laffite had never envied a man as much as he envied this pompous ass. He didn't like the feeling. It wasn't over until a death. Laffite could wait. He was much younger than Dubois.

Maurice loved taking Celestine and little Philippe for walks around the city. They'd visit all the shops and buy things they needed, with Maurice introducing his son with the pride of all new papas. He never told his wife, but it was his statement to Jean Laffite that his family wouldn't buy the contraband products of a pirate. His money would only go to the New Orleans' businessmen's purse.

These were some of the dearest days for Celestine. It became their custom when he was in port, to have their afternoon shopping and visit with people on the street. Maurice carried Philippe until he got so big, he insisted on walking. Exchanging news and gossip with neighbors and friends was a delight for her husband after spending long months at sea, he became known as a loving husband and the perfect family man.

Chapter Seventeen

1812

Maurice didn't want his portrait painted, but Colette begged and cajoled and Celestine begged and cajoled and finally Philippe begged and cajoled. He couldn't fight them all.

Colette was becoming a very good portrait artist and brought her paints on this trip. If Maurice knew he was going to be badgered by his family he would've thrown the damned canvases and paints overboard.

They were at sea for many months and finding it hard to keep their boredom at bay. Letty and Philippe had begun to get on each other's nerves. Pierre and Maurice were spending more and more time with the crew in their mess area playing cards, drinking good rum and smoking the cigars they bought in Havana. His nights with his wife were still well worth bringing her on this voyage and he loved waking with her next to him each morning. She could make him laugh at nothing and find beauty in things he'd never even noticed in his world at sea and in some of their ports of call. Her knowledge of history and the flora and fauna of the areas they visited was amazing and he found he was learning along with Philippe and Letty each day.

Marguerite hadn't made this voyage; she was too busy working with her women's charities. Josef was left to take care of the house. He was glad to stay on dry land. He had enough of the sea life in his long years of exile and now that his mother was dead, he had no reason to go to Port-au-Prince or any of the islands. He chose to stay and be with Augustine and Marguerite and take care of the house.

He was inventing a spraying bath at the bottom of the big cistern by the stable as a surprise for Papa Maurice and Tante 'Tine. It was an idea he'd been thinking about for a while. He was six feet and four inches;

too large for the tub baths and he didn't like waiting for the hot water to be boiled. He was fine with the tepid water in the big cistern on a summer night, and in the winter; the cold water was refreshing and good for the skin. He knew his Papa Maurice would love it, he didn't know about Tante 'Tine, she loved her hot bubbles and good smelling soaps.

He was glad to have the big house to himself. More and more the Laffite brothers were leaving him in charge of the blacksmith shop with some of their slaves and he could work on his inventions with the hot iron and metals and not be bothered. He was twenty nine years old and was in love with the same woman for years, but she wouldn't marry him. He'd decided he'd wait. What choice did he have? He didn't want anyone else and he couldn't force her. He slept at her little house in rue de *l'Hopital* most nights and would go to work from there. Once the family left, he moved her to the big house on *rue du Maine*. She wasn't at all pleased, but she wanted to be with him.

Colette had her easel and canvas set up on the deck and Maurice sat in his big captain's chair with Philippe standing next to him with his hand on his shoulder. Colette began her masterpiece, but kept sighing louder and louder.

"For God's sake what's wrong, woman?" A woman's sigh was a real thorn in Maurice's side. *If a woman had a gripe, let her voice it and not wait to be asked.*

"You both look like you've just lost your best friend. Can't I have a nice smile?"

"Don't be ridiculous, woman, you aren't supposed to smile in a portrait; it distorts the face." Maurice didn't know much about art, but he knew that much.

"Oh Posh, I want to see you two smiling."

Letty came running out on deck in her 'mermaid' outfit. She'd taken her mama's skirts and belted them around her ankles and was doing a funny, swimming 'dance' behind the easel; blowing out her cheeks and puckering her lips like a fish. Maurice and Philippe both started laughing at her antics.

"That's it. Keep it up, Letty." Colette had what she wanted. It only took her a couple of weeks of one-hour sittings a day with Letty and Celestine taking turns at the mermaid dance. Pierre's mermaid was the best and neither Maurice nor Philippe could stay in position long enough with Pierre's mermaid's antics. The whole crew left their work to enjoy his fine dance and theatrics.

The portrait was finished and she named it 'Smiling at the Mermaid'. Celestine loved it. It became her favorite possession. Maurice thought it was the silliest thing he'd ever seen and made him look like a fool.

A few days before they sailed back into New Orleans, Maurice went to bed later than usual. He'd had a few brandies with Pierre and the time got away from him. When he entered the big cabin it was dark. No candle or lamp was lighted and he didn't want to light the lamp and wake his wife. He stumbled over his big chair and cursed as he stubbed his toe on the leg of the table.

"Captain Dubois?" The voice was Celestine's, but low and sultry. It was giving him an erection; he hoped it was intended to do that.

"Please don't be angry that I stowed away on your big ship, Captain Dubois."

He heard the match being struck and saw the lamp begin to glow. He turned to see Celestine sitting up in bed in nothing but a lacy corset cover and white stockings held up by blue ruffled garters. Her hair was down and she was spread legged with her heels pulled up to her beautiful ass. She blew out the match with puckered lips, "Shhh." And the flame went out.

"Celestine? What are you doing? That's positively indecent." He was breathing so hard he couldn't undo his breeches and he was fumbling with the buttons.

"Please don't punish me for stowing away on your big ship, Captain. I'll be good." She was swinging her knees in and out exposing herself. He couldn't move.

"Please don't spank me, Captain. I promise I'll be good. I'll do anything you like, just don't spank me." She slapped her bottom and ran her hand down into her center.

"Oooh God, wife, what are you doing to me? " He was going to have a heart attack. He heard about mistresses and Courtesans doing this for their men, but Anna had never done it. He was going to get this treat from his woman. He didn't know if it were the thought of her being a little waif under his power, or the idea of spanking that delicious bottom, but it was powerful stuff.

"I need a spanking, Captain. But, please don't hurt me. I'll be good and I'll make you feel sooo good." She was running a wet tongue around her lips, breathing the words in a soft whisper.

"Yes… well… young lady… you've been very bad." He was no good at this. He sounded fake and it was taking the wind out of the sails she'd hoisted in him.

"Come to bed, Captain. You don't have to tell me how bad I was. I know I've been bad."

She turned to the side of the bed and reached out for him. He got into bed and sat up against the pillows and she crawled across his naked lap on her stomach. He became the stern captain she wanted and gave her a few good spanks. She jumped and wiggled at each blow and her soft stomach on his erection was doing amazing things. He gave her a few more and she wiggled and bounced on his erection, until he was spanking her and moving himself under her. He'd never been so aroused or wanted to made love so passionately. She begged for mercy and promised never to stow away again; he literally couldn't get enough of her. She was the naughty girl at her best and twisted and fell with her mouth on his erection, then said she was sorry and didn't mean to disrespect the big Captain and his mighty cock. Her 'punishment' went on until they were both spent. It was the best sleep he'd ever gotten.

He was exhausted the next morning and dreaded the same old questions. Where the hell did she learn this? He only knew about it from talking to seasoned sailors and bar buddies. He turned to her and gently awakened her by shaking her shoulder.

"Wife? Pierre and Colette?" She woke just enough to know what he was asking.

"Yes. You spank too hard. Colette didn't warn me about that. We won't be doing this too often." She rubbed her bottom.

"Well, don't stow away on my big ship anymore, little girl." He was laughing and stopped when he saw she was serious. "Oh, my love, here, let the big, mean, Captain kiss it for you." He turned her upside down with his mouth on her center and that started a whole new series of events.

They returned to New Orleans that spring and Maurice was worried about his next voyage. British warships and French warships and privateers alike were attacking merchant ships. He was worried getting his family back to New Orleans safely. He thought about not going at all, but there was a huge need with the merchant ships being robbed and the sailors pressed into service on the navy vessels from all countries.

He'd make one last trip and honor a contract he signed before the last voyage. He wasn't worried about the privateers, they knew his ship and knew to leave him alone; he certainly didn't worry about Laffite's, La Diligente, he wouldn't attack le Celestine; that'd be bad manners. Maurice knew the man to be very well mannered even though he was a murderous pirate calling himself a privateer. He wouldn't leave Maurice's wife a widow; there was an honor unspoken between the two competitors. It was the English Warships that worried Maurice. They could steal a man's cargo, press his men into service as sailors and offer the Captain a cup of tea as his ship was sinking and not think a thing of it. They'd been doing it more and more frequently.

He wanted to make this last trip and then dock le Celestine until he could see what this war was going to do. He had plenty of money; he could wait the war out and enjoy home life for a change. He'd started the big house about a mile up River Road before this last voyage and wanted to get his family out of the cramped city and into fresh air in the country.

They returned to find the widow's walk already complete and he hoped Celestine would enjoy it while he was gone. She and Philippe could watch the stars through the big glass he installed and they could all three be watching the skies together each night; Maurice from the deck of his ship and his family from the roof of the new house. He loved the image. She'd be able to move in while he was gone and he could come home to a busy wife and be in her way and underfoot. The thought amused him.

He only had a few days at home before he'd head back out and he wasn't looking forward to being alone on the water, even though it was to be a short two months or less. He'd grown used to his friends and family running around the big ship and keeping him and his crew company.

He and Celestine had spent the night making love. They couldn't get enough of each other. It was like their first nights being married. They spent time laughing at the antics of their son. Philippe discovered the spraying bath and had taken so many baths in the last few days that Josef was worried he may empty the big cistern before the next rain.

Maurice was never happier, and his cock more tender from the long night. He loved feeling what she'd done to him, hopefully it'd last a day or too as a gentle, and very tender reminder of the night.

The family saw Maurice off from the levee and Celestine went with Josef straight to the big warehouse. Celestine was happy to be home and start on the new house. There was paint to be chosen and furniture to be delivered from the big warehouse where Maurice had it stored. They'd handpicked every piece from all over the Atlantic seaboard and Europe. She had summer rugs from Haiti so the big open rooms would smell fresh like the tropics and hand woven wool and silk rugs from France and the middle-east for the winter. She had mahogany pieces for Philippe's bedroom. There were rosewood beds with matching dressers and armoires the size of small rooms, and marble topped bases to go under the big beveled mirrors, some as tall as ten feet. She'd chosen French designs for Marguerite's bedroom to remind her of the big homes in her native Port-au-Prince. The big ware house was full; they'd brought back so much she couldn't remember most of their purchases. She was looking forward to re-discovering each treasure as she and Josef went through the big buildings.

She didn't miss Philippe until evening and 'Rite came to the warehouse to see if he was with his mother. She'd looked everywhere and he was nowhere to be found. Josef hadn't seen him since Maurice left. They all came to the same conclusion together. He was on the ship. She knew it. Oh God, how long before his father found him? How far out to sea before he could safely turn around and bring him back?

They rushed back home for Josef to get a man to go with him down the river. They had to wait until morning. Josef would start at dawn.

She heard Philippe's loud mouth coming into the carriageway and the three ran to see what was happening. Jean Laffite had him over his shoulder walking with him into the courtyard.

"Did you lose this, Mme. Dubois?" He dropped him into Josef's arms and gave Marguerite, Philippe's small bundle of run-away supplies.

"Philippe? What does this mean? Where'd you go?" He was crying into Josef's chest and wouldn't look at his mother.

"Young man, speak to your mother or I shall feed you to the swamp and not look back." Laffite was an angry papa barking at his young.

"I wanted to go with papa." He was sobbing on Josef's chest.

"What'd I do without you, little brother? You have to stay here and help me look after your mama and 'Rite." Josef was taking him upstairs to his room and Celestine watched as her young, sad son was taken upstairs. She was beginning to cry herself.

"I can't be mad at him, Jean I wanted to go also." She gave an embarrassed laugh. "Where'd you find my son?"

He looked at her; she was still the most beautiful woman in New Orleans by far. He'd missed seeing her while she was gone on her sea voyage. Her face had seen some sun and salt air and it gave her a healthy glow and complimented her eyes. Her age was showing in her face and replacing the young innocence with an exotic beauty. He was getting an erection and would give himself away if he couldn't control it

"Your husband sent him with Pierre David in a dingy and asked that I return him to you. He was found on the ship in your husband's closet. I suppose he'll be going to sea one day, Madame. The apple doesn't fall far from the tree."

Jean felt it was a compliment that Captain Dubois had trusted the safe return of his son to his care. It meant there was a strong bond between the two men; a bond of respect in an adversarial friendship.

Celestine reached up and kissed him on the cheek. "You have saved me again, Jean, thank you, sir." She was glad her husband had trusted her old friend with their son, it meant a lot to her.

"Captain Dubois asked me to give you this, my dear." He handed her a little box. "You're not to open it until he returns."

She was confused, but thought it a good omen that Maurice knew he'd be returning. She wouldn't open it, it could bring bad luck.

Maurice trusted Laffite with Celestine's son. It would give his son a life-long protector if anything happened to him on this voyage. It'd compliment Laffite and make him an ally if *le Celestine* ran into trouble in these waters. He could've turned the ship and gone back up river, but this was a decision he thought best. Pierre assured him Laffite was more than happy to return Philippe to New Orleans, and considered it the honor Maurice had hoped; so his son was safe at home.

He was proud of his son's bravery in stowing away on his ship, but it worried him that he was so selfish as to leave his mother unprotected. The boy was a constant joy and a source of pride, he wished he had ten more, but Celestine hadn't conceived and they'd decided to enjoy the one son God gave them.

He knew the warships were following him. He'd seen them two days before on the horizon like greedy, ugly buzzards on a dead tree. He only carried eight fourteen pounder cannon and that was a sling shot compared to these mighty warriors. He could try to outrun them, but the wind was not in his favor nor theirs. He held chapel with his men and asked for a safe return to their families. He knew there were times when a man does his best and trusts God will do his; he wasn't taking any chances. He kept awake as long as he dared and would only sleep an hour or so each night. The wind was beginning to pick up and he was glad to head out and away from the big ugly ships following him. He was lighter and should be able to out distance them.

Pierre said he'd take his shift and insisted Maurice get some rest.

Within two hours Maurice was awakened by cannon fire. He ran on deck and grabbed the big glass Pierre handed him.

Here it is, he thought. How did they get so damned close?

The fire wasn't aimed at *le Celestine, La Diligente* was between Maurice and the warships and they were firing on Lafitte.

He ordered every sale to be raised, if Lafitte could distract them, surely he could outrun them.

La Diligente had already done considerable damage to one of the ships and was about to board. Maybe Laffite knew the warship was carrying gold or maybe he just wanted to own a warship for his ever growing fleet of privateer vessels. Either way he was in it to the death.

Maurice drew a sigh of relief. Thank God for *la Diligente*, if she could hold them long enough, *le Celestine* would be safe. Maurice didn't know for how long, but at least a skirmish would be avoided. He'd owe the pirate now for sure.

"Sail, HO, Man of War, Captain." A frightened voice called from the crow's nest.

Maurice looked off the bow and another warship was coming straight for le Celestine.

"Where the hell did that monster come from?" Maurice knew he'd have to stand and fight, he couldn't run directly into the oncoming ship and he sure as hell couldn't go around it. Pierre walked up beside him and put his hand on Maurice's shoulder. Maurice reached up and squeezed Pierre's hand to reassure him and then began to bellow orders to his crew. His confidence was running on high and his men felt it and began to ready the big ship for battle against the devil himself.

Josef would never see his father again. He knew it when they all waved as he sailed down the river. He tried to hide it. He tried to warn him, but he wouldn't be warned. He made Josef promise he wouldn't say anything to worry the family and Josef kept his word. He woke many weeks after Maurice had sailed and knew his father was no more. His beloved Papa Maurice was standing over his bed asking him to protect Marguerite and his wife and son. He watched as Papa Maurice walked into the beautiful sky above a calm sea with a man who looked like Philippe. He heard Papa Maurice laughing and calling the man 'Papa'.

Josef got up and threw his stones on the floor of the little house.

Augustine was just waking up and knew Josef was working his gris-gris looking for something in his stones. He was crying because he saw the battle and the men dying. He saw Laffite and his men board the big warship and kill the British sailor, but it was too late for *le Celestine*, she'd been hit too many times and the men were flying over the sides and swimming to the boats that had fallen or were lowered into the water.

He could hear screams from below deck and Papa Maurice trying to get to his men. He saw Pierre try to follow Papa Maurice but was picked up and thrown over the side by his Papa Maurice. He saw the ship go down and Papa Maurice being hit by a falling mast and then he saw Laffite with a horrible gash to his leg picking the men out of the sea in *La Deligente* and out-running the other damaged warship. He saw his papa Maurice die a very brave man. He saw Pierre, half dead on his way to give the bad news to Tante 'Tine.

Josef wouldn't be there, he couldn't bear the sadness. He'd stay with Augustine and sleep and not think. He couldn't stand losing this father he'd known and loved. He didn't think he could live through it. He knew he was weak, but so be it. But, Augustine insisted he go. She couldn't believe he wouldn't go. Hadn't his father asked him to protect his family? He had to admit, she was right and he wouldn't let Papa Maurice down. He'd go to his old room and be there when Pierre came in with the horrible news. He walked across the courtyard and smelled the coffee under the banana tree. He'd have to hide his face; but it was too late. She looked up at her handsome step son and knew. She screamed; "No, Josef, NO, NO fix it. Josef, quickly go get your father, you can do this, you can fix it. JOSEF do as I'm telling you. Go GET HIM." She screamed.

She was up close to him now and whispering in his face and holding onto his collar. "You can fix anything son, you know you can. You must go find him and fix him and bring him home to us." She stood back waiting for a response. "You must do this, Josef, you have to, please." *She was begging him. He could fix it. He could go and find him and bring him home to her. He could always make things right. Everyone knew Josef could fix anything. He was big and he could keep this from happening and she had no idea how or why she thought he could, but she wouldn't accept what his face was telling her.*

Josef put his arms around her and let her scream into his big chest. She was angry with him for not helping his father and his heart was breaking. His chest had a gaping hole where his heart used to live, and his stomach was trying to crawl out through his throat but he had to be strong, didn't people understand; being big doesn't necessarily mean you can carry the sorrow of the world?

Marguerite was running down the stairs to see what was happening and Philippe was up and running after her. The neighbors were looking in the gates to see what the screaming was about and began to part as Pierre walked through the gates and across the courtyard. He was dirty and bloody and he had two men with him and they were all trying to steady each other. He saw her and began to cry. He passed out and the men took him upstairs and put him in the room she showed them.

"I'll make him well. I'll take care of him. I can make him well and he and Josef can go and get Maurice and bring him home." *She had to make him well, she had to make him well, she had to make him well so he would get Maurice and bring him home.*

"Quick, 'Rite, bring the bandages, Josef get some hot water and show the men the kitchen so they can have something to eat. He has to get well, so he can go find Maurice."

One of the neighbors had gone for Dr. Pabon and another had said they would go find Mme. David and bring her back. Pierre was waking up.

"Can one of you go for Captain Dubois; he must know about this, he can help?" She said it so innocently, Pierre looked around for Maurice, but then realized she had gone to a place in her head where she felt safe and wasn't coming back for a while.

The next few months were agony on everyone. The man was such a force, the entire group of family and friends felt the loss. Even his crew who escaped being pressed onto the big war ships were finding it hard to leave the side of his family. The house was full of people night and day. Most of the men wouldn't leave her side and allowed her to talk about the Captain incessantly. It made them feel strangely safe and they understood her need to keep him alive through her conversations.

She thought she was being very brave. She finally acknowledged his death and could begin to grieve, but it was the brandy she had begun to drink on an hourly basis; her bravery was a drunken bliss and she didn't know it. She wouldn't allow the men to talk about the battle or even the day of the battle, but they needed to talk of it and relive it and exorcise it from their memory. One by one they began to leave and seek solace elsewhere, they couldn't help the woman, and she couldn't help them. Her son was trying to cope with the loss of his father and the loss of his mother's sanity and had begun to sleep curled in his father's big armoire among his clothes.

"Get up, Celestine." She recognized the voice, it was stern and angry.

"Get up and get out of that bed." Who was angry with her, didn't they know she had lost her husband to the sea and to the bloody British warship?

She felt the cold water being poured over her head wetting the whole bed. She gulped for air and looked up to see Rev. Mother and Ste. Mary Clarisse and two novices in her room.

"I should be ashamed of myself. Is this what you've become? Will you be taking in sailors on the levee next? When Marguerite came to tell me, I didn't believe her, I thought she was carrying tales, but it's worse than she said. Look at your son, Celestine. Look at him."

Celestine shook her head to clear the fog and saw her pointing to Maurice's armoire. Philippe was curled in the corner under one of his father's jackets asleep, sucking his thumb and crying in his sleep.

Her heart was breaking, this was worse than losing her husband. What'd she done to her brave little boy? The same little boy that'd tried to stow away on his father's big ship was cowering in the bottom of his father's closet because his mother was too selfish and drunk to take care of him? She ran to the boy and gathered him to her. Josef brought in a tub; the novices were filling it for her bath. She took Philippe back to her bed.

"How about a nice hot bath, son? Things are going to be fine. Mama is here, my angel." She got him undressed and wiped his face. She smelled like stale liquor and unwashed body, but Philippe needed her. She'd deal with her pain after she took care of her baby boy. How could she've been so selfish? Her pain could wait.

"Finish your baths, both of you and then come downstairs, I have things to say to you." The Reverend Mother walked down the stairs. Celestine felt safe watching the long, black dusty skirt follow the woman's feet down the stairs in her very sad and lonely house.

Celestine looked at her son. There was a new camaraderie between them, just the two of them with Josef and Marguerite against the world; depending on each other. Josef had Augustine and Marguerite had her little family.

"Philippe, are we in trouble?" She smiled at her son.

"I hope not, mama, she can be awful mean to a little boy when he's been bad, or steals oranges from her tree." He was smiling back at his mama. Those were Maurice's eyes looking back at her. Had she never noticed how much he looked like his father? How we take things for granted on a daily bases. It took them over an hour before they were both dressed and presentable.

"Celestine, Philippe. Do you know how Captain Dubois died?"

They didn't; they just knew *le Celestine* was sunk in the Gulf by two British warships and half of his crew had survived. Some were picked out of the Gulf by the ships and those men were now part of the British Navy against their will. The others went down with Maurice and the ship.

"Please, Reverend Mother, don't. I can't bear it. I can't and Philippe shouldn't have to."

"Yes, he should and so should you. Captain Dubois went down with his ship because he wouldn't leave his men trapped below deck to die alone.

He could've easily stepped into the last life boat and lived, but there were men calling and screaming from down below and he wouldn't desert them. Pierre tried to stay with him, but he threw him overboard and the lifeboat pulled him out of the water. Your husband stayed with the ship and called down to them to be brave that he'd save them. Maybe he thought he could save them, maybe not, but he made sure his men died with dignity, not frightened and alone. Now, is this the way he'd expect his wife to act, or his son? Is this his legacy?"

Celestine took Philippe on her lap. She was astonished. Why hadn't anyone told her this? She remembered she wouldn't let anyone talk to her about the ship or his death. Of course she felt better knowing her husband hadn't died in fear and was a hero to his men.

"Has anyone told you of Laffite's part in the battle?" Celestine's heart caught in her throat. *Was Jean responsible for Maurice's death? She'd kill him.*

"He came to their rescue and tried to out maneuver one of the ships and was seriously wounded. If he hadn't shown up when he did, there'd be no survivors and your friend Pierre would be with your husband. Your husband did serious damage to one of the ships before he was hit with the fatal blow, but the Warships were better equipped for battle than *le Celestine*. Laffite's *La Diligente* did it's best to save the two.

"Where is Captain Laffite?"

"No one knows; he's in 'seclusion'. I'll leave you to your grief. I should think you'd be proud of your husband, my dear and know he's with our heavenly father."

Mother Superior took Celestine's hand and pressed a rosary into her palm. Celestine recognized it as one of the Reverend Mother's own from her childhood in France.

Mother Superior left Philippe and Celestine with the information still circling in their heads and waiting to be processed. She suddenly remembered the little box Jean brought her when he returned Philippe. She walked up to her bedroom and got it from the drawer in her dresser and brought it back down to the table.

"What's that mama?"

"I don't know, son we'll find out together." She opened the little box. Maurice' wedding ring, his big gold watch and diamond stick pin greeted her with a note."

Wife, keep these safe until I return. Philippe, take care of your mother and stay away from big ships on the sea.

Love to you both, Husband and Papa.

She'd die later; she had a child to comfort.

A few months later, Philippe went to stay with Letty to get a new perspective on life outside the big grieving house on rue du Maine. Fresh country air and his best friend Letty was the best thing for him.

She found Josef at Augustine's house.

"Where is he, son?"

"You can't go alone, Tante 'Tine. He's much better. Tante 'Tine he doesn't need a nurse."

"Tell me where he is. I'm sure he can use a friend."

Josef took her. He didn't know if it was a good idea, but she needed the male attention. She could call the man a friend all she wanted, but Josef knew what she wanted, he couldn't blame her; Papa Maurice was a powerful force for a woman to do without. He could feel how much she needed it; he'd even told Augustine his predictions. Josef knew Laffite would keep her safe; if she made a fool of herself, no one would ever know.

They rode horses across Bayou Savage into a place called the Rigolets, between Lake Bourne and Lake Saint Catherine south of the big Lake Ponchartrain and headed toward the settlement of Biloxi. He took her out to a camp on the lake surrounded by water and bits of island. Josef left her with Pierre Laffite and said he'd be back for her. He knew she'd be safe, but he wouldn't if he were found by one of the men who didn't recognize him. There were so many more men in Laffite's world than before, and many couldn't be trusted.

Pierre Laffite took her into a large room off a main parlor and shut the door. Jean was sitting at his desk and acted surprised to see her.

"My dear, how good of you to come. How are you, my pet?" He had the same smiling hazel eyes, but he was not the happy man she remembered.

He got up and walked over to her. He knew she was coming, his men told him before she arrived that she and Josef were on their way. He was walking with a painful limp. He walked up to her and took her little hand and kissed the palm. There was so much love and tenderness in his voice; she thought she couldn't bear it.

"I tried, Celestine." He spoke so softly she almost couldn't hear. "I swear I tried, my love. I thought I could save him." He looked into her beautiful blue eyes and hated the hurt and pain and loneliness she carried like a penance. He'd find a way to get that look out of her eyes, he had to.

She went into his arms and buried her tears in his chest breathing in his scent. She longed for his safety and his comfort. His strong arms wrapped around her and held her so close she could die and be happy right in this moment. He picked her up and walked with her to the bed; got in next to her and cuddled her into him.

"I'm here, my pet, your Jean is here." She sobbed all afternoon. She hadn't felt this safe since Maurice left her bed. She didn't want to leave him. This was where she belonged now. Josef came to get her, but she didn't want to leave.

"Don't send me away, Jean. Please. Please." She hated how pitiful she sounded, but she couldn't help it. He took her face in his hands.

"I'll come to you, my pet. Go with Josef and I'll come to you, I promise, *ma deese*."

She got her cloak and went out to Josef and her horse. She'd made a fool of herself. She'd never begged a man for his company and now she'd embarrassed herself and tarnished the memory of her brave husband. This man would never come to her. He was wanted by the police and he certainly couldn't be seen in New Orleans. She'd never say her life couldn't get any worse, because fate would show her it could.

She couldn't look her Josef in the face, he knew her humiliation and she wanted his quiet respect more than any man she knew.

"I know you loved Papa Maurice, Tante Tine. Sometimes we all need a strong heart to lean on." He'd never judge her for her needs. If he didn't have Augustine, he wouldn't have gotten through his loss either.

Celestine and Josef rode slowly back into the city and she wondered if she'd ever stop missing her husband and the life they had together. She rode into her carriage way and she could smell some of 'Rite's good jambalaya on the fire and thought for the first time in months how hungry she was. Maybe it was a sign she'd live. She gave Josef her horse and walked back to the kitchen. It was familiar and warm and 'Rite was sitting peeling apples for a pie. She was so pretty. Why had some young man not scooped her up? She'd make someone a wonderful wife? Celestine was reminded that she had people in her life that loved and needed her.

"It smells wonderful, darling. What time do we eat?"

"Anytime you're ready, Tante 'Tine. I thought I might bring some up to your room later." She was smiling a strange smile and looking very impish. *What wasshe hiding under her thought bonnet,* Celestine wondered to herself.

Celestine pulled herself up the stairs to her bedroom. Lately she hated going into it. She knew it'd be empty and his things were locked in

the big armoire and the bed was too big. She opened the door and saw
the black jacket on the back of the chair.

"Oh, Jean, you came, you came to me." She was smiling and crying at
the same time.

"Didn't I say I would, woman?" Why did his women doubt him
when he told them something? He never said 'yes' when he meant 'no'.
It took forever for his women to know that.

He pulled her down on his lap and she reached her mouth up to his
and she couldn't get enough. His kiss touched her soul and awakened
something she'd tried to stifle. She was pulling his shirt over his head.
She stopped to take in his beautiful chest. The black soft curls took her
breath away; the thick hair almost covered his whole chest. She reached
for the buttons on his breeches and he laughed and pulled her hands
away.

"Slow down, my pet. Wouldn't you like to work into this?" He was
worried she'd stop and realize what she was doing as a new widow and
shy away.

"Ah, you don't want me? "

Oh damn, she was frailer than he thought. She was a large
broken barrel of changing emotions and he could tell he was in for a
surprise a minute.

"Stop. Of course I want you, my pet, now slow down. Stand up and
let me see you undress. I want to see you naked." He was going to have
to take over, humor was always good and she was in no condition to
keep a decision longer than the thought it took to make it.

She stood and took her clothes off so fast, she knotted a corset
string. She was pulling and twisting it and making it worse. He got up
and turned her around. He was trying hard not to laugh.

"Stop, move your hands. Stop or I can't get it lose."

She finally stopped and let him undo the knot. He was trying not to laugh and he was trying not to throw her on the bed and enter her; he wanted badly to do both.

"Now, let me see you, my pet." She was naked and turning slowly in front of him for his pleasure. She liked being told what to do; it took her mind away from everything except the task at hand. He couldn't catch a breath. She was even more beautiful than he imagined. Her skin was the color of rich cream and her breasts were full and shapely with large rose colored nipples. He could see ribs under her breast going into the smallest waist imaginable. Her flat stomach and perfectly rounded butt looked like half an apple when she turned to the side. But his heart caught in his throat at the beautiful blonde hair covering what he desired most. His mistresses were beautiful, but he'd never seen blonde hair on a woman's privates. He didn't know what to kiss first. He had to stay in control, whimpering at her feet wouldn't bode him well.

"Now come and help me with my breeches and mind, be careful of my leg."

She bent down and unbuttoned his breeches and reached in to find what she wanted. He wasn't as large as Maurice, but well-endowed and hard as cypress. She couldn't wait; she wanted to taste him; breathe him; devour him. She had to fill up the gaping hole in her empty soul where the cannon ball blew through le Celestine and landed in her own gut tearing out all reason and happiness.

She gently pulled his breeches down and saw the big rapier scar across his thigh. It was still soft and pink, and would be tender but not sore. She gently licked her warm tongue across the soft skin of the scar and felt the difference in skin between the scar and the leg itself.

"Oh Jean, you were hurt trying to save him." She was dragged back to her husband's brutal death. She stood up and looked for her wrapper; *Jean had to go home, he shouldn't be here. She was Maurice's widow and she shouldn't have a man in her bed.*

He saw her eyes go back to the bad place and he wouldn't let that happen. He couldn't let her think of the scar or the battle; she needed this more than he did and he needed it desperately. He stood up and brought her back down to him and kissed her for a long time and softly spoke.

"Shhh, relax Celestine, let me hold you and make love to you. Shhh. I know what it's like to lose a love, my pet. I know." He could feel her relax into his chest.

"Oh, Jean, yes, please make love to me." She reached up for his kiss.

She relaxed again and he could tell she was back into pleasuring his body and being pleasured and moving out of her thoughts and the pain. She looked into his eyes with a bittersweet smile.

He'd never been so hard in his life. This woman was all he'd dreamed she would be and better. His plans for the gentle love making of a woman in mourning were fading as he tried to get enough air in his lungs. She went back down his chest and stopped at his nipples and drove him crazy with her suckling and pulling his hair with her mouth, dragging her tongue across his belly and down to his erection. He had many women do this, but never one who committed to giving him pleasure through her pleasure. He'd always had to ask for this treatment and buy expensive gifts and explain the technique.

She was getting enjoyment out of his cock in her mouth and going down her throat. He was about to spend just looking down at the soft blonde curls surrounding his groin and falling across his thigh and the big scar. He thought it couldn't get any better and then she was reaching for one of his nipples and tweaking and gently pulling as she was going down to his seed and then gently coming back up to the head and down again. Her saliva came from nowhere and kept him wet and slippery and he was ready to spend and he tried to tell her and move her head but she wouldn't stop. She wouldn't move her head. She reached down and cupped his seed gently then added pressure and more pressure still. He released and she was drinking him and swallowing him and continuing her gentle, steady movements until she felt him make his last plunge into the back of her throat. He took her head in his hands and gently pulled her off of him. She pulled her head up and lay on his stomach and breathed him in and got up and sat on his spent cock and put her head into his chest and whispered:

"I love you, Jean. I need to love you. Please don't leave me."

He had to think. He wasn't prepared for this. He was prepared to take this woman and ease her suffering and help her get over her husband, but he wasn't ready to fall in love with her. He had to think. He was getting hard again with her ass on his spent cock and just like getting her to move her head, it was too late. He knew he loved her from the first day in the pirogue coming down his bayou; lying to the authorities over slaves that didn't exist. He'd dreamed of her long blonde curls falling and covering him; mixing with the black hair of his chest just as they were now. He was madly in love with her and it could be his undoing, but he couldn't do a damned thing about it.

He picked her up and walked to the bed. He put her in first and then got in on top of her. He kissed her breasts and took as much as he could in his mouth and played with it and sucked at it and ran his tongue around the velvet softness of the nipple. He reached his hand between her legs and felt the little nerve of pleasure and watched her face as he brought it to life. He wanted to taste it, but he also wanted to watch her face as he entered her. It was a favorite thing of his. He could always tell if a woman liked his cock by the look in her eyes. He could tell a fake and he could tell the real thing. His energy was too much for some women and he wanted to make sure his woman was enjoying him. If she wasn't he had other tricks up his preverbal sleeve he could use to make her happy. A man wasn't a real man if he couldn't make his woman happy.

"Do you want me, my pet?" He'd dreamed of saying that.

"Yes, please, oh please, Jean. I want you, Captain Lafitte." She was breathing the words more than speaking them. He wasn't expecting those words. They sent new waves of pleasure over him and he thought he'd release from her soft voice whispering his name. He entered her and watched as her eyes went soft and desirous of more. Her long brown lashes closed slowly over her eyes and then opened again as he went further. She was already in an ecstasy he hadn't expected but was sweetly providing. He began his strokes and watched to see how they were received; she still wanted more, he went deeper and stronger and she wanted more. He was driving himself harder and deeper and she pulled her legs around the small of his back and pulled him in deeper with the heels of her feet. He could feel her legs holding him in a strong caress and he was harder than he remembered since he was young and lived with the granite erections of youth.

"I need more, please, more Jean, please. Fill me, please; harder." He took her legs from around his waist and looped her knees over his arms and brought her hips up higher to receive him and went in deeper. She still needed more and he was afraid he was going to hurt her, but she didn't care, she couldn't get enough. He picked up her legs and put her ankles over his shoulders and went in as deep as he could reach and he'd hit bottom minutes before, but she wanted more and he was surely hurting her. He had to stop. He was going to hurt her. He stopped and pulled her legs down beside his.

"Celestine, I'm hurting you. Stop this."

"No, no, I can't stop. Please, do this for me, Jean, Please."

She flipped him over and got on top of him before he realized it. *He was more than twice her size and she'd flipped him, for God's sake. Who the hell was this woman he thought he'd tame and own like the other women in his life?*

She took him in her hand and inserted him into her wet warmth and began her strokes and he went deeper and she came down harder. After what seemed like a long time, he finally had to spend and he couldn't wait for her. He was breathing hard and every muscle tensed and he bucked and shivered into her. She held her breath and tensed; she felt the release come from her toes into her groin and up into her chest. Her hips bucked and she fell into his chest; she kept moving and bucked again gasping for breath. She held his hips and leaned back onto him and came forward. It started again and she was going into another spend. She didn't know she'd ever feel such ecstasy again after Maurice.

Jean felt she was having more than one release and he stopped moving so she could move at her own pace on him and finish her ecstasy. She fell onto his chest and fell asleep before he could move from under her. She was going to be a sweet challenge; this woman and her insatiable energy and appetite. He had a whole new respect for Captain Maurice Dubois.

He gently rolled her over and pulled her into his chest and fell asleep and neither woke until the sun was coming up.

"I guess you think I'm a bit brazen?" She sounded so sweet; he couldn't believe it was the same hellcat that almost neutered him the night before. His laughter could be heard down to the kitchen.

"My God, woman do you come with splints and bandages? You nearly killed me."

He rolled over and entered her again and this time he was gentle. She was tight and wet and cinched him in and curved herself around him; she took him into the center of herself and reached up for his kiss. She put her hands around his arms and kissed his tight muscles and arched her back and shuddered and bucked into her release.

She was so sweet he thought he'd die with his love for her. She felt him tense and take a deep breath and he bucked into his spend and she was receiving his seed and held him close to her as he bucked again.

"Ahhhh, Ahhhh." He yelled it. He hadn't had such a release in years. He wasn't usually verbal in a release; but he couldn't help it. New things were happening to him with this woman and he'd have to be ready for anything.

She was holding in a laugh.

"Is there something amusing you?" *What was next with her? How'd she gotten under his skin this comfortably?*

"You really are a pirate." His head came up off her breast and his frown was visible.

"What did you say to me, Madame?" Was he hearing her correctly?

"You really are a pirate, you said 'Aaarg'."

"I did no such thing, how dare you?" He was searching her eyes.

"Yes, you did, you said Aaarg. And you said it very loudly. ARRRRGH."

"Is it your custom to torment the man who gives you pleasure… and nearly ruptures himself doing so?" He was beginning to see her gentle amusement.

She was laughing now. She hadn't laughed this much in too long.

He began to laugh. *She was adorable.*

"I believe I said, Ahhhh. I have no recollection of an 'r' or 'g' at the end, my pet."

"No, I'm pretty sure I heard an 'rg'." She was going too far, she had her laugh, he was still a dangerous man, shouldn't tweak a friendly bear.

She became quiet. He laid his head back down to listen to her heart.

"Jean? Do you think I'm sinful to want you so soon after losing Maurice?"

"I'm a pirate, my pet, I don't judge other people." She couldn't believe he said it. She couldn't believe he'd ever say it. She didn't know what to think.

He rolled off of her and she turned on her side to look at and admire him.

"You did say, Aaarg."

"I did not."

"Yes you did."

"Celestine!!!!" He reached over and slapped her bottom. "Stop tormenting me, woman." He pulled her into his stomach and kissed her. "Just know a privateer loves you."

She could torment him for the rest of his life and he'd never have enough.

Chapter Eighteen

Josef brought one of the big Haitian grass rugs from the warehouse and cut it in sections and wove it in the iron scroll work on the big gates. It hindered the breeze but it made for complete privacy in the courtyard. Jean could sit at the dining table and not be afraid of being seen from the street. They could enjoy dinner as a family and no one would be arrested.

Celestine hadn't been able to go to the new house. She didn't know if she ever would again. It held her dreams and the future she and Maurice had been building. She missed him terribly in this house, but the thought of walking through those beautiful rooms without him by her side was more than she could stand. She was looking at offers from people who wanted to buy the place. She knew she'd sell it. Just thinking about walking around the widow's walk and not seeing his ship coming in would send her into tears for days.

Josef had seen Papa Maurice around the house. He was waiting for his wife; he told Josef. He didn't seem to mind that Laffite was in residence, Josef figured those feelings didn't matter once you were on the other side. The ghost would warn Josef of upcoming storms or people trying to take advantage of 'Rite and her beauty and innocence. There'd been several men interested, but none had been anything but fortune hunters looking for the money in her dowry from the white Captain.

She was so trusting and so good; she'd let anyone talk her into anything. Papa Maurice told him about Augustine and her reasons for not marrying him. She was afraid of his gift and his powers to see things; she thought it was voudou, and it scared her Catholic senses. Once he knew that, Josef explained to her that it was a gift from his mother and they'd come to a decision. He'd start going back to mass and they'd be married. He couldn't understand why he hadn't seen it himself. Maybe he was too close and loved her too much.

Augustine never conceived and they both wanted children. Josef still worked in the blacksmith shop and followed the Laffite's and their lives. He knew Jean bought and sold slaves and he knew Tante' Tine didn't know this. It wasn't his job to tell her. He couldn't stop the man and it could only mean trouble for his family if Laffite was angry with them. There was only so much a man could do to keep his family under his own control. Laffite's brother approached Josef one morning and told him of one of Jean's mistresses dying and leaving three little girls with no one to care for them. The man thought it'd be an excellent idea if Josef and Augustine adopted them. He'd spoken to his brother, Jean and he thought it a wonderful idea as long as Josef didn't change their names. He also thought Josef was a savior to do this for him and the girl's mother.

Josef spoke to Augustine and she was thrilled to take them and went to meet the woman, Mary Anne.   She wisely and lovingly began a friendship that lasted until her death. The girls got to know Augustine through their mother and felt safer going to her and Josef after she died. Laffite made sure the girls were financially secure, but Josef and Augustine would be their 'parents'. Josef and Augustine were impressed with Jean's loving attention to Mary Anne and his kindness to her as she was dying. Laffite loved all of his children and it was a huge compliment to Josef and Augustine that he'd trust them with his little girls. Josef's life was getting better and he wanted to find a larger house for his soon to be new family.

Celestine liked her life, love wasn't the word. She loved Jean in her own way and liked his living with her even though it was on his terms most of the time. He came and went as he pleased and she'd learned not to question his life. Sometimes he'd come from his home on rue Royale and sometimes he'd come straight from Barataria.

The war with the British was gearing up and he was getting more and more involved with the whole business. She wanted no part of any of it. As far as she was concerned they could rot. The whole British fleet was not worth a pair of her husband's boots. She had no love for the bastards; one just had to ask to hear her say it.

She was asleep when he came quietly into her room. She could smell him from the door. She recognized the smell from a swamp bath she'd been given years before.

"What on earth? Why do you smell like swamp?"

"Sorry my pet, I had to swim part of the way back to you." He was undressing.

"No, you don't; go downstairs and get under the spray; clothes and all; I'll bring you your dressing gown and a bathing towel." He was still wanted by the police, he probable did have to leave his boat and come by swamp to her bed.

"For God's sake, woman, does a little nature bother your senses?"

"Yes, my love when it takes away your natural scent; you stink."

"Damn, when did a man's profession offend the delicate senses of his woman?"

"Hush, Jean, you'll wake the house." She followed him downstairs and watched as he undressed by the cistern. Josef had the tub under the spray so Philippe could shower without using all the water.

She got in the tub in her chemise and pulled him down onto her lap. They'd never taken a bath together; it could be fun she decided. She took the good clove soap and ran it over his hair and filled it full of soft foamy bubbles and then ran her hands down his chest and soaped the black curls and on down as far as she could reach. She handed him the soap to reach farther down. He pulled her arms down to his groin and gave her the soap. She felt the cypress knee he called his cock and was once again amazed at the hardness. She watched him wash his legs and feet as she tried to keep his manhood from slipping out of her hands. Her arms were not long enough and she was half losing him under the water. She pulled the little chain to get enough water to rinse his hair and his body and he walked out of the tub and wrapped the towel around his waist. He reached back in and carried her wet and dripping back upstairs and removed her wet chemise and laid her into the soft eiderdown of the big bed. He got in on top of her. He was kissing her breast and her neck and she was dying from the scent of the clove soap and thoughts of Maurice. She could close her eyes and it was her husband and not Jean. She was back in Maurice's arms and he was making sweet gentle love to her and he was not dead and she was so happy she could burst. Jean pulled up on his elbows to look at her and saw her eyes were closed. She was moaning and gasped when he stopped stroking into her. She was kissing his shoulders and running her tongue down onto his chest. It only took him a few seconds to see what she was doing. This was a first for him. He'd never been in someone's fantasy before. He didn't like it. Had she done this to him before? He didn't think so; he'd watched her face and enjoyed the look in her eyes as he made love to her. It was the bath and the soap; he'd smelled the soap in Maurice's armoire once when it was opened. He'd let her have this one. She may not even know she was doing it, but it'd be the last. He spent on purpose and got out of bed. He got a fresh set of clothes out of the big armoire that had become his and left without a word. She was lying on her back as he left; crying and allowing her heart to break into a thousand pieces. She did it again, she hurt the man she loved by having another man in her mind.

Jean didn't show up the next night, or the next and on the third day, she was barking at everyone. She barked at Philippe for not eating his breakfast and she barked at 'Rite for over salting the fish and she barked at herself for being so foolish. She went to the shops and bought some beautiful soft linen and died it dark green. She made the shirt with the big sleeves that he liked and the neckcloth had his initials in black thread. (J L B)   The green shirt would make his hazel eyes turn as green as the velvet leaves of the big magnolia tree and twice as beautiful.   She put Maurice's in her chemise drawer next to her father's; two of her most favorite things along with Maurice's wedding ring and watch. Both would be saved for Philippe on his coming of age.   The diamond stick pin, she'd given to Josef.

Jean would be back.   He had to come back; she wasn't ready to lose both her men.   If she had to, she'd go find him herself.

She heard the children first.   Josef and Augustine were walking into the courtyard with three of the most beautiful little girls she'd ever seen. They looked to be around ten, five and three years old.   They had creamy skin with black soft curly hair falling around their shoulders.   She walked down the stairs to see what was going on. They all had varying degrees of hazel eyes and long dark lashes.

"Tante 'Tine may we present our girls?   This is Alex, Marie and Tina and they are ours."

She caught her breath; these beautiful children could only be Jean's. She looked up at Josef.

"May I speak to you, Tante 'Tine?   Augustine, would you take the girls to the kitchen, I believe 'Rite has some cookies."   Augustine took the girls around back to the kitchen.

"Tante 'Tine, these are Laffite's girls, but their mother has passed and they are going to live with us and be our family."

"That's wonderful, Josef. He's given his consent?"

"Of course, he was happy for it. I would've told you sooner, but I didn't know what you'd think."   He couldn't tell what she was thinking. It was a big step for him and Augustine but Tante 'Tine's new grandchildren were her lover's children. She would be their grand-mere, step mother. Their little family just kept getting stranger and stranger.

"I'm so proud of you. I'm thrilled for you and Augustine. I wish your father could see."

"He does, Tante, he does, we talked about it." He knew it always made her nervous when he said these things, but it came out before he thought. She knew Josef saw Maurice on occasion, he told Marguerite and she told her. Celestine thought she saw him once on a rainy afternoon while she was reading to Philippe in bed. She caught something out of the corner of her eye and looked to see him sitting with his wonderful smile aimed at her and his son leaning back in his big chair by the fireplace. She knew he wasn't there; it was her loneliness for him. She wished she could see him like Josef did.

The girls came from the kitchen and Celestine was introduced to Alex and Marie and little Tina hiding behind Josef's big leg. Celestine was in love. She looked over to see her son was also, he had his eye on Alex and she swore he was about to swoon. They'll be great friends she thought. She had no idea she was looking at her future daughter-in-law. Life could get stranger; all she had to do was wake up each morning. *She wondered if families two hundred years ahead would have these strange family groupings; or was it just a gift from her husband.*

Jean woke her up several nights later. She hadn't heard him come in; as usual. Usually she wasn't a sound sleeper, but he could come and go and never wake her. He took her in his arms and cradled her and he smelled like Allspice and lavender and the scent was wonderful. It suited him. He handed her a box of soaps.

"These are for the boudoir, and I've left some by the spraying bath. Don't ever mistake me again, Madame." His eyes had turned dark brown, almost black.

"No, my love." She cuddled into his spicy scent and wanted more of him. She could tell he missed her; he fumbled taking off her night gown and almost tore it trying to get it over her head. He wanted to take her and make gentle love to her, but he was about to spend and couldn't get into her fast enough. He spent before he had taken a dozen long deep strokes.

"I'm sorry, my pet; but I've really missed you."

"I didn't go anywhere, you did."

"Oh no, Madame. You left me while I was inside of you?"

"Oh, yes… Jean; I'm so sorry."

"Do you have any dead husbands who smell of Allspice?"

"No, not as yet." She laughed.

"Good." They lay in each other's arms.

"Do I lie here and wait days so you can empty into me and leave me wanting?"

"Relax, woman, I haven't left your bed. Give a man a chance to reconnoiter." He put her hand on his beginning erection and moved it up and back down. She took over and went down with her mouth. She'd never had a semi-soft erection in her mouth; she loved feeling it come alive. He remembered why he'd missed her so terribly. He stopped her after a few minutes, turned her over and brought her hips up to him and entered her from the back. She could feel him all the way to her center. She liked this position, it was new and seemed kind of naughty and it suited her. He waited for her to spend before he emptied into her. He got up to pour himself a drink of whiskey.

"Where were you?" She'd never asked, but he'd never been away this long. "Jean, why are you so sad, my love?"

"I love you, pet; don't ask me questions. I don't want to get in the habit of lying to you." He'd never tell her he was with his dying Mistress and his heart was broken at her death. His children would be part of Celestine's world now and he'd only see them when he visited in her home. It was not something a father wanted to discuss.

She got up and went to the armoire and pulled his new shirt and neckcloth out and handed them to him. He looked at her and smiled.

"I'm usually the one giving gifts, my pet. This is new to me." He put the shirt on over his head and it did just as she had desired, his eyes were dark green and sensual.

"You made this for me?" He took her in his arms and kissed her tenderly.

"I'm in love with your daughters." She nuzzled her face into his sweet smelling neck.

"Me, too." He answered casually.

"I want one of my own."

"Josef has three that should be enough for you, my pet." The thought of losing her in childbirth suddenly became a possibility and he couldn't think of it.

She saw he didn't want to discuss it.

"Don't shut me out of your life, Jean."

"You are my life, Celestine. Everything else is what happens on my way home to you. Leave it." *Jean realized he'd never given this woman who carried his heart a gift. She had everything, how had he not thought to give her some little token of what he felt. He could be an ass; he'd have to remedy that.*

Chapter Nineteen

1814

Colette saw the wanted posters. She tore one down and brought it to Celestine.

"Do you see this? Do you see with whom you're cavorting?"

"Colette please, did you think he was a Sunday school teacher?"

"What would Maurice say?" She couldn't seem to get it across to her old friend that the man was a murderous thug and dangerous to have around her son.

"Don't play that card; I know what I'm doing."

Colette had become horribly judgmental of Celestine and her liaisons with Lafitte. Celestine really had nothing in common with the woman any more. She'd been hanging around with other women artists who wore men's clothes; Colette had no room to talk about liaisons.

Giving up Jean at this point would be as hurtful as giving up Maurice again. She had no intentions of it. She loved him; not like she still loved Maurice, but she loved him with whatever pieces of her heart she had left. He'd saved her many times and shown his loyalty, he wore a huge scar from trying to save her husband, for God's sake; it wasn't likely she'd see him as a thug. Besides, he smelled really nice lately. She loved the spice scent M. Chenier had created for him. A mixture of Allspice and lavender, it made her dizzy with lust for the man.

She'd seen the posters; she'd also seen the ones Jean had put up in response. Governor Claiborne offered a five hundred dollar reward for Jean Laffite. Jean Laffite offered a reward of fifteen hundred dollars for Gov. Claiborne, fair enough. It was a joke on Jean's part, but few people found it funny. Celestine found it hilarious. She heard rumors that Jean was infatuated with Governor Claiborne's beautiful, third wife, Suzette. She sent Josef to find out if it was it true.

There was only one true love in Laffite's life and her name was Celestine Dubois and Jean had better understand that; or his privateer ass wouldn't be worth the five hundred dollar reward the Governor was offering. Celestine was firm on that.

Colette had been acting strangely for some time now. It started on the long voyage. They'd all started as the best friends they'd been for years, but Colette had spent so much time with one of the sailors who was also an artist that she'd been absent from many of their games and dinners. Pierre seemed to understand; he knew how much his wife loved her new found talent and she couldn't get enough. Maurice kept an eye on the goings on. He wouldn't have his crew member make a cuckold of his friend Pierre, but Celestine laughed at his fears and kept him from acting on the foolish accusations.

Pierre was coming around more. He thought of more and more reasons to come into town. Celestine couldn't blame him; her house was now overflowing with laughing, happy children and the odors of good things coming from Marguerite's kitchen. The only thing it lacked was her husband.

She'd hired help for Marguerite and a groomsman so Josef could tend to his family and not worry about the stable. The children loved Josef and were already calling him, Papa'sef and they were calling Augustine, Mama 'tine. Jean hadn't been around with the children there and she wondered what he'd think seeing his children so happy with their new home. She hoped he'd be pleased.

Jean had indeed seen his girls happy with their new home. He knew they were in good hands and he should let them know he was still part of their lives, but it was still too hard for him. He'd have to wait until he could be glad to see them and not let them see his pain in losing their mother. He and Mary Anne hadn't been intimate in a few years, but she was still a very loving part of his life. She depended on him and enjoyed his visits. She'd taken a lover and he was glad she had someone. Their friendship was very dear to him and he'd miss her gentle scolding when he told her about Celestine and how he didn't know what to do with her. She'd been adamant that he should marry her before her reputation was totally destroyed and her son was made an outcast. He felt being married to him would go worse for her and Philippe. They'd never agreed on the matter. He missed her now. He wanted to tell her about the war coming and his plans to help make this new country and get full pardons for his men and get his ships back from that bastard, Paterson. Celestine couldn't talk of it, it made her go to a place in her head that shut him out and locked the gate.

He'd tried to tell her how important it was for him to partner with General Jackson; but Claiborne and Jackson were both totally against it. She'd turned a deaf ear.

He was thinking of Celestine more and more. He really thought that bedding her'd take some of the energy out of his pursuit, but it'd made it deeper and stronger and he had to admit he was crazy about her. Maybe he should marry her. They didn't have to live in New Orleans; they could live anywhere she wanted.

Josef hinted to him that she was jealous of Suzette Claiborne. Good; wouldn't hurt her to keep on her toes. He wanted to keep the control in this affair and he'd let his guard slip too many times. If she ever really knew her power over him she'd tire of him in days and he'd be back in the swamp. She could have any man in New Orleans; she just didn't know it yet. Mary Anne was right, she was already being thought of as a very high-class courtesan and many had wondered what Laffite had done to keep her so long. He could tell a person it almost takes two cocks.

He'd used Suzette Claiborne to get to Governor Claiborne and might again, but she was no Celestine, not even close.

He wanted to give Celestine some little trinket she'd like. He'd embarrassed himself when he realized he'd never been generous with this woman who'd been so generous of herself with him. There wasn't much he could do to top naming a ship after her, hard act to follow for sure. Too bad; her name on one of his ships would please him very much.

He decided it was time to buy a house for Josef and Augustine. The one they were in was too small and they were doing an excellent job creating a happy home life for his girls. He knew it'd please Celestine, but he was going to do that for his girls anyway. He was getting an erection just thinking about Celestine. He'd be in her bed soon for sure.

Pierre was worried about his friend. He and Josef talked about it. The affair with Laffite hadn't dissipated like both men hoped. She was more involved with the man than ever. Colette had been right to worry. His reputation was dangerously close to destroying anyone who knew him; especially a respected Sea Captain's widow.

Josef broached the subject to Laffite about Celestine not liking Mrs. Claiborne, thinking it would drive him away. A man like Laffite didn't need clinging women, if Celestine got too jealous and demanding, he'd disappear. But it had worked the opposite. Augustine had fussed at him all night for doing such a stupid thing. He got the point; he was no good at this stuff. Josef thought the man would take himself elsewhere once he'd won her, but he'd moved himself into her affections and had no intentions of leaving. Josef could feel the man had even thought of marriage.

Pierre was dealing with his own personal problems. His marriage was over and no one knew. The reuse of the sailor on the ship had given him an excuse when the time comes to walk out, but the little queer sailor had nothing to do with it. His wife had been in love with Celestine since they were kids and he thought he could fix it with his love; he thought she just needed a patient man who could provide her with a safe bed. He was wrong. He'd first noticed something was different when Colette asked so many questions about sex. He'd get excited telling her things; thinking she wanted to learn to please him, and of course, he fell for it every time.

He made it his business to learn new techniques and bed games to share with his wife thinking she'd come to him. He'd talked to seasoned sailors and friendly whores in the saloons; he could write a book on his creations in the bedroom. But Colette was just getting information to take back to her friend. She finally admitted that talking about sex was the closest she'd ever get to her friend's affections, and it hadn't worked. Celestine had no idea where Colette's affections lay and so as the years passed, Colette stopped. Pierre managed to cajole her and offer gifts for her sexual affections, but he grew tired of the charade and stopped after Letty was around three. He'd been lucky one night on the big ship, but he knew it was a spit in the dark and would never happen again; she'd lain with her eyes closed and God only knew who she was thinking of, it certainly wasn't her husband. Everyone important in his life had been in love with Celestine. He loved her as a friend and for years had been jealous of her hold on his wife. Now he saw her as a safe and happy haven and he didn't want this pirate messing with her heart and head and certainly not her reputation, it could affect Philippe and Letty also.

He wanted to move in and be a part of the weird group they called family, but that'd be entirely too strange. It was bad enough he was trying to find love for himself and not destroy his wife and child in an annulment or divorce. Colette found a group of women artists who accepted her and he suspected showed her more than acceptance. He couldn't judge her, he knew how hard she tried to be a wife for him, and if it wasn't in her, then so be it.

He'd talk to Celestine himself about getting rid of the pirate. Sometimes a person just needs to see from another's point of view in order to put things in perspective. *He knew that was bullshit even as the idea was forming in his head.*

Celestine wanted to know what was wrong with her darling Pierre. He'd been moping around her courtyard for days. She knew Colette was involved with her portrait painting and that was fine, but she should cherish Pierre. He was one husband any woman would be lucky to have.

Letty loved playing with the other children, but Celestine thought she should go home sometime. She'd gotten too bossy with Philippe and he and Alex had been trying to get away from her. Celestine left them alone, to work it out; she just didn't want little Letty getting hurt. Letty thought of Philippe as hers, but then so did Alex.

She hadn't seen Jean in a few days and she missed him. Maybe he'd come to her tonight, he'd never been gone from her bed more than a few days and that was only when he was angry.

The house didn't quiet down until late. Josef had taken the girls home after dinner and Philippe and Letty stayed up playing cards until Pierre made her go to bed. She loved her evening coffee with this friend. It was part of what made her life so nice. She'd ask Pierre tonight what was going on with him and Colette.

Suddenly the big gates flew open and men were rushing into the courtyard. They had guns and they were looking for Laffite. She had to stay calm, there were children asleep and this would terrify them.

"We know he's here Mme. Dubois, you can't hide him anymore."

"Gentlemen, we're alone here except for children sleeping upstairs. What is the meaning of this?" Pierre had never seemed so calm to Celestine. He was grace under fire.

"Capt. David, we're looking for Laffite, we mean no harm to your children."

Letty and Philippe had come onto the gallery and Letty was screaming for her papa.

"See what you've caused, Sergeant?" He ran to get Letty and take her back to her bed.

Celestine was still standing at the table aghast at the intrusion and the men with their guns. Is this what Colette had warned her about? She had to warn Jean.

Pierre came back downstairs and escorted the Sergeant upstairs to look in the empty rooms and see for himself Laffite was not hiding in the house. One man checked the kitchen and the stable.

"Please leave my house." Celestine had finally found her voice. "My son lost his father only a year ago and he is very easily shaken."

"We apologize for any inconvenience Mme. Dubois, but it is well known the pirate resides here most evenings. Please tell him we'll be back."

Celestine's knees gave way and she fell into her chair. She had no idea she was so watched and her actions were so known. She could die of humiliation. Maurice had lived his life exemplary from such scandal and now in one year she'd brought this down on his house. She'd die of mortification. Her sweet Jean, how could they be in this fix?

She sat looking into her cup, seeing nothing, hearing nothing, feeling nothing.

"It's true, my darling, he's a very dangerous man. Just because you know him in the bedroom of a night, doesn't mean he hasn't slit someone's throat in the swamp in the afternoon. Celestine, you have to wake up, my heart. He's offered his services to the American forces and Gen. Jackson won't even meet with him. Gov. Claiborne wants him to hang. These are good men, darling, they know more about him than you and I." Pierre didn't know any other way to say it. She had to see the truth.

"I'm going to bed, Pierre. I have to think about all of this. Would you close up the house and lock the gate?" She walked wearily up the stairs.

"Yes, my love." He could die for what he'd just done. He hated himself for doing it, and if she ever found out, she'd never speak to him again; but he had to. Damn it, he just had to.

He prayed that seeing the children so frightened would open her eyes. It could easily have been real soldiers, it was just a matter of time, but they wouldn't wait for him to take them upstairs, they'd barge into any bedroom with guns loaded and apologize later. He watched her walk into her room and close the door.

Celestine took off her clothes and got in bed. She was tired and scared and humiliated and she missed her men.

Pierre had told her before the men broke into her home that she was getting a reputation as a courtesan, Jean had called her that also. Was she? Maybe; she liked men and she liked their touch and she was never getting married again. But, her lover was wanted for God's sake. His brother was in the prison three blocks from her house for God's sake and he'd be trying to break him out any day. Well, not if she got there first.

"You're not going to let a few little men with guns scare you; are you, my pet?" He was getting undressed and climbing into bed. She grabbed him and buried her face in his chest and pulled his big arms around her and didn't move for a very long time. She'd just had a hideous revelation. She liked being in danger, it made her desire him more than ever. What the hell did this mean?

"Take me, Jean, take me now. I can't wait. I've never been this ready to release. Did they chase you? Did they follow you here?" She was struggling trying to find him under the covers.

He took her hands and stopped her. He pulled her head up to look at her.

"My God, woman you're on fire." He moved on top of her and entered her so fast she gasped. He couldn't get enough of her. This was the most thrilling thing he'd ever known. His woman was hot as fire thinking he could be murdered in her bed. He took a few wonderful strokes and stopped.

"Wait." Something's not right with this, he thought.

"What, what, don't stop please, Jean don't stop."

He looked down into her face.

"What exactly about this makes you desire me, my pet? My imminent death; or discovering people know we do this each night?" He looked closely for the answer.

"What, what are you talking about, why'd you stop?" She was searching his face.

He rolled off of her.

"Celestine, what part of the danger makes you want to release so quickly?"

"AAH, just knowing that any minute we could be… well, just knowing that the police… ah. What the bloody hell do I know, this is new for me too you damned, pirate. Now don't stop until I release." *By God, she was magnificent. He had a huge erection and he may as well give it to her as not. If he had to go, so be it, he'd die with his cock in the most wonderful woman in the world. How did such a dainty little woman get such a mouth? Takes most people years at sea to perfect.*

"Corsair, Madame." He whispered in her ear.

"I don't want to hear another sound from you unless it's 'ARRHHG'." She was too serious to hear the humor in what she said.

He was trying to stroke and laugh at the same time. He couldn't get enough; he felt like he could go for hours.

She finally released and fell to the side. She was breathing hard and fast. He released and fell onto her chest.

"Jean, we can't do this anymore." She knew it when she came to bed and he was waiting.

"I know." He didn't. He didn't want to think about it. After the trouble with the British was over, he'd come back. He had to come back. He'd kill people if he knew he could never come back. He knew the men weren't soldiers. He'd never seen some of them and others he knew to be friends of Pierre. But they could've been and they could arrest her and hurt Philippe and his daughters. He'd come back when the world was back to normal.

He turned to her.

"I love you, Celestine. You know I'll be back; when it's safe for the children."

He took her in his arms and kissed her and started at her creamy neck and tasted her all the way down to her stomach. He went back into her and started his slow long strokes and kissed her breasts and her neck. She was releasing and crying and he promised he'd be back after the war. She held on to his big arms so tight her knuckles were white and he released and emptied himself in her center and wanted to crawl in and stay with his seed.

He left before dawn. Even Pierre hadn't seen him come or go. She stayed in her room all morning and smelled his clothes and took the neckcloth she made for him and folded it next to her father's and her husband's and she hoped this one would be the last in her collection.

She got up in the late afternoon and saw the boxes on her dresser. Two small velvet boxes lay on a card. She sat at her dresser to open them. One was a diamond ring the size of a robin's egg set in platinum filigree and was the most beautiful thing she'd ever seen. The other box held a gold charm on a beautiful gold rope chain. The charm was no bigger than her thumb; it was a dainty little ship and engraved on the bow: *'le Celestine'* and on the other side *'La Diligente'*. *She thought she'd die, how can her heart be breaking again, she had none left. She read the note.*

My Pet,

Aaarg, I love you.

J. Lafitte

She called Josef into her room and they spoke for about thirty minutes. He left quietly with a somber look. A man on a mission.

She went back to bed and slept for two days.

Pierre was watching. She'd made a decision and she was sleeping to heal, thank God, he'd gotten through to her. Josef told him Laffite had come and she'd sent him away, he didn't think it necessary to tell him the man spent the night.

On the morning of the third day Josef knew what to do. He opened her door and told the kids she needed to wake up. Suddenly she was attacked by five sets of hands and feet and elbows jumping on her bed and laughing. Marguerite had a huge breakfast for her downstairs on the big table and she pulled herself out of bed and went downstairs. Josef and Pierre hauled the tub up to her room and Marguerite prepared a nice hot bath. She wanted to thank Pierre, but each time she looked at him, she'd tear up and couldn't speak. She'd get through this. Maybe Jean would come back to her once all this mess had calmed down. Yes, that's it, he'll come back. He's not dead. She perked up. He's not dead, just wanted by the police and the American Militia and the United States Navy, and the British Navy and the French Navy and the Spanish Navy, not so bad. He's not dead.

She ate everything on her plate.

"Josef, I need to talk to M. Dubonnet this morning. I want to rent the big house on the river to some nice family."

"Pierre, would you go with me to the warehouse?

I want to pick a few things to keep and then I want to sell some things. Is the warehouse costing us anything? If it isn't then let's leave things for the children to choose from once they're older. It's a shame to sell some of the things."

Pierre and Josef were thrilled, their plan had worked and she was back. What they didn't know was that she'd decided to live as a very expensive courtesan and the devil take the gossip and Creole society. She'd have favorite clients and the first would be her handsome Jean. *I would like to have him right now served up for breakfast, oops, I hope I didn't say that out loud?*

She went upstairs to take her bath and his soaps were gone, she looked over at Marguerite.

"I'll get you some more; he'll want these when he comes back." She knew how to play this game too.

The talk of the town was Pierre Laffite and three Africans escaping from the prison in the Cabildo. It was a mystery never solved. Many were accused but none arrested. The question on everyone's lips was how it could happen with so many guards and the heavy chains that shackled the men to the iron bars. Someone must have known a lot about ironworks and how to pass the guards without anyone being hurt.

Celestine gave it no thought. It was none of her affair. She was busy looking through the condolence letters she received after Maurice was killed. She knew there was one from Maurice's old friend. She just had to find it and read it in the clear light of day with an open heart and mind free from mourning. There were so many, she didn't know why she kept them, but she was glad she did. Maybe Philippe would like them one day, or Josef or Marguerite. It took her a couple of hours as she began to read some and got carried away with the sweet sentiments. She marveled at the amount of friends her husband had. She finally found it. She sat at Maurice's big desk and wrote the notes. She'd ask Josef one more favor before she asked him no more. The last one had been too dangerous and she was feeling guilty that she even asked it of him.

Josef answered Celestine when she called him from the gallery. Another favor? He was getting used to doing her dirty work. He didn't mind, she'd never ask him to do something that wasn't good for someone else.

She was his girls' grand-mere and that pleased him enough to do anything she asked. When she asked his help the other night, he'd already thought of it; the Laffite's, especially Pierre Laffite had been good to him and his family and the girls' Uncle' shouldn't have to rot in prison over a political matter and that was what it was, really. The Governor wanted his brother not him. It was much easier than he anticipated and it cost less than Tante 'Tine had given him for the bribes.

The jailors could've asked a lot more. The chains were no problem; his big wire cutters hidden down his long pants leg, had been honed by him and had a special strength developed in his own work-shop. He wouldn't get the jailors in trouble by using their keys. Pierre Laffite was too important a prisoner and they could lose their jobs.

This new favor was an easier one. Deliver a letter to Andy Jackson and one to Laffite. How hard could that be? He had a vision as she handed him the letter. He saw many men being brought into their courtyard on stretchers. But he also saw the courtyard free of bloody men and his family happy. He took that to mean there would be war, but none of his people would be harmed. He liked visions like this; when he was warned of events, but then assured things would be well again.

He took the letters. On the third day he returned to *rue du Maine* to find Marguerite had baked one of her wonderful persimmon cakes and set out coffee things for guests. She'd prepared a cold supper for the big table in the main drawing room and was setting out cups, saucers, small plates and cutlery. The drawing room was beautiful. The candles were lighted to give the room an intimate feel and there was pre-Christmas greenery on the little mantle with a soft friendly fire in the fireplace. The small kitchen arm Josef had installed in the parlor fireplace was holding the coffee pot, simmering and inviting; the aroma filled the house with its spicy goodness. He loved the allspice Tante 'Tine used in her coffee and he knew it'd be hot, strong and black. She'd set out her best crystal decanter full of some of Papa Maurice's finest brandy, but only two glasses. He wondered if this little party had anything to do with the letters he'd been delivering the last few days. She was coming down the stairs in her finest black silk dress, looking like the beautiful queen she was. She may be in widow's weeds, but she could turn any head with her looks and when her eyes lighted on you, a man was as good as under her spell for life.

"Josef, hurry and dress, I want you here in the courtyard in case of trouble. My guest'll be here, God willing, any minute."

Fifteen minutes later, Josef had finished washing his face and hands in the kitchen and went to answer the bell on the big gate. Celestine had only lighted part of the carriageway so the street wouldn't see her guest entering. Josef opened the gate and ushered General Jackson into the courtyard. What the hell was she planning? Josef was trying to keep his calm.

Within seconds Celestine appeared and took his hand.

"My husband was a great admirer of yours, General Jackson." He bowed and kissed her hand.

"Your husband saved my life when I was a foolish young boy, Madame Dubois. I have followed his career for years and when time permitted we wrote to each other. I was most distressed to hear of his murder by the British. I am at your service."

"Please, let's go into the drawing room and have a cup of Marguerite's good coffee." She ushered him in and waited for him to adjust to the warm, family atmosphere of the room.

"I understand dear Rachel is not with you this trip, General Jackson. How I would like to meet her. She must be most wonderful to capture the heart of a man such as yourself."

"She is that and more, Mme. Dubois." He laughed. I'm the winner, here. I'm not worthy of her. Thank you for inquiring."

She'd done it, she'd pleased him. She knew the gossip surrounding his beloved wife and the snubs. If Celestine ever decided to marry a politician, same could be said about her. Rachel had divorced a bad husband, Celestine was a widow with a pirate as a lover, one could toss the charges in the air and both would land like a rotten egg in the puritan society in which they lived.

She heard the bell on the big gate. Her heart almost stopped; what had she done? Was she out of her mind? These matters were none of her affair.

"Ah, there's my friend now. This friend almost lost his life trying to save my dear Maurice. I think you two will be good friends."

Josef opened the door and Jean walked into the parlor and up to Celestine.

"You sent for me, my treasure?" He started to take her in his arms when he saw Jackson standing by the fireplace.

Both men gasped, and went for their weapons, but their hands froze as she gifted each with an inquisitive look and then the smile again.

Celestine took Jean's arm and led him to Jackson.

"Jean, General Jackson was a friend of my husband's and I believe owes him a great deal. Is that correct, General?" She flashed her smile and turned to Jean.

"Jean, you tried to save my darling Maurice and I think somehow, that means you two have something in common through my beloved Maurice. I don't understand these things, but it just makes sense to me that you'd like a nice chat, maybe remember my husband and what a patriot he was? *Nez pa?*" She turned and walked to the French doors and opened them.

"Excuse me, gentlemen, but I have children waiting for a bedtime story. Please enjoy your visit. Marguerite has provided a cold supper and some refreshments. Take all the time you like."

She was out and across the courtyard. Josef had to catch her before her knees gave way.

"Oh, Josef, what have I done?"

"You've either gotten these two egos together for the good of each, or I'll be looking for places to hide the bodies in the swamp. Either way, I'm proud of you, Mere'tine." Celestine thought she'd die with love for this big gentle son who just called her mother.

There were no bodies to bury and Jean stayed for two days after the general left. He knew it'd be months before he could come back to her. None knew Anna's prediction to Maurice had just come true. His friendship with little Andy Jackson would change history.

Chapter Twenty

The disgusting war was over December 24th, 1814. But on January 8th, 1815 the last bloody battle at Chalmette had been won in less than three hours. The Ursulines' prayed all night to the statue of Bon Succor and were being called miracle workers once again.

General Jackson with the American militia and his comrade Jean Lafitte were the victors. The wounded began appearing late afternoon.

Celestine's house was full of wounded soldiers picked from the battle field by Josef and Pierre. Some were slaves that'd been with their young masters and were not allowed in the hospital and some were Indians who needed mending but not surgery and Marguerite had volunteered the house for them to recuperate. Marguerite had two young novices from the convent helping her mend and tend; bathe and care for the wounded men.

Celestine had just finished making a cot in the courtyard when she saw familiar boots coming in the gate. He was supporting a young man as big as himself with a slash in his neck and the young man's slave was following behind with a beautiful horse helping as best he could. She motioned for him to bring the young man to the fresh cot and called for Marguerite to bring some bandages for the young man's neck injury and get his information. She was trying to keep busy and not die from the desire she was feeling for this man who'd been her lover. He looked tired, but he still had those wonderful eyes and she could tell her yearning to touch him was more than matched by his.

He grabbed her hand and stepped into the stable.

"Oh God, I've missed you." He breathed into her mouth as he pulled her so close she could smell swamp, blood, horses and raw, male sweat.

She felt his erection and knew she'd die before he could find a way to get back to her.

"I'll be back when I can, my pet. I promise." He was kissing her again.

He took her face in his hands and said. "Celestine, I promise."

"Please, Jean. I miss you so much." She knew he'd not be back for a long while. His eyes were already thinking of things he had to do. She was begging this man to come to her, again. She'd never do that with another man; but then, she knew she'd never want one as badly as she wanted her Jean.

"Tanti 'Tine, this man needs you." She walked over to the cot and looked down at the man Jean had just brought in. He was a very handsome twenty five year old Captain waiting for something wonderful to give him reason; someone to save; battles to win.

"Did my man get something to eat? He's been all day bringing me here. His name is Franklin, mam, and is there food for my horse?" He'd used all the energy he could afford to sit up on his elbows long enough to speak.

"Yes, your horse is in the stable and Franklin's in the kitchen now, eating some nice rabbit gumbo my daughter made this morning. Shhh, lie back and let me tend to your neck."

His neck was bleeding again and Celestine reached for the bandages and began to dress his wound. Her tears were falling on the young man's face and throat. He looked up to see the sad face of a beautiful woman who needed saving right away.

"Am I dying?" There was a smile in spite of the sad question.

"No, this is very shallow, just bloody and probably very painful."

"Oh, mam, you were crying so hard, I was goin' to write a letter home to my mama." She laughed and looked back into his smile. He could turn a few heads. Her family told her the pirate was dangerous, Jean wasn't even close to what this young man could do to a lady's heart.

"I'm so sorry, I just lost a friend." She wiped her eyes with his sleeve. He held up the other arm for her to use that sleeve too and she laughed.

He'd never seen a more beautiful woman and he just made it his business to make sure she never cried again. He guessed her to be around twenty nine or thirty, he liked older women, they didn't giggle and hide behind those stupid fans when a man tried to make conversation.

"Andrew Harmon Down, Mam. I'm with the Kentucky Riflemen Militia out of Paducah. We sent them scrambling back to their ships today, I reckon." *He'd talk even stranger if she'd keep that light in her blue eyes for him. His fake country accent was amusing to this little French lady. If he could make her laugh he wouldn't see the faces of the men he'd been killing all morning.*

"Don't mind my sayin' so, Mam, but I hate the bloody British. Hang the lot of 'em if it were up to me." *He could see her smiling now. She really was amused; he knew he could do it. He was always able to make a lady smile; he was famous for it back home.*

"Andrew H. Down, from Paducah, Kentucky, would you please stop talking, you're making your neck bleed again and I hate the sight of blood?" She reached down and kissed him gently on the lips and lingered a second longer than necessary. *He was so sweet she could eat him up with a spoon and honey. Some lucky girl was going to have her hands full one day if he didn't already have one.*

He was bigger than he looked lying on the cot. His arm came up and around her waist and pulled her down on top of his chest and kissed her as she loved to be kissed. She was breathless.

"Fine, a fine thing to do; now you're bleeding again."

"Don't mind my say'n so, Mam you're sure in the wrong profession if you hate the site of blood." *He made her laugh this time. You're doing all right old man.*

"Josef, would you come redo this bandage for me, please." She looked down at him and winked, *wait until he sees this nurse; he won't be trying to kiss this one.* Andrew looked up to see huge Josef with the kind eyes laughing directly in his face.

"Now, let's see if you can behave yourself a minute or two."

Franklin came out of the kitchen laughing and eating a huge boot of hot French bread.

"You dead yet?" He laughed down at Andrew.

"Nope, just a wound to the heart and pride, ole man. Did you see her Franklin; I think she may be Mrs. Andrew H. Down, before this war's over."

"Nope, but there's one in the kitchen I be takin' home."

Celestine was tired and her clothes were bloody and she smelled like the herbs and salves they'd been putting on the men all day. She just wanted a hot bath and sleep.

Philippe and Letty had gone up to Colette's and she wondered if she'd made a mistake. Maybe Philippe needed to see this and help, but the war was too close and no one knew how it would end. This morning she was terrified she'd be doctoring the British if things went badly. But, Philippe was fourteen and it was time he stopped being her baby. She walked into her room and Pierre was lying back in her tub enjoying the hot water.

"Oh, Pierre I'm sorry, I didn't know you were…" She looked over at her old friend and shrugged, he was still a handsome man, just sadder around the eyes. She adored this gentle man, her best friend. He deserved a wife who adored and worshiped him. She went over to the bed and got out of her clothes and got in with him. He'd used the lavender soap she loved and the whole room smelled fresh and clean.

"How many people do you think this old tub will hold, my darling?" He took the sponge and washed her back.

"Ooh, that feels so good. I know I shouldn't be interrupting your bath, but I can't wait for another one to be filled and I can't stand myself any longer." She leaned back into his chest and didn't care anymore about anything except getting clean and sleep.

"Don't get upset, Pierre, you're like a brother to me."

"Brothers and sisters don't take baths together at this age, my darling. Unless; you come from up around the hills; do you come from up around the hills?"

"Hush and wash my back again, that felt good. Turn around I'll get yours for you."

What kind of room did she think there was in this tub. They'd already lost half the water to the bedroom floor when she got in to HIS nice bath. Pierre was trying not to let her see or feel his erection. He'd told her about Colette. What part of not having sex for many years had missed her reasoning?

Celestine got out of the bath and dried off. She went to the armoire and got her nightgown and put it on and climbed into her big bed.

"I had to give the cot to a new wounded; you'll have to sleep with me tonight. Don't mind, I won't bight you too hard." She'd have laughed but she fell asleep.

He waited to hear her breathing and knew she was asleep and got out of the tub. He thought he'd spend trying not to watch her as she dried that incredible body. He put on Laffite's dressing gown and went to the door and told Josef he was through with the tub if someone wanted to come and get it, otherwise he'd bring it down in the morning. Josef and Franklin came up the stairs with buckets and started emptying the big tub out of the big window onto the little spot of grass below by the stable. Pierre pulled the screen over to the bed so Celestine would have some privacy in her sleep. Running a hospital wasn't always as private as one hoped. Josef carried the tub downstairs and Franklin followed with the buckets. Pierre knew they'd set it up in the big kitchen for Marguerite and her novices; they were full of blood and sweat and would be glad to get it.

Pierre didn't know what else to do so he got in bed and tried to stay as far over to his side of the bed as he could get. He was awakened by Celestine gently crying and hiccoughing in her pillow. He reached over and pulled her into him.

"Shhh, Pierre's here, darling. Don't cry, you know I don't like to see tears." She went back to sleep hiccoughing into his chest. How much was a man supposed to stand? Why did his wife have to like women and what the hell was he doing in bed and bath with Celestine? Too many questions. Sleep Pierre.

He was awakened later by her moving in closer to him. She was snuggling. He knew snuggling when he felt it. This wasn't her moving about in her sleep. He was hard so quick he thought it might fly off his groin and hit something and he could swear he heard a 'boiing' as the damn thing stood up. He bent to kiss her. He gently kissed her lips and pulled away, he went back for another. He was hungry for her mouth and tried not to be too rough as he pulled her into him and opened his mouth and covered hers. His tongue found hers and he realized he hadn't made love to a responsive woman since before he was married. He was not going to be able to go as gently as he thought she needed. He had to remember himself, this was not his wife. This was Maurice's wife.

"Oh damn, Celestine I really didn't think this would happen, I didn't plan it I swear. Are you sure we should…" She had covered his mouth with the next kiss.

"I planned it, my darling. You need this, my friend and so do I. Let me do this for you."

It could've been minutes or hours but the sun was coming up and he was totally spent and felt good about life. He'd turned her every way imaginable, she'd danced naked for him and taken him in her mouth and made him spend into her throat. He'd licked and tasted every inch of her until she spent. He'd used her hand on himself and she'd used his on herself. They'd laughed and had fun and laughed again. He looked over at her and she'd enjoyed it as much as he. She'd used every trick he'd ever taught Colette and for the first time, he knew how wonderful they were.

Celestine liked being a courtesan. She decided she'd give a free one or two or three to an old friend, on occasion and Pierre was definitely an old friend.

He had to look at his friend's widow anew. He had a new and very healthy respect for the stamina of a Sea Captain and a pirate and decided he was among good men and true. He never knew women could enjoy the act as much as she; and she told him it was because of him. He felt like a man, a good strong healthy man and it changed his whole outlook on the world. He never dreamed all the things he'd told Colette about love making would one day come to him with Celestine. *She's calling herself a courtesan now, I just call her amazing.*

Marguerite was a happy woman, she wanted for nothing because she didn't know what she wanted. She had her family and the little sisters in the convent; her kitchen and the children's laughter. She'd been courted by some of the free men of color in the city, but they wanted a good wife and a warm body in bed. She'd never been in love with any man. That'd mean she'd have to leave the life she had and she wasn't going to do that. Some had wanted her only for her money. Her Papa Maurice left her a wealthy woman and she could do anything she ever dreamed of doing and she was; she was taking care of her family.

She'd raised Philippe as if he was hers and Tante 'Tine knew it and loved it. Philippe had called her mama many times and didn't realize it. She couldn't understand the world. She didn't understand why her mama needed to heal mean men and she certainly didn't understand why men needed to own other men. She didn't understand why white men thought themselves better than anyone else. It just didn't make sense to her. She didn't know how people could believe in God and think as they did.

Until she met Tante 'Tine she thought she might be slow or daft and didn't catch on like other people, but Tante had explained that she was right and other people were wrong. Tante 'Tine pointed out that her Papa Maurice and Pierre were good examples of that reasoning and Marguerite began to look for white people who felt the same way. She only found a few and they were mostly nuns.

There were things that happened in the square in front of the Cathedral that she was not allowed to see. Even at sixteen when she considered herself a woman, Papa Maurice had forbid her going anywhere near the square when there were people gathered there. But one day, she'd been reading and walking and she was on the square before she realized. There were slaves standing on a tall platform; shackled together. The stench was horrible. The fear and evil were so strong, you could see them rising from the very earth. She froze and couldn't think. She couldn't move and she couldn't stop staring at these beings like herself who'd been born in the wrong place at the wrong time and were suffering at other men's hands and beliefs.

There were mamas with babies and old people wetting themselves from hear. Suddenly a big arm had come from nowhere and grabbed her from behind and around her waist and tucked her up under his arm and was walking toward home. She watched the muddy sewage, trash and dead animals stuck in the muck of the street as his big boots got closer to home. She saw the bottom of the big gate open and the bricks of the carriageway and then the courtyard and she was plopped down unceremoniously at the big table. He was standing in front of her, his blue eyes dark with anger.

"What have I told you, Marguerite? Answer me. What have I said about that place?" He went to the gallery and called up.

"Wife, come get this girl before I kill her." He was too angry to deal with her. Tante 'Tine came running down the stairs.

"What's wrong, are you all right? Have you been hurt?" She was looking Marguerite over and checking her out.

"Tell her where you were. Go on, tell her." He'd taken a step back. Josef had come from the stable when he heard the commotion.

"Tell your brother. What am I going to do with you, child? What have I done that you torment me and disappoint me so?" Celestine stepped in front of him.

"Hush, Maurice you go too far. What has the child done that's so terrible?" She was searching his eyes.

"I forgot, Papa. I forgot and I was reading and walking and then I couldn't move. It was horrible, Papa, don't be mad at me." She began to sob. He had her in his arms so fast Celestine felt a breeze from his movement.

"Oh, baby girl I'm not mad. I just can't stand that your sweet, gentle heart would see such things. Please don't go there again, please, my little girl. You're the only little girl papa has and I don't want you to see such things." He had her sitting on his lap and she was too old and she wished he'd let her grow up.

She thought of it the other day in the kitchen and she'd give anything to sit on that big lap of his once more, just for a scent of his cigar or a look at his smile. Josef sees him and told her he stays around the house, but she didn't have Josef's gift. She only knew she missed him so much it hurt and she couldn't even let herself think of her mama and the times the four of them shared in the little house in Port-au-Prince. She watched men building and making her own noose, didn't he think she was stronger than his little baby girl? But once she was older and raising Philippe she understood what he meant. The fact that she'd seen her own noose was the very reason she should never have to see horror again. She was so busy with the hospital in the house she'd not had time to think of her past much or her future. She thought this the perfect hospital. People came to heal and no one died. She had perfected so many of her remedies that the men were healing faster than they would've at the big King's Hospital. She was proud of her accomplishments in her medicines and cures.

If Papa Maurice had lived, she was perfecting a potion for Tante 'Tine to have more children. She was learning from an old Indian woman at the market who knew every plant known to man and she told her of a potent mixture that would give a woman many children. Marguerite had believed her and was prepared to start Celestine on it when Papa Maurice was next home and they moved into the big new house. She was mad at herself for not giving it to her before; Tante 'Tine would have a child now for Marguerite to raise and spoil.

Josef's girls were being raised in this little village they all called a family and they were doing very well. It took Marguerite a long time to pry the memory of their mother out of their heads and into conversations. She knew they needed to talk about their loss and remember their mama. Her papa Maurice loved to hear them talk about their mama. She and Josef could make him laugh remembering the antics they put their mama through. It kept her mama close to them on those long months at sea. Papa Maurice was a wise man; he knew what he was giving them. Marguerite had done the same for Mary Anne's girls. The one she had a problem opening was Marie; she was a papa's girl. She lived, ate, drank and breathed news of her papa. One of the girls told her he visited here at Tante 'Tine's sometimes and she began to watch Celestine's comings and goings. She followed her around until Celestine fell in love with the child. She spent more and more time with her and the two were inseparable at times. Celestine was teaching her to sew and help her with the quilts she made. Marie loved the stories the quilts told and was planning one for her papa using material died the same color green as his favorite shirt.

Once Jean stopped coming around and the war was so bad, Marie began to lose her hopes of ever seeing her papa again and she began to show sadness in her eyes way beyond her years. Marguerite watched as Celestine tried everything to bring back her happy little Marie, but she couldn't. They'd all gotten so busy with the hospital no one noticed the little girl sitting under the big banana tree cutting quilt squares day after day. She'd cut the material and stare at the young soldiers as they came into the courtyard. Marguerite loved her little girls and would make sure Marie was happy soon.

Franklin walked into her kitchen the first day he was there and stole her heart. He fell into rhythm with the work being done and took over many of the duties the young women were sharing which took them away from the wounded. He'd work and flash Marguerite his beautiful dimpled smile and she couldn't think. She began to find more and more reasons for going into the kitchen. At the end of the first evening she went in to close the kitchen and prepare it for morning. He'd already done it and was waiting for her with a cup of hot chocolate. She'd never been so pampered. He flashed his dimples and gently picked up her hand. "These be the hands of a goddess." He kissed the back of her hand.

"You have rescued us, Franklin. Thank you for all your help. Where'd you come from, did God send you to us."

Marguerite had never talked to a slave before. She naturally assumed they all walked around like the ones she saw in the city under someone's scrutiny and control. She heard rumors that the convent had slaves, but she'd never seen any and prayed it was rumor.

"I'm here with Captain Andrew. I belong to him and Cedar Plantation in Kentucky. We just down here getting' rid of the British so dis country can go on ahead with itself."

Franklin thought she needed to be kissed. He wanted to taste that beautiful mouth and lick the bit of chocolate off her upper lip. He'd flash her as many of his dimpled smiles as it'd take.

She couldn't believe he was a slave. He was well dressed but dirty from the battle and Andrew's blood. He spoke like the country people coming into the market to sell their hides and greens; he could be one of the free men of color that courted her. She could live in those dimples, just give her a pillow and a blanket and she'd never come out again. She couldn't fall in love with this man. There was no future. She'd die of a broken heart thinking of him in Kentucky as property of some white man. But right now, he was at her table and he was leaning in to kiss her and she was tingling all over.

Chapter Twenty-One

The war was finally over and Laffite had not come to her. She had to get on with her life, she'd see him again; she knew it in her soul. Most of the young soldiers had gone back to their homes. She and Pierre were still sharing the same room and were quite comfortable together. *Colette was a fool.*

Celestine was putting things away in the little linen's room when she heard the door open and shut. She tried to turn around but he was holding her from the back.

"Pull your skirt up, quick, we don't have much time." It was Pierre and he was about to enter her through her skirt if she didn't do as he said. She gathered up her skirts and he pushed her gently against the wall and raised her hips and entered her with one stroke. He was reaching around and into her dress for her breast and she was breathing into the wall and loving this. It was pure naughty and they could be caught; just her cup of tea. She spent much faster than she expected and he kept on until she was worried someone would come in, or they'd be missed, but then she spent again and he followed.

"Now, that should keep you happy for a while. I know it will me." He buttoned himself, kissed the back of her neck and walked out without her seeing his face.

Now, that's the way to have an affair, she thought. Nice and easy, enjoy the fireworks and back to work.

She saw him later helping Josef bathe a patient and he smiled an innocent smile like he hadn't seen her since last night. Pierre was becoming a most interesting friend. *Colette was a fool to let him get away.* She was discovering she loved having sex with him. There were no cumbersome emotions or blinding love. They were two old friends enjoying a toss in the hay and each other's company. She'd save her deep emotional fulfillment for Jean and her memories of Maurice. If she were going to live a life of a Courtesan, she couldn't let love get in her way. Pierre was good practice.

She was wiping down the big table when she saw her little Marie under the banana plant with Jean's shirt. She grabbed her heart.

"Oh my sweet, baby girl, come here." The child got up and walked over to Celestine.

"Let grand-mere hold you." She gathered the child and the shirt up in her arms and sat with her at the big table. "Tell me what's wrong, baby girl?"

"I miss my papa." The tears started and she knew what the child was feeling, she'd missed her own papa since the day she was born and she knew Maurice had felt the same. But, this little girl had known and loved her papa, so her missing him was by far worse than what Celestine and Maurice felt. Alex had Philippe and baby Tina had Papa'sef and the attention of everyone in her little village, but Marie had held herself away from the acceptance and Celestine saw why.

"Are you a papa's girl, my angel?" She understood; she wanted the child's papa also.

"Grand-mere's going to get your papa for you. Will you trust me?" The little girl was beside herself, she was perking up and smiling and hugging Celestine's neck.

"Yes, Grand-mere, I'll do anything you say, I promise. He needs me, I know he does." Celestine knew he probably did.

"Now, it'll take a few days for my plan, but if you'll trust me, you'll have these little arms around his neck before you know it. Now you mustn't tell anyone; not even Alex, do you understand?" Now, let me see your quilt. How're you coming on your squares?

The child would do anything she said. It took Celestine less time to think of a plan than she ever imagined.

Andrew Down was coming down the stairs from the nice room he'd been renting from her until he could get back to Kentucky. He could have left sooner, but he was smitten with Celestine. He had no intentions of leaving without her love. His scar was going to be a rugged addition to his handsome self. He saw her looking at him and his heart must have jumped because he was beside her in no time. Had he jumped the stairs?

"Andrew? Do you know where Captain Laffite found you when he brought you here?"

"Sure do, he fished me and Franklin out of the swamp down by his place on Grand Terre."

"Could you and Franklin take me there?" Please let him want her enough to say yes.

She was waking up to her power over men and she not only loved it, she was about to make it her profession. She needed this exercise as much as the one with darling Pierre.

"Now, come on, Mam, why'd you want to go down there? You don't know what it's like in those swamps and some of his men might cut you up for crab bait. Now, that'd upset me, Mam and I'd have to kill more than my share." She loved listening to his funny bragging and she knew in her heart it was probably more factual than he let on. She learned from Marguerite that the big scar on his leg was from a war in Haiti he and Franklin fought.

"I just need a big strong man to help me find Laffite, will you help me, please?" She reached down and brought his hand up to the outline of her breast and held it over her heart. His head was spinning. This was a dream come true, he was touching her breast. When he bent down to receive her kiss, his chin met the steel of her knife and he carefully pulled his chin back up and stared down the bridge of his nose at this beautiful woman holding his very life in her hand.

"I'm not good with dangerous places, Monsieur please do this for me."

"Oh shit, Mam, put down your knife and we can talk about this." He couldn't lower his head; a knife blade was ready to enter his chin. Gently removing his hand from her breast, he looked down trying to decide if he should overtake her, or just go with her plans. He chose life; his hand came up fast, took her knife and turned her around with his arm pressing into her neck, her own knife at her throat.

He was getting dizzy from the jasmine scent of her hair.

"Let her go, Andrew. Let her go." It was Franklin he'd seen it all from the arch leading into the stable. He walked over slowly and slapped Andrew on the back of his head and Andrew's eyes focused and he realized he was about to strangle and cut the throat of this very beautiful woman.

Franklin turned to the woman.

"Mam, it ain't good to challenge a soldier so close out of battle… Mam." Franklin had to admit, these New Orleans women were some kind of different. The black women were beautiful and the white women'd kill you soon as look at you.

Celestine looked at both men.

"You'll do nicely. Will you take me?" She'd seen exactly what she wanted to see and was strangely aroused by the attack.

Going into dangerous waters she had to know who could protect her and how well. She knew she could take care of herself but not against so many.

"Mam…" Andrew looked down at her and her eyes had softened and she was looking at him like she could make love to him right there in the courtyard. He was damned if he understood this whole place. He'd at least keep his dignity.

"I'll have to think about it." *Some dignity, you idiot. I should walk away and go back to normal people. But those eyes; I walk away from that and I'll never forgive myself. My life's at least worth a night with this amazing creature.*

Celestine knew he'd take her to Laffite. She just wanted a little fun and she had to know if the man was a warrior like she suspected or a little boy playing soldier. She'd wait; he'd be knocking on her door in a few days. She'd get rid of Pierre for awhile; she needed to be 'alone' for this maneuver. She'd see what Andrew's next move was before she made hers.

Andrew waited the first night for her to come to his room. He was disappointed, but he figured it was too soon. The next day she flirted all day with another young man still mending from an arm wound. The second night he knew for sure she'd come to him; she had as much as promised him with those deep blue eyes. She didn't. The next day she wasn't around and by evening he saw her riding into the carriage way on her horse. She was dusty and sweaty from her ride and he wondered where she'd been and with whom. A few minutes later, another young soldier rode in and took her horse from her and went to the stables. Andrew was ready to kill someone. He'd decided she was his and he didn't have to share the knowledge with anyone else. His word was law in his world and there was no reason for him to change that now. He went to his room to wait. She'd played with him long enough, she'd be in soon. He felt it; he wished for it and he counted on it.

There was water running under his window and outside the little stable. He looked out to see the dressing screens hiding the little spray bath from all but his window. She couldn't see him watching and he felt like a cad watching her bathe but he couldn't stop himself. He watched as her creamy skinned body lit up from the moon. She'd tied her hair but loose tendrils fell out of the blue ribbon and blonde curls were blowing around her face from the river breeze . He was about to die with desire. She dried herself and put on her wrapper and walked back up to her room. He was damned if he knew what to do. He'd taken baths in waterfalls back home, but he'd never seen a beautiful woman bathing in one. The intimacy and personal nature of it made him desire her even more. He was in trouble. He could take her to the damned pirate or he could get Franklin and get the hell out of this city in the swamp while he still had a shred of dignity. Oh hell, he knew he'd take her, but by damn she'd have to ask.

The whole next day he spent trying to hide his erection. Each time he passed the cistern his damned cock'd raise its head and want to burst one of his buttons. She was nowhere to be seen all day. At dinner, the conversation was lively and the food was delicious. He found it difficult being around these strange people but he couldn't leave. She was driving him crazy and besides, Franklin was falling in love and wasn't ready to go.

She flirted with Pierre all through dinner and Andrew wanted to smash his face. Maybe she'd decided not to go find the pirate and he was just an unwanted guest in her house. He'd offer to take her in the morning. Andrew fell asleep in his dressing gown in the chair by the window. He awakened to her soft lips on his.

"Andrew." She was whispering into his mouth.

"You knew I'd take you, didn't you." He said still trying to catch his breath.

"Yes. Did you enjoy my bath last night my handsome man from Paducah, Kentucky?" Hearing she'd known he was watching, made him so hard he could break logs.

"Did you touch yourself while watching me, my treasure?" she whispered in his ear, her warm breath caressing the soft skin of his lobe. She slipped out as quietly as she'd come in.

No, but I damned sure will tonight, he thought to himself.

She went back into her room and found Pierre asleep on her bed. She took the little tassels from her drawer she'd been saving for this very moment and tied his hands and feet to the bed posts. She gently sat on his chest and waited for him to wake up. This particular exercise he'd shared with Colette and Celestine years before.

He smiled and moved to put his arms around her and discovered he couldn't. She started at his ears and went down his throat to his chest; to his stomach; into his groin and gave him the most pleasure he'd ever had.

She'd wanted to do this forever, but with Maurice's past he'd be too angry and break the bed to keep the control.

With Jean, he'd never allow himself to be put in such jeopardy; he'd leave and never return.

With Pierre, she was in complete control and he loved it. The success depended on the man and his trust of the woman and his desire for pleasure at any costs. He considered it worth the possible danger of a house fire. She woke early and didn't wake him.

Andrew and Franklin woke at dawn. Celestine dressed in some of Laffite's breeches and his green shirt and wore her own riding boots and put her hair up in a black scarf. They'd be gone a couple of days, but she'd promised herself and a little girl she'd bring back a papa.

They had no problems on the way down to the bayous and spent the night with her sleeping in the boat and the men by the fire. The mosquitoes got so bad she joined Andrew and cuddled up to sleep next to the fire and away from the biting insects. She could feel him wanting her, but there wasn't much he could do with Franklin five feet away. She knew he was well endowed when he pulled her down for a kiss the first day he was brought in to her courtyard. She was looking forward to enjoying it in the near future.

She could see the lights of the big house before they got to the landing. There was music and laughter; what the hell was being celebrated? If he were able to celebrate, why'd he not come to see her and his daughters? She left Andrew and Franklin to watch the boat and honestly thought they'd stay behind. It's amazing what Celestine didn't know about men outside the bedroom.

She walked around the big house to find his room and saw the big shutters were closed but there were lights and movement inside. She wondered if she should walk right in. What if he had a woman in bed; what if he had a favorite mistress with him? What if she'd been replaced? She hadn't planned on this. She didn't know what to do.

"Why don't you walk in through the front door? Like you're welcomed?"

Andrew was whispering in her ear in that stupid southern accent.

"Better than catching a man with his pants down." Franklin was in the other ear.

"Drop your weapons and turn around." It was a familiar voice.

Her voice caught in her throat and they turned around. Pierre was standing with the biggest smile she'd ever seen.

"I like Andrew's idea." He whispered.

She was getting angry. She'd embarrassed herself with her lack of planning and now she looked like a fool instead of the *femme fatale* she'd tried so hard to portray.

"Bloody hell." She exclaimed and opened the shutters and walked in through the big window, her entourage following.

Jean was sitting in his tub smoking a fine cigar and sipping from a glass of wine. He was startled but kept his composure as no other man could or would.

"Welcome, my pet if I'd known you were coming I would've taken a bath."

He was laughing but his eyes were dark as night. The men stepped back out into the night and Celestine was left standing in his clothes watching his angry eyes watching her from his bath.

"Oh hell, Jean, I've made a bloody mess of things." She wanted to cry. She'd have no power over him now to insist he go back with her.

"Take off my new green shirt, woman, I didn't say you could wear it. And take that stupid rag off your hair." He was so glad to see her he couldn't breathe, but he couldn't let her know. If she knew what she was doing to his calm, she'd be coming in unannounced twice a week. She walked over to the tub and took the sponge. He was pulling his shirt over her head and reaching for her breast; he almost broke the little ship charm moving his hands inside the shirt.

"Be careful." She snapped and held it up so the shirt didn't break the chain. He smiled; he was pleased she was wearing it. She didn't tell him she never took it off. She'd saw his erection and watched the anger in his eyes change to love and lust. Thank God, his feelings for her hadn't changed. She hoped the other men weren't getting an evening's entertainment. He got out of his bath and went to the bed and held the covers open for her.

She walked over to close the shutters and latch them. The men were standing around the fire with some of Jean's men. She was glad to see Andrew was such a patient gentleman and Pierre, well, she should've known he'd follow them.

She turned and got in next to Jean and buried her face in the curls on his chest. She breathed in the scent of Allspice and man and felt a deep contentment which she knew was temporary at best.

"I've come on a mission, my love. Marie sent me." He was up on his elbows looking down at her.

"Is she safe, is she well?" His eyes were full of fear.

"Yes, Papa, she needs to put her arms around your neck and let you know she still loves you. She thinks you need her. I would've brought her but I thought the trip too dangerous."

"So it is, my pet. I'm glad you came alone... with your brave knights." His eyes were smiling again.

"I'll come to her soon, very soon. Please tell her that for me. I've missed her little eyelash kisses. Is she happy?"

"Jean, she's so wonderful you can't believe, but she wants you to need her, my love." She loved that he loved his children so much.

"I do, she's right. I need to see all three of them. I'll come sooner than soon. I promise."

He wanted her now and talking of his children was putting out fires he didn't want to put out. She was here in his bed and he'd missed her more than she'd ever know and … she was here in his bed… he was the luckiest man alive. He went into her kiss and took her gently but passionately and made love to her twice. It was time for her to go back. He gave her more clothes, and kept the green shirt.

Franklin sat by the fire half the night watching Andrew and Pierre pacing back and forth. This woman was something else. She had a pirate in bed; a young Sea Captain pacing not fifty yards from the pirate's bed and a spoiled young, very rich Kentucky planter pacing in one hundred dollar boots around the mud in the swamp outside the pirate's bed. She must be damned talented that's all he could figure.

Pierre felt his time with Celestine was over. He needed to move on and find a mistress. He wouldn't divorce Colette, her reputation was hanging on by a thread at best since she and some of her friends had started wearing men's clothes. He knew what kind of woman he wanted, but she was busy with her pirate at the moment. There must be more Celestine's out there. He was still a good looking man and he could please a woman better than most men, he'd recently been reminded of that. He had money and a generous heart, how could he fail?

Andrew was at a loss. Should he kill the pirate and take his woman or do the right thing and wait and forgive her? He'd never had such a dilemma and if he had to talk with that ridiculous accent anymore he'd go mad. Franklin was already looking at him like he was insane every time he opened his mouth to speak. He needed to give Franklin his freedom. He was more friend than slave, but if he did; the man would stay in New Orleans and marry Marguerite and he'd lose him. He wasn't ready to lose Franklin, they'd been together since birth; he was the brother he never had, his best friend; he'd think about it. Besides, it wasn't being selfish, Franklin had it pretty damned good. They'd saved each other's life in two wars, they were friends damn it. He didn't want to lose him, he was his best friend, damn it. Besides there were laws and paperwork to be considered with permission from the government.

Chapter Twenty-Two

Celestine was exhausted when they got home. Marie was waiting for her in her big bed. Marguerite said she'd fallen asleep waiting for her. She got undressed and went downstairs to take a spray bath with the screens covering all sides and came back upstairs. She pulled the little girl over close to her and fell into a deep sleep.

Jean woke her at dawn and motioned for her to get out of bed. He was in his dressing gown and slipped in next to Marie. Celestine kissed him and went downstairs to make some coffee.

Franklin was coming out of Marguerite's bedroom scratching his head and trying to wake up. He jumped three feet when he saw Celestine sitting at the big kitchen table at the same time the whole house was awakened by Marie's screams of joy. The girls came from all over the house to see papa.

Celestine's bedroom became a playground. She took a tray of coffee up to her room; stood in the door and admired her man. He was covered by little girls' kisses and ruffled nightgowns. She carefully handed him a cup of coffee then Josef took the tray and took a cup and gave one to Augustine. There was a strange Christmas morning atmosphere in this growing family in this very happy house.

Celestine noticed Philippe standing over by the big armoire. Her heart cried for him. His papa'd never come home and his girlfriend had another man in her life and it wasn't Josef. Her baby boy was becoming a young man with young man's problems. Where had the time gone, a couple of minutes ago he was a little boy stealing oranges from the Reverend Mother's trees.

Jean had taken over the celebration and had gifts for all the children, including Philippe.

"Alex, go to the kitchen and ask Marguerite if she'd like to come on a picnic with us. Then you can help fry some chicken and maybe make some of those meat pies Papa likes so much."

Alex ran and grabbed Philippe and they ran down the stairs. Celestine needn't have worried; her little boy's favorite girl hadn't forgotten he needed attention too.

"Marie, take Tina and you two get dressed for an all day picnic. Papa's taking you out to the country."

"Josef, you and Augustine get dressed; we're buying a house today."

Josef looked over at Augustine and she shook her head 'yes'. Josef wasn't sure he liked someone else buying his house, but that was part of the deal and Jean insisted; it was in their agreement.

The room was empty except for Jean and Celestine.

"So, woman, looks like we may have grandchildren one day. Young Philippe is smitten with my Alexandra." He was smiling into her eyes with the greatest pleasure.

"We'll be crawling with them and you can bounce them on your old worn out knees." She laughed, she hadn't thought of that until he said it. She loved the idea.

"Woman, lock the door, we don't have much time. Come let me pleasure the hell out of you." She locked the door and jumped in bed next to him. His mouth was the most wonderful thing she'd ever tasted. He got out of his dressing gown and pulled her gown over her head and they were spent before the little knock on the door.

"Yes?" Jean gently called to the door lying on top of her.

"Papa, should I wear my blue or green dress?" He looked to Celestine who mouthed, 'green'.

"I love the green dress, my petal." They heard little bare feet running down the gallery.

"Who's been wearing my dressing gown, my pet?" His realization was turning his eyes cold and black.

Celestine looked over at this dangerous man, this man who'd murdered people not at war, this pirate who should've been hanged several times, the pirate who'd almost ruined the merchants of the city by selling his stolen goods cheaper, this wonderful father of little girls. She was so full of love she thought she'd die of it.

"Don't ask me questions, my love. I don't want to get in the habit of lying to you." She pulled him over onto his back and sat on his erection and began to pleasure herself.

Laffite's mighty laugh woke Andrew.

Andrew came to the door of his room. She has that damned pirate in her bed again. It was time for him to take Franklin and go home. This was a losing battle and he should know when to quit and go home. Too bad, it could've been great. He was still mesmerized by her, when she spoke at dinner he couldn't get enough of her laughter, when she walked across the courtyard to the kitchen, it was music. She was so much better than the man in her bed. Why was she wasting herself on him?

Andrew should be grateful to the man for pulling him out of the swamp and bringing him here to be healed, but he only felt deep jealousy and resentment to the thug. There he said it, the thug. Just because the man had manners and dined like a gentleman didn't make him a gentleman.

Andrew called down for Franklin. Maybe Franklin could talk him out of killing this man who was probably better in a duel than he. Franklin was busy killing chickens for a picnic. Andrew would have to wait.

Jean was up and dressed trying not to cross his legs too hard over his tender privates. He'd forgotten how long it takes to kill, pluck and fry chickens and maybe 'pleasure the hell out of you' was too exact a term for this woman. Whoever the hell'd been wearing his dressing gown hadn't done a thorough job, she was on fire this morning and she nearly killed him; he should find the guy and thank him for leaving the best for him. *He was a very happy man with a sore cock.*

He was having more coffee on the table downstairs when the girls came back with the picnic. He'd hired a closed carriage for the day. It wouldn't be a good idea driving around the city with his family so exposed. Besides, he had other children he needed to see, and he didn't want them seeing him with the girls. They were off in a cloud of laughter and fun.

Andrew had reluctantly given Franklin permission to go help Marguerite with the picnic. Franklin, Josef and Marguerite were driving Celestine's carriage behind Jean's with the food and essentials. Josef had mixed emotions watching Augustine with Jean and his little girls.

Celestine wanted the girls to have this day with their father so she hadn't gone. The morning had been the most perfect day since the perfect mornings with Maurice and the kids when they were young.

She was adjusting to the bittersweet moments in her family's happy life missing Maurice. She'd finally learned to live with the knowledge she'd never get over missing and wanting him. Alex asked her if she'd ever get married again. Celestine had to think about it. If God had wanted her married, he wouldn't have taken her husband, so the answer was, 'no'. She'd not be getting married again.

Andrew waited for the happy crowd to leave. He came down and went into the kitchen. He knew he'd have to get his own breakfast if he wanted anything to eat. She was taking hot biscuits off the fire and she was so pretty with her sleeve covers and blond tendrils hanging on her damp forehead he thought he'd melt. There was absolutely no way he could go back to Kentucky until he'd had her in his bed.

"I thought you might be hungry. I hope you like hot biscuits and ham?"

"Ohhh, yes." He breathed in a huge sigh. He'd had enough of the good seafood and fancy French dishes for a while. Biscuits and ham was the very thing he needed and missed.

"Here, I made this strawberry jam myself."

He'd have to marry her. He didn't know how; but he'd move heaven and earth to make it happen, but first he had to get her away from this city and that damned Laffite.

He walked over and put an arm around her waist and pulled her close to him. He was coming down to her mouth when she lightly pulled away and went back to the big cabinet to get a *serviette* to go next to his plate. She couldn't be in love with the pirate if she came down here and made me biscuits. In his world the lady of the house who was waited on hand and foot, didn't cook for a man. He didn't need a virgin; he was fine with a confused widow. He'd heard about widows and their needs after having a husband, otherwise she wouldn't be sleeping with different men. Marguerite told Franklin who told Andrew; the pirate reminded Celestine of her late husband. Andrew decided the biscuits meant he was still in the running, and if not, he'd enter the race.

"Why won't you let me kiss you, Sugar? Why're you torturing me? Have I done something to offend you?" He was coming back to her and was going to try to kiss her again.

She couldn't help her reticence; she was so in love with Jean at this moment she couldn't think straight. She could still feel him between her legs and it was a sweet pain she wanted to carry all day. She wasn't even sure she'd made the biscuits correctly.

"I'm sorry, Andrew what did you say, darling?" She knew he'd been talking, she just hadn't been listening.

He'd made a mistake; she wasn't as confused as he thought. She liked having men in her bed whether she'd been married or not.

"Never mind. I think it's time I went back to Kentucky. Did I tell you; women up there don't bed pirates who remind them of a dead husband. Women in my part of the country don't share their beds with their best friend's husbands and they don't take showers so a man can watch and nearly die with a desire you won't let him quench." He turned on his heel and walked out of the kitchen. She picked up a plate and put two biscuits and some ham and preserves on it and looked around to see where he'd gone. She was holding it when he stomped back into the kitchen; took it and stomped back out.

A man has to eat, thought Andrew. A woman had never made him so angry. Come to think of it, no one'd ever made him so angry. She was obviously playing him for a fool.

Celestine wondered what'd gotten in to Andrew, he seemed angry about something. She floated back up to her room and crawled in to Jean's big dressing gown and inhaled the spice and lavender. She thought she'd take a nap, but she couldn't get Andrew out of her head. What was he going on about? Torturing him? Who was torturing him? His accusations began to come back and she was beginning to hear what he'd been saying. She sat up in bed. She was outraged. Who does that country bumpkin, peckerwood think he is? *Damn 'Kaintuck'.*

She threw Jean's robe back onto the bed and slammed the French doors against the walls pulling them open so violently and rushed out and down the gallery. She burst into his room. He was packing his things.

"How dare you, monsieur? How dare you come into my home and accuse me of having sexual congress with my friend's husband and Laffite? You monsieur, are no gentleman and if you spied on me while I bathed, then you're a thug and a cad. If my husband were alive he'd kill you, monsieur. Please leave my house." She was breathing from her bosom and was going to faint with this anger. How dare he assume what went on in her bedroom. How dare he judge her, he who came into her home and allowed her stepdaughter to feed and heal him; he, with his expensive boots acting like he was the king of the world? He, whom she would've taken to her bed and given the greatest pleasure of his young boring, little life. He, who owned his best friend and wouldn't set free.

Maurice would've thrown him over the side of his ship as so much trash.

Andrew looked over at the alabaster breasts heaving with anger. All he had to do was replace her anger with desire and he'd be on top of the world.

"I'm leaving, Madame; I won't be but a moment. If you'd be so kind as to let Franklin know I'll be staying at the Planters and Strangers Hotel on *rue des Chartres*, I'd be most grateful. And if your husband were alive, I'd hope you'd behave yourself, Madam." He'd finished packing and turned to her with a slight bow and tipped his hat as he put it on.

She was still heaving and hadn't gotten the apology she deserved.

"That's it then? Have you no apology for the hostess who took you in and healed your wound and made you a part of this home?"

"Of course, Madame, please tell Marguerite how much I appreciate it. And that I apologize for not saying good-bye."

He was down the stairs and around to the stable saddling Captain before she realized he needed killing. Where had that adorable accent gone? Who the hell is he anyway? She wouldn't kill him today; her anger had turned to disgust. The disgust had turned to ugly dislike and she just couldn't be bothered. The only saving grace for young Andrew Horrible Down was Franklin. He was worth more than a hundred of the spoiled young planter.

The picnic was a huge success and Josef found a house he and Augustine and the girls all agreed on. It was off of St. Charles Avenue and close to the river and much bigger than Josef ever imagined he'd own, but he owned it. It was in his name and he was a home owner. They'd gone by the office of M. Dubonnet and Jean made arrangements for the house to be paid in full and signed the papers over to Josef Dubois.

Celestine said a reluctant, bittersweet good-bye to Jean and he headed back into his world. Again she was left with a soft longing for a man she loved. Marie wouldn't leave her side; the two now had something in common, their undying love for the same man.

Franklin came back to a house turned against his master. What had the idiot done now? Sometimes he thought Andrew just didn't have good sense. He was with a woman who could shave some of his rough edges and make him the real man he always wanted to be and he'd pissed her off. She wouldn't even let the family use his name. Marguerite would find out for him. He needed to know Mme. Dubois' side before he heard the distorted side from Andrew.

He was ready to go home. He loved Marguerite, but until Andrew gave him his freedom there was nothing he could do. He and his Marguerite had even talked of his running away. She had the money to get them as far away as needed until he could find work. Neither liked the idea of leaving her loved ones behind. Franklin knew she'd never be happy. There was a big problem; as it turned out, the wonderful Marguerite would never leave this house and her family. She was what his mama used to call Andrew's Aunt Violet; a "contented old settler". She loved her life and had no intentions of giving it up, even to save Franklin. He'd gotten into her bed and cuddled and kissed her for nights, but that's as far as she'd allow and he was about to explode if he didn't get home soon to his little friend in Paducah. Marguerite had shyly offered to buy his freedom, but there was so much wrong with the idea, he wouldn't hear of it. He didn't want to wake up a few years from now a free man with a very resentful wife he couldn't repay. He may be a slave, but he wore the pants with his women. He was firm on that. Andrew would do the right thing, sooner or later. Then he'd come back and claim his love.

Andrew was pacing up and down in his hotel room. What had happened? One moment he was about to take the most beautiful woman in the world to his bed and the next moment he was pacing alone in this hotel room. Women, why'd she been so damned angry? Everyone knew the pirate was in her bed. Hell, he'd watched her go into the man's private rooms while he was bathing. Did she think him blind? He knew she was sleeping with Pierre, and as much as he didn't approve, he felt that was more from loneliness than love. Andrew stopped dead in his tracks. Had she given pleasure to all the wounded soldiers? Maybe he wasn't special after all. Maybe she was one of those women he'd read about and she couldn't stop herself. The scientists have a word for women like that.

He could hear Franklin's boots in the hall. He opened the door.

"What have you done, Andrew?" Andrew was pouring them both a glass of whiskey.

"She's crazy, Franklin. She's really crazy. We shouldn't be in this city, these people don't think like we do, Franklin."

No, they don't, thought Franklin, they think I should be a free man.

Andrew took his glass of whiskey and sat down in the chair by the big window.

"Did you know she wanted me to apologize to her for telling her the truth; the truth Franklin?" He was still unbelieving of this woman's reasoning. Franklin was shaking his head. Where to start? Did he start by telling this lunatic that you don't mention a widow's peccadilloes, ever? Should he start by telling him that calling a man a pirate and berating his mistress, is not a good idea as the man has been known to kill men for using that title. Not to mention everyone in the city knew the man was in love with this, his favorite mistress and he'd probably defend her honor in a brutal manner… to the death? Or, should he just start by telling him how incredibly insensitive he'd been to a lonely young widow trying to find some happiness. She was married too young and was given too much responsibility brought about by her husband's good deeds in adopting two Haitian children, but she was dealing the best she knew how. He thought he'd start there and work backwards to Andrew's being a total ass.

Andrew let him speak until he'd finished explaining to him how he was a total ass in his dealings with this woman who wanted nothing more than to make him a better person. Andrew went into a deep depression. This, this is why he couldn't let Franklin go. How could he be allowed in the drawing room if Franklin didn't kick his ass when he was being one?

Chapter Twenty-Three

Andrew accepted the invitation to the ball Governor Claiborne was giving for General Jackson's great victory. Claiborne invited half the city and many were young officers who helped win the battle. He would go. It'd restore his ego; one thing Andrew knew was how well received he was on a dance floor and how women; married and single alike would be following him around all evening. He sure wished Mme. Maurice Dubois could see him then. Going to a nice big party'd give him something to think about other than his horrible behavior; maybe seeing himself in some young belle's eyes would soothe his hurt pride.

He'd written a note of apology, passed it by Franklin, who in turn passed it by Marguerite to go along with a beautiful diamond necklace. He knew he'd never be forgiven, even though Marguerite told Franklin it was the sweetest apology she'd ever read. From Franklin's point of view, Andrew was a drowned man and should just remove himself back up to Cedars and home. Franklin enjoyed kicking Andrew's ass; it put his life in a strange but fairly satisfactory balance. Now that Andrew decided to attend this damned party, he'd have to stay a few days longer and not have the release he'd been expecting. Andrew knew Franklin was hurting. He'd seen him mooning around and not showing any satisfaction or light heartedness after nights spent with Marguerite; it didn't take a brilliant man to figure he wasn't getting into the young woman's 'good graces'. He could identify with that.

Andrew thought of having a new formal suit made; but decided to have his uniform instead. He had the leather fringed breeches and jacket of the Kentucky Militia made by a tailor in the city, bought new boots and hired a beautiful Phaeton then went to the little shop on rue Royale. M. Chenier created a personal scent for him. M. Chenier asked questions about his life and where he was from. He walked around Andrew darting in to sniff and then backing out and back in, creating a strange dance. Andrew guessed every profession had its own oddities. The man came up with a wonderful scent of cedar with a hint of spice and tobacco. Not something Andrew thought he'd like until he smelled it and realized he liked it very much. It reminded him of summer evenings on the big front porch with a good glass of Kentucky Bourbon and a fine cigar after a beautiful dinner. It reminded him of friends and family enjoying the fresh smell of the cedars coming from the grove on the hill and watching the moon on the Ohio River. It reminded him of home.

Franklin thought he'd be sitting out with the other footmen waiting for the white folks to have a good time and drink too much, but Andrew surprised him. He got down from the little sporty carriage and handed Franklin a wad of bills and told him to go find some relief. He was tired of seeing his eyes bulge.

The two men had a good laugh and Franklin was up and gone before Andrew reached the top of the stairs.

Captain Andrew H. Down, Kentucky Riflemen Militia, your Excellency; announced the liveried footman at the big entrance.

Heads turned as the most impressively handsome soldier in the room went down the line of the Governor's reception. He was introduced to and found himself in the company of men he greatly admired and respected. He was glad he'd come; he'd almost changed his mind. He looked around at some pretty young women and thought if he played his hand discreetly, there may be a loose lady here who wouldn't mind a toss in the preverbal hay with a good smelling young Captain such as himself.

He was spotted by every matron in the room with an eligible daughter and all the eligible daughters spread their fans in unison and the eyelashes began a chorus line of demure battings. Every married woman with a boring husband was staring at six feet two inches of Prime

Kentucky beef walking into their romance hungry midst. *Piece of cake,*
Andrew thought, I'll have spent by midnight, maybe twice.

He could feel the eyes and hear the twitters; this was familiar ground,
he'd come of age in this atmosphere, he could take a deep breath and
begin his search for beautiful prey.

"Madame Captain Maurice Etienne Dubois, your Excellency."
Andrew caught his breath. He turned as did everyone in the room to see
her standing at the top of the grand staircase. She was standing graceful
and beautiful, a dainty grand duchess in her widow's black silks and laces.
No woman in deep mourning had ever been so alluring. Her blonde curls
were lightly cascading from their enclosure on the top of her head and
small pins of diamonds sparkled in her hair. She was magnificent in the
shimmering dress, the border under her breast and down the front and
along the hem sparkled with thousands of tiny black onyx beads. The
dress was cut so low it was almost indecent and Andrew's diamond
necklace was her only adornment. Its radiance almost overshadowed by
the woman herself.

It never dawned on Andrew she'd be invited. He realized he knew
nothing about this beautiful woman. General Jackson was walking up
the stairs to escort her personally as an old friend. Who the hell was she?
There were twitters and gasps and neither Celestine nor Andrew knew
her entrance was the second scandalous event in the grand ballroom this
evening. Jean Laffite and his wounded ego had left the ball only twenty
minutes earlier and sworn to leave New Orleans and never return.

Fate has a way of stepping in and saving people from themselves.
Her already ebbing reputation wouldn't have survived dancing with the
pirate all evening. She would've left on his arm and not cared what
people thought; but she had a son and someone was watching out for
him and his acceptance into society.

Andrew didn't know Laffite had been there, nor did he know what
disaster was averted with his leaving or what it would've done to his

plans for this woman who had captured his heart. He only knew she was by far the most beautiful woman in the room and she was wearing his necklace. He was in love. He was in lust. And he was in terrible trouble. Where to begin? Ask her to dance? Ask her to forgive him? Ask her if she liked the necklace? Ask her to marry him and have his children? So many questions and it would take only one 'no' to dash his heart and send him home with his tail between his tall muscular legs.

His new breeches were feeling too tight and he realized his erection was stretching the seams and wanting desperately to come out and play with her. Play hell, the damned thing wanted to come out and ravage her, he went behind a large palm to adjust his breeches unseen. The Kentucky prime beef was about to show his true colors and some of the women would faint with desire and some from fright. He finally got it under control and turned back to the dance floor.

"You might try hiding that monstrous pride, you'll frighten the virgins." She said, breathing close to his ear.

He almost spent from her warm breath.

"Is it for me?" She whispered.

"Of course! Do you actually think it could be for anyone else with you in the room?" He barked. He couldn't play anymore games. He just wasn't good enough. He couldn't know that because of her, one day he'd be one of the best.

"If you ask me to dance, I can help you disguise it." She was teasing, another good sign.

"Are you sure we should, I mean, your being in mourning? People will say bad things and I'd hate that, Sugar."

"Captain Down, I assure you, my reputation can stand my dancing in widow's clothing better than my friendship with Lafitte." She really didn't give a rat's ass anymore about this silly town and its gossips. If anything, Maurice would love to be at this dance showing her off to polite society, but since he couldn't be here, she'd do it herself.

"Shall we dance? I don't think this'll hide my dilemma, Sugar. I think we're making it worse."

They were both laughing and her laugh went over him like warm molasses on one of her hot biscuits. Celestine had no idea he'd be here or she wouldn't have worn the beautiful necklace. She would've waited and worn it for him in a more 'personal' venue.

Marguerite told her of his dilemma and of Franklin's disgust with the man's manners. Marguerite had also told her how much in love Andrew was with her and how badly he felt over his behavior. Celestine understood that. She too had over reacted as she tends to do when people accuse her with the truth. It'd given her a wonderful idea. There were too many men in the world that had no idea how to treat women or pleasure them or even enjoy their intimate company. Thanks to Andrew, she'd decided on her calling. She hadn't thought of him until she was standing on the landing being introduced and she saw him across the room. He was the most handsome man in the room and he made her head swim with his broad chest; slim waist and those long legs. She knew how well endowed he was and in that respect he could stand beside Maurice and Jean as equals. He'd be her first client, whether he wanted to or not. She could reel him in like a fish and he wouldn't know he was in school until he was ready to graduate.

"I wish I knew you wanted to dance tonight, I'd have escorted you myself." He was looking down into those bewitching eyes and knew he'd already said the wrong thing.

"Where's your knife, Sugar; would you like to cut out my tongue or my heart?" How could he assume to escort her without asking? She was not his to order or demand or assume.

"Andrew, relax. I'd love for you to have asked me to this lovely dance." She was smiling at his acknowledgement he'd just corrected on his own. She was going to love her new profession. How was she any different from Anna? Look what the woman had done for her wonderful Maurice? Anna just made bad choices in whom to save.

General Jackson and Rachel were walking their way. Celestine met them and took Rachel's hand. She didn't wait for an introduction. She felt such a kindred soul to this woman.

"How nice to see you. Are you enjoying your stay in our strange city?" She laughed.

"It's wonderfully strange. You are Celestine. My husband told me about your 'war effort'? I also owe your husband a huge dept. Have you ever questioned why those two fools tried to join a war when they were barely ten years old? I must say, they were lucky to survive at all." She was a delight. Celestine had missed the company of truth saying women.

"I have a little boy, who tried to stow-away on his father's ship once. I'm told girls are much easier to raise." Both women laughed good naturedly.

"Mrs. Jackson may I introduce Captain Andrew Down?" Andrew took Rachel's hand and kissed it with a slight bow.

"It is my pleasure, Mrs. Jackson. I am a great admirer of your husband."

Rachel smiled a delightful smile and turned back to Celestine.

"I shouldn't take your time; my husband's been wanting to dance with you since you were announced." She was laughing as only a wife assured in the knowledge of her husband's love can, when facing such a beautiful woman.

General Jackson walked over and took her hand and led her to the dance floor. Her reputation had just been given a second chance. If the great general could approve of her dancing, the crowd would look the other way. Andrew reached for Rachel's hand and informally led her into the Virginia reel. Both couples were at home with the tune and the dance. The remainder of the night, Andrew had to stand back and watch as Celestine danced with the line of men waiting to ask. He started out hopeful and expectant, but now he was miserable and wanting her to come back to him. Finally in self defense, he began to dance with the young women blushing behind their fans, and before he knew it, he was having a good time. Knowing she was watching him, made for a better time. He'd been right; his prowess on the dance floor and in a ball room was quite impressive and he'd use it to his benefit. Of course so was hers and it was killing him watching some of the young studs and lecherous husbands pulling her a little too close in the new dance, the waltz, but he could wait, many of the young men didn't know the new dance yet and had to wait on the sidelines. There were no competitors here he couldn't disarm with a well-placed frown or phrase.

It was getting late and people were beginning to leave. She was talking to a young man by the stairs. *Oh no, that little thinks-he's-a-stallion isn't taking her home, she's mine now, by God.*

Andrew stood at her side holding her wrap and walked her up the stairs before the young man could ask.

Oh shit. Franklin's not back with the Phaeton. He hadn't told him a time.

Andrew picked her up in his arms and walked the few blocks to *rue du Maine*, his new boots could take the mud and sewage better than her dress and slippers. He walked across the courtyard and deposited her onto a chair by the little table under the banana tree.

"Andrew?"

"Yes, Sugar?"

"Will you take this back to the party? It's not mine, darling." She handed him the wrap and smiled sweetly at his mistake.

"Mine matches my gown and has my name embroidered in the back."

"Of course, Sugar." His face was as red as a freshly boiled crab and twice as hot. He couldn't even think how he made such a blunder and she was still smiling at him. Franklin came rushing down the street with the Phaeton and he jumped in the back.

"Back to the party, Franklin your idiot has done it again."

Andrew sent Franklin happily back to the hotel and walked back to Celestine's with her wrap. Why'd she not corrected the mistake standing at the stairs?

She didn't want to embarrass me in front of the other people standing around. He needed some of her manners. His mother had tried and his father had tried, but they were old fashioned and people were different now. People were being more honest and not hiding behind parlor games. But this woman wasn't playing a game, she was well mannered and when was that ever old fashioned? Yes, he'd marry her and she could teach him some manners.

He walked back through the big gates and up to the gallery and around to her room. He took his boots off before he reached her door, no need to ruin her pretty rugs. If he were lucky maybe she'd at least kiss him goodnight.

"Come in, my darling." God he hoped she didn't think he was Laffite.

She was lying in bed with her hair falling over her shoulders onto her full creamy breast. Her nightgown was so low and sheer he could see all of her underneath the silk; his diamond necklace caught every flicker of the candle light.

"Undress for me, Andrew H. Down, Captain from Paducah, Kentucky and let me see all of you, my darling." She said seductively.

His hips jerked involuntarily and he knew he wasn't going to last long enough to enjoy this for more than a few minutes at best. He'd never last with her soft French accent whispering her desires to him and that body like a goddess. He took off his coat and put it over the back of the chair. He caressed her with his eyes while he was untying his neckcloth and taking off his vest. He watched her desire for him growing in her breathing. She was mesmerized by the look in his eyes and not his body; this was a new seduction he'd never tried. He walked over to the bed and reached down and kissed her. He pulled his suspenders down and let them fall over his hips.

"Undo my breeches, Sugar; I've got something for you." She reached over and unbuttoned him and pulled his pants down and he pulled his shirt over his head. His chest was smooth and smelled of cedar and a hint of his pipe or cigar, she couldn't tell which one. She couldn't wait any longer. She was melting from the desire in his eyes as he undressed.

He felt the warm wet mouth on his organ before he could reach to kiss her again. He was going to die and it was going to be the most wonderful thing that'd ever happened to him. When they find his body, his mother will die of embarrassment and his father will be ashamed and he just didn't care. He leaned back into her pillows and stroked her blonde curls with his big rough hands. He'd never had anyone do this for him before. He'd read about it in dirty novels, but he didn't know real people did it. He was about to spend and he couldn't imagine putting his spunk in her mouth; he tried to stop himself and then he tried to move her head, but she grabbed his hands and held them against her breast. He let himself go and he plunged into the back of her throat and she was still going and moving and he plunged again and knew he'd do anything she ever asked of him and if she wanted that damned pirate tonight, he'd go get him. Oh God, don't let her want the man. He prayed.

Celestine got up and washed her mouth at the bowl. She loved his scent. She couldn't get over what it did to her. He smelled of fine cigars and spiced rum on a cedar filled Christmas day. She was leaning back on the pillows waiting for his next move. He rolled over on top of her and tried to enter her with nary a 'by your leave' or 'may I' or 'want a kiss?'.

"Andrew, did you enjoy my gift to you just now?" She knew she didn't have to ask.

"Ohhh yes, Baby, you know I did. Yes." He was still trying to enter her and she was turning so he couldn't have access.

"Do you think it'd be nice if you helped me get as aroused as you?"

What did she want from him, he was trying to enter her? What more did she want? He'd show her pleasure soon as he entered her and showed her what he had. She'd sing a different tune then, by God.

"Caress my breast, Andrew. Kiss my neck, do something nice to arouse me and make me desire your entry." She was going to have to take him one step at a time. She was realizing how fortunate she'd been to have three seasoned lovers who knew how and insisted on making their woman happy.

"Andrew, if you think you're a good lover, good for you and your fumbling, but leave my bed. If you wish to become a wonderful lover to a future wife and keep her pleased, then do as I say. Which will it be?" She was not going to subject herself to this and be his punching bag. She was beginning to wonder about the young belles of the county and how many had subjected themselves to Capt. Andrew Down and his battering ram. She reached up and caressed his chest and felt both nipples and tweaked and pinched slightly and ran her hand over his stomach; he was beginning to moan and breathe deeply.

"Does that feel good, my pet?"

"Ooh yes, let me in, Baby and I'll show you what I can do for you. I want you so much." He was nuzzling her neck and brought her hand back up to his nipples.

She pinched his nipple so hard he yelped like a stray dog.

"Leave my bed, you ass." She was up and throwing his clothes over the railing into the courtyard. He was as flaccid as he'd been hard a moment before. He grabbed his shirt and held it in front of himself and was walking out the door when he saw Franklin sitting in the courtyard talking to Marguerite, looking up at him and shaking his head. Andrew had done it again. He turned back into the bedroom and closed the door.

"Celestine, tell me what to do. Don't throw me out of your life. I'm the biggest ass in the world. Please baby, don't give up on me. Sugar? Please."

It worked. If there was one thing Andrew knew how to do it was cajole and beg a woman to get what he wanted, he just hadn't known until now what he actually wanted. Celestine had never been called 'Baby' and 'Sugar' before. She liked it; it was foreign and gentle and not like the sweet French endearments of New Orleans. It was a nice change having an American man and wondered if that was the cause of his rough love making. Everyone knew the Americans moving into the city by droves were coarse and not as refined as the established French and Spanish families. No one could say they weren't good looking, but none would be as wonderful as her American Andrew once she'd completed his schooling in *l'art de l'amour*; he was going to be the best of both worlds or she'd give up her new profession and sleep in all day.

She had him sit on the big chair and she sat gingerly on top of him. He'd have to earn his entry and then she'd be in control of when and how deep. She took his hand and opened her legs and encouraged him to feel her. She showed him how to move his fingers and where to put his thumb. He shyly wanted to see for himself and she lay with her legs spread on the bed and he could examine for himself. He wanted to taste her and she showed him the little nerve bud and how to find it and massage it with the tip of his tongue.

The biggest gift to Andrew was seeing her feel the pleasure he gave her with his hands. He thought he'd drown in his love for her as she softened her eyes with each touch and she moaned into his mouth. He saw a woman receiving pleasure and he never even knew they could or should. When he was finally allowed to enter her he watched her face closely to see what she was feeling. She was in a silent ecstasy that he was creating and he almost spent too soon. The first night he spent three times and he couldn't believe how much he didn't know about making love or having sex or getting in touch with a woman. Everything he knew about a woman up until now he could put in a little gold sewing thimble. He was embarrassed by his first night's fumbling; but she told him about calling herself a harlot in front of Maurice's crew and how she nearly died of embarrassment. He thought how adorable she must've been. He shouldn't be jealous of a dead man, but he was.

Chapter Twenty-Four

Celestine didn't see the calling card until she walked into the music room the next morning. When had he come, why wasn't she told? She was terrified he'd come while she was with Andrew. She couldn't bear it if she'd hurt him again. Pierre was coming into the courtyard.

"Celestine, come out here, you'll want to hear this."

She walked out and took him back to the kitchen to get them both a cup of coffee. They came back and sat at the little table under the banana tree.

"Now, what's so terribly important, Pierre?" She was preoccupied worrying about Jean and when she'd missed his visit.

Pierre told her how the city was buzzing with Jean Laffite's exit from the ball over a mistaken insult. It was a terrible mistake, but Laffite felt a slight and left early. Some were saying he'd vowed to move out of New Orleans for good.

"What'd they do to him, Pierre? Tell me." *Who did she have to kill?*

"I told you, my darling, it was a mistake. Laffite walked up to Claiborne and Jackson and the Generals Coffee and de Flaugeac to be introduced, and was greeted warmly by all but de Flaugeac; he didn't see Laffite's outstretched hand and turned his back. At that slight, Laffite stood up very straight as you know he can, my darling and introduced himself as, 'Laffite the Pirate' and left the ball."

"Pierre, he called himself Pirate? Oh God, he must've been hurt; he'd never say that."

"They apologized but it did no good. He may've been embarrassed at his own premature reaction."

Celestine was dying, her man needed her and she was dancing at a party, the very party he'd just left and she was having a good time with people who'd just criticized and insulted him. She'd go to him. She'd go alone this time. She knew the way and she knew how to hire a pirogue, she'd done it before. She'd not disguise herself, her man needed her and she'd go as herself and walk in his front door and let him know that he was respected and loved and very appreciated.

When Andrew woke in the afternoon alone in his bed wanting her, she was gone. No one knew where, but she'd dressed and left about an hour before he came down to the kitchen. He walked into the music room and sat at the piano, it'd been a few years, but he could still impress the ladies with a little ditty. He was in the middle of a Mozart piece when he saw the card on the little table inside the door. No, please God, don't let it be. He walked over to see his worst nightmare come true. Laffite's beautiful signature was curving and waving up at him in grotesque mockery. No, sir. No, damned sir, the pirate wasn't going to take her away now that she was finally responding to him. The son of a bitch'd die first. He needed Franklin. He needed his advice before he raced into the swamp and killed people.

Franklin moved them out of the hotel and back into the house on rue du Maine. He knew Andrew; after what he'd seen the night before, there'd be no need for the hotel. Andrew could deal with the bill later. They almost missed each other on the street, but Franklin turned back and called to the preoccupied Andrew.

"Where you goin? I done moved us out." Andrew turned and started walking back with Franklin.

"She's gone to Laffite. I'm going after her."

"No you aint, we goin home where we belong."

"I can't do that, Franklin. You know I can't. She could be in trouble. I'm going, if you want to come do, if not, stay. It's up to you. But I sure wish you'd come."

"Andrew, you done chased this skirt all over town, she don't want you, boss. She wants the pirate. Some folks just like danger and she's one who can't get enough of it."

Andrew walked back into the carriageway and into the little stable and saddled Captain. He'd go alone. She could be in trouble and he couldn't live with himself if anything happened to her. Whether she wanted him or the pirate; didn't matter as long as she was safe. Who the hell was he kidding? Of course it mattered, but he couldn't stand it if anything happened to her now that he had her in his life.

He crossed the river on a flatboat and headed south to Bayou Barataria. He'd hire a Pirogue at Little Lake and go the rest of the way from there. He was worried about Captain, he was a thoroughbred and not meant for this terrain, but a horse had to do what a man needed him to do. He reached Little Lake in the middle of a full moon; he could go all night with the light it was creating on the water. He rented a boat from a man living in a little raised house on the bayou and paid him to stable and feed Captain. He walked down to the water and stepped into the boat.

"Wait for me, you ain't goin alone, you dunce." Franklin was getting off a big skiff. He signaled for the two men in the big skiff to head back.

"Who're your friends, Franklin?" Andrew was never happier to see anyone in his life.

"Two of Marguerite's old suitors. Shut up, Andrew." The two men started on their journey toward a wounded pirate's lair.

Celestine arrived at the big house at dawn of the second day. He wasn't there. No one was there. The place was disserted and lonely except for the barracks full of men and women waiting for their ill fated and horrible destiny on the other side of his big compound. She'd never been told of these people or their misery. She only saw the house and grounds empty and couldn't believe he'd leave without saying good bye. But he'd tried to say goodbye, she was dancing and having a good time when he'd come to her, and now she'd never forgive herself. She wore a dress he particularly liked and now it was soiled from the swamp and sleeping in the little boat. Her hair was a mess and she smelled like mud and soured Jasmine cologne. She'd really done it this time. When would she learn to stop running into unknown situations without a plan? How old did she have to be before she could consider herself a mature woman with good judgment? Now she'd have to turn around and go back the long disgusting bayous to home and clean clothes and the humiliation of people in her life knowing she'd openly chased a man. The Reverend Mother told her girls; "If you're chasing a man, someone's running away." That was never truer than this moment. She sat on a step of the huge gallery and gave into her tears. Didn't matter, no one was here to see or hear; maybe an old alligator or two, but they'd be welcomed company at this point. She cried until her face was so puffy and red it hurt. Her head was beginning to ache and her pride was screaming at her. She wanted Maurice. She wanted him so badly she couldn't breathe. Why'd he gone and gotten himself killed, the bastard? He'd been warned not to go and he'd gone anyway and now see where she was and it was all his fault. Women can always find a way to blame a man when they've knocked themselves so low it looks like up from a turtle's belly and Celestine was no exception. She was hungry and she needed a cup of strong coffee before she dragged herself back to the family depending on her to be calm with good sense.

She walked around to the big kitchen and there were barely coals left to start a fire, but she managed to get some water boiling for coffee. There was bread left on the table and some warm cheese. She drank her coffee and ate some cheese and a piece of the bread and put her head on the table to rest a moment. The coffee needed to do its job and return some of her energy and the food might keep her head ache at bay.

She was startled awake by horrible screaming outside the big kitchen door. An animal was being killed and the large cat doing the killing was screaming even louder than its victim. She got up from the table expecting to see Jean and his men killing supper or worse, but as she got halfway to the door, the big black swamp panther had dropped its newly killed wild pig and was watching her. He was prepared to trade the pig for bigger game, or keep her from stealing his dinner, she couldn't tell which, but either way she was part of his hunt now and there wasn't anywhere for her to go. She reached for her knife, but it wasn't in her stay. It was on the table with the cheese. She hadn't bothered to get a knife from the kitchen when she ate her supper. Stupid mistake for a person who brags they can take care of themself, she thought. She began to back up slower than she thought was possible and the cat was on to her tricks; he was crouched low and inching forward ready to spring. Who'd tell Philippe? Would he go through life ashamed of his mother for putting herself in this situation? The thought only lasted a second, but in that second she'd reached her knife and caught the big cat in the leg. *Oh my God, I've made it angrier.* He was twirling around and trying to get the knife from his leg when she saw the kitchen knives on the big cupboard. She reached for another one and knew it wouldn't fly as true as her own, but she gave it a try and cut the big panther's ear off and again the damned thing wasn't giving up, just getting angrier still. He screamed and lunged and she fainted as she heard the gun shot booming from behind the cat.

"See, Franklin, I was right to come by damn." He was gathering her up in his arms and walking with her back to the boat.

"I give you this one. She'd a been et, that's for sho."

"Oh ye of little faith, maybe you'll listen to me next time."

"Shut up, Andrew, we got a long trip back."

Franklin walked back and took Celestine's knife out of the dead cat's leg. He put it in his pants, thought about it and drove it into the bullet wound of the big cat so it appeared the animal was killed by her knife. The kitchen was covered with the cat's blood and Franklin figured it was probably normal for the pirates' life that something was covered in blood. He didn't have to clean it and that suited him just fine. *Laffite needs to know what he missed.* Franklin had developed a liking for Mme. Dubois and her bravery. If she had the guts to come out into this pirate's din alone and defend herself against a damned Panther, she should at least get credit for the pelt.

Celestine woke in Andrew's lap. He looked down at her scared, dirty, little face.

"You're safe, Baby, you're with Andrew now. You need the privy?" She shook her head, 'no'. "Lean back into me, Sugar and go back to sleep." She didn't know if she'd die of love for this new man in her life, or die of embarrassment at the circumstance in which she'd gotten the three of them. She decided to shed her tears and let time and Andrew take care of the rest. Andrew loved feeling her tears through his shirt wetting his chest. He'd been a hero and saved his woman from death by Panther. She'd think twice from now on coming into the swamp alone with her little knife. Why'd she think men carried guns? If little knives would suffice, why be bothered with heavy fire arms? Women, God's tormenting mystery for men to try and solve. She slept until they stopped and Andrew picked up Captain. She wanted to sleep on the little boat back to the big river with Franklin, but Andrew wasn't taking any chances, he put her on the saddle in front of him and she was soon asleep with the rocking motion of Captain's big easy strides. She didn't wake up again until dawn and Andrew was handing her down to Franklin in the big carriageway.

Franklin took Captain to the stable and Andrew took her upstairs and put her in his bed. He was taking no chances on Laffite coming to her bed unannounced. He was undressing and washing himself in the bowl on the commode when he heard her stir. He turned to watch her looking around, confused. He got in bed and took her into his chest. She looked up at him and pulled his head down to her kiss. He took off her clothes; got the sponge and bowl from the commode and washed her face and hands. He put her head on his big chest and his hand over her ear.   She could feel and hear his heart beating and smell the cedar and tobacco; she was safe and fell back to sleep.

Andrew was awakened in the night with her mouth on him, his erection was going to be considerable and again he pictured his parents finding him in bed with a smile as big as Kentucky and he didn't care. He'd rescued his damsel from a swamp Panther and she was rescuing him from himself.

They were dressed and having breakfast at the table in Andrew's room and she was trying not to relive her humiliating ordeal when they heard boots running into the courtyard and the voice screaming.

"CELESTINE. CELESTINE." The great voice bellowed. He was running up the stairs to her room and they heard the doors fly open and hit the walls. "CELESTINE?" He was running back out and around the gallery. He kicked the doors to Andrew's bedroom open and Andrew was already up waiting for him with his sword drawn and ready.

Celestine was sitting at the table with the most frightened look Jean had ever seen on a woman.

"Thank God; you're all right. I thought you dead, woman."

He looked around the room and saw Andrew, every muscle in his body tensed and ready to kill. Laffite took it in and let it register.

"Relax young man. I just came to return your knife, Mme. Dubois." His face showed no emotion and she was dying for what she was doing to him.

"Andrew would you give us a moment?"

Andrew couldn't believe his ears. She was asking him to leave so she could be alone with the pirate.

"Take more than a moment, Madame Dubois. Take as long as you like." He walked out of the bedroom and down to saddle Captain. He'd pack when he could get back in his room, but his horse'd be ready to leave after he'd told her what he thought of her.

"Jean, I can't do this anymore. I went to you because I missed you when you called before and I wasn't here. I can't. I just can't. I love you too much and I want you in my bed every night. I'll never have that and this obsession is getting worse and I can't do it anymore." She began to cry. How many tears did she have left to cry over this man she desired more than any other man since her husband?

"Andrew followed me and saved my life. I can't keep expecting men to come after me and rescue me from myself. That's what happens with this strange love I have for you. I can't control myself." She was crying and talking and trying to make him understand. He reached over and took her on his lap and sat with her and caressed her hair:

"Oh, my pet. Don't you know it's not our time? Don't you know we're passing in the night like two dangerous ships on a beautiful moonlit sea? I love you. I'll always love you. All of my children should've been born to you. I'll come back to you, my wife. I'll come for you when we're safe and I'll take you wherever you want to go and we'll live to be very old. We'll remember these times and tell our many grandchildren of our love." He kissed her sweetly and walked out of the room down through the courtyard and out of her life and she thought she couldn't bear it. He wasn't dead. She stopped crying. He wasn't dead. As long as he wasn't dead, there was still a chance they could be together one day. He'd come back for her and they'd sail around the world. Until then, she could have her career and make herself happy. He wasn't dead.

Andrew waited for her to leave his room and walked back in and packed his satchels. He had to get back to some kind of normal life or he'd go crazy. He was raised the only son of a wealthy land owner, he was king of his own castle. He'd never been denied anything his heart could wish and he was allowing himself to be thrown around like a bad pumpkin by this little French woman. His father'd be ashamed of him.

He'd been taught not to let his pecker rule his life and so far his pecker had almost gotten him killed and caused him to fall in love with a wanton woman who could kill him in his sleep and eat breakfast off his ass if she so desired.

God, I'm so in love I could die, he thought as he walked down to the stable to get Captain.

She couldn't let him go yet. Her heart was breaking and Pierre was gone up river and she couldn't sleep alone missing a man again. It was too painful and besides, she hadn't finished with this young stallion and she'd grown fond of his humor and stories of his life at Cedars Plantation. She couldn't have her beloved Maurice and she'd done the mature thing with Jean; Andrew would be her prize for doing something grown up in her life. She watched him come back up and pack. She had to think fast. He wasn't going to come to her room and say good-bye, so she wouldn't be able to talk him into anything. She had one last idea and prayed it'd work. He walked into the stable and reached for Captain's reins. His heart was breaking. He'd send a man around to get Franklin and tell him to meet him at the boat with his things.

She came out of the stall totally naked on her beautiful bay, Rosebud; her blonde hair cascading down and around and over her creamy breasts. Lady Godiva of New Orleans.

"I thought I'd ride with you as far as the boat, my darling." She pulled Rosebud up next to Captain.

"What the hell are you doing, Celestine?" He wanted to grab her down and take her on the hay of the stable.

"I told you, my darling; I'm going to ride with you."

"Damn it woman, stop this foolishness and get in the house. Everyone'll see you, where's Franklin and Philippe and Marguerite?" She sat up straighter on Rosebud.

"I sent them away just as I did Jean, my darling."

"Get down, Celestine. Don't challenge me on this or you'll find yourself naked in the streets facing the charges alone while Captain and I board a boat going up river." She knew he wouldn't. He knew he wouldn't. Even the horses knew he wouldn't.

"I'll take my chances. Don't underestimate Rosebud, she's carrying a lighter load and she can be very fast. Shall we go?"

He decided he'd challenge. Not a chance in hell she'd leave her courtyard naked. He walked Captain to the big gate and she passed him and opened it herself. He was down and closing the gate and had her off the horse and over his shoulder and up the stairs to her room before she realized anyone looking in a crack of the gate would see her naked bottom being carried up the stairs. He threw her onto the bed.

"What'll it be, Celestine? If you really want me to stay, I won't play seconds to any man, Celestine. Not Laffite nor Pierre nor anyone else you want to bring home for your pleasure. That's final." He was looking down at her and wanted to cover her with kisses and bury himself in her and never come out again. She'd won her man and he was spectacular in his response. Yes, her American man was going to be someone to be reckoned with in any situation with any woman.

"What's it gonna be, Sugar?" He softened his approach and bent down to her. He was dying for this woman and he would marry her.

"I don't want to answer that, Andrew. I don't want to get in the habit of lying to you." He was out the door and over the gallery railing, riding out the gate on Captain leading Rosebud behind him before she could tell him it was a joke. Franklin came that night to bring Rosebud back. Celestine was broken hearted. She begged Franklin to tell her where he was, but Franklin swore he didn't know. Celestine knew he was still in the city. She saw Franklin in the market two days later. Maybe Andrew had gone on ahead and left Franklin to come on another boat?

On the fifth night after Andrew's sudden departure, Celestine smelled turpentine and walked downstairs to see where the acrid smell was. Over the fireplace in the drawing room was the most beautiful portrait of Jean Laffite she'd ever seen. His hazel eyes were looking into the future; into a distant horizon following the sun's path on a calm sea. He was wearing the green shirt and his eyes were kind and loving.

"The damned paint isn't dry, so don't touch it." Andrew was sitting at the piano and began to play a gentle Chopin for her. She sat across from him and admired his grace and beauty. His generosity in commissioning the portrait for her was the second sweetest thing a man had ever given her; surpassed only naming a ship for her. If this young man could understand a woman's feelings that well, he was going to make the best husband in the world. At that moment in time she was in love with him and would do whatever he wanted. He finished the Chopin and she took his hand and walked him up to her room. She closed and locked the door and thanked him for the gift all night long. The next day she went downstairs and made breakfast and took it back to him and thanked him for the diamond necklace... all day long.

Andrew stayed in New Orleans four more months. His father wrote several times wondering when he'd be home. He knew he had to go back, he'd run out of reasons to give his father for his absence. He had to decide how to approach his parents about marrying Celestine. He loved her, but he had concerns about her not conceiving since Philippe, and he wanted children. He caused his own dilemma by falling in love with her, but that didn't stop his heart from feeling what he felt. He'd wait a few more weeks and see what happened. He met a nice young man, Elliott Dubonnet, the son of Celestine's lawyer who introduced him to some young men his own age. He enjoyed the horse racing and fencing exercises he was so fond of back home. Captain could still outrun any of the nags these men called fast and he had another race tomorrow morning out by the lake. He'd ask Celestine to come and bring a picnic and they'd make a day of it. He loved looking over at her sitting under the big oaks with her little parasol protecting that beautiful skin from the sun and pretending to enjoy the races. She was so patient with him and his new cronies. It just made him love her more.

Celestine knew it was time to give him up. She loved having him around, he was still magnificent and she could love him if she let herself, but she'd never marry him and move to the country. Besides, she liked being a courtesan, whatever that really meant. She thought she knew, but if she were going to do what she planned, she couldn't keep one client forever. She made the decision in the market the week before when she was picking out greens for Marguerite. She turned to see him handing a little boy a beautiful peach. She almost lost her calm. It was so dear and beautiful just like her Maurice.

She decided it was time for him to find his life. She began to wonder if she was falling in love with the Maurice she saw in him or young Andrew himself. Marguerite told her she only loved Laffite because he reminded her of her life with Maurice. Andrew's life would be sweeter because of her and it'd bring joy to whomever he chose to wed thanks to her. Her knowing that would have to be enough.

He had his friends now and she'd suggest he go to a few of the balls and parties they were always offering. If he didn't find anyone to his liking, then maybe they were meant to be, but he needed to see for himself what was in the offering.

M. Dubonnet approached her about his shy son Elliott and she didn't question how he knew of her new profession, but if she were going to have one, someone needed to know about it and send young hopefuls to her. She met Elliott when he came around to visit Andrew; he was around twenty three and nice looking. He'd make a very sensitive lover and she liked that. She'd had her rough pleasure with Jean and she had her hands full with Andrew and his mighty prowess. It'd be nice to have a quiet sensitive man for a change. She'd write to M. Dubonnet and they could discuss it further.

Chapter Twenty-Five

Josef came into the courtyard frantically looking for Marie. She'd run away again. This was the third time in two months. He didn't know what he was going to do. He'd tried to reach Laffite a month before and had written to two addresses but had no answers. He was praying she had come here to be with Marguerite in her big kitchen.

The child loved to be with her grand-mere and Tante Marguerite. Josef knew partly because she was hoping to see her papa. He'd come to the end of his rope with this child. He stayed frightened that she'd be hurt or stolen and he had a special feeling for this little girl whose past was so like his own. She'd be stuck to his side one day helping with his inventions and wood working and the next, she'd be holding one of her papa's old shirts and hiding from everyone in the house. He should've seen the signs; the days with the shirt meant an escape was imminent. Her mood swings were troubling to him and Augustine and they had spoken to Pere Antoine. He'd suggested they keep close watch over her and see if she'd outgrow them or send her to live with the little sisters. Augustine wouldn't hear of her leaving home to board with the little sisters, and Josef agreed. He didn't know how he'd missed her this time. He'd been so careful. His father's heart was gripped in fear wondering where the hell she could've gone. Any rumor about a Laffite sighting from any of her classmates at the Ursulines Day School and that's where she'd head.

Andrew was turning into *rue des Chartres* from the Canal Road, when he saw the little waif walking fast from doorway to doorway hiding as she went into the heart of the city. He followed her on Captain to see where she was headed. She walked into the street to cross to another doorway and she almost fainted when she saw him looking down from the big horse with the frown she deserved. She started to run and Captain caught up to her quickly. Andrew reached down and scooped her up screaming and kicking.

"Stop it, Marie, you're scaring my horse." He knew Josef and Augustine had been having problems with her and he could see for himself how troubled she seemed. She stopped screaming but continued to struggle and Andrew put his arm around her so tightly she couldn't move and began to ride down the street. He turned into *rue du Maine* and went into the carriageway. Josef ran up to Andrew and reached up for his child.

"Hold on Josef, this child doesn't want to live with you and Mama 'Tine and her sisters anymore so I'm going to take her to the bayou and find Laffite and give her over to him. Please tell her sisters not to cry and miss her too much and I'm sure she won't mind giving them her toys since she won't be needing them any longer." He looked down at Marie.

"You won't mind will you, Marie?" She looked up at Andrew and didn't answer. She was thinking and wondering what she had gotten herself into.

"Now I know you must've been beating her pretty bad for her to want to run away, so when I get back, you and I are going to have a talk about that." He looked back down at Marie.

"Does Mama 'Tine beat you too or just Papa'sef, Sugar?"

"They don't beat me." She said in a small voice.

"It's all right, Sugar, you can tell Andrew the truth. I know when your papa asked these folks to take you and love you and raise you he didn't know what he was doing, so he'll be very angry when he finds out how miserable you are. Maybe he'll come and beat them for beating you."

Celestine had come from the kitchen with Marguerite and she stood next to Josef. What was Andrew doing to this baby? She looked terrified. Josef was looking up at his little girl with big fake, sad eyes.

"Now, Marie you know your papa loves you and he's very busy and probably out at sea on La Diligente, but he can sail back into port and stop everything he's doing and come get you. Now, he may have to give up his work and stay home so you can see him every day, but we can bring food for you and your papa and you can sleep under the French Market at night. Now, I'm warning you he may not be happy to see his little girl so needy. I'm sure he's asked you to be brave before, but he didn't really mean it, right? He can't expect you to be brave. You've lost your mama and now your papa, oh by the way, did you know Papa'sef lost his mama and papa too? Of course his papa can't come and get him and he depends on his girls to love him and be there for him, but since he beats you and is horrible to you, you don't care."

"He doesn't beat me." She was screaming and reaching out for Josef. Andrew let her down and she fell into Josef's arms.

"I'll take care of you, Papa'sef. You need me. I won't leave you alone, I promise." She was holding on to his neck and crying as only a heart broken little girl can. Sometimes a child just needs to be needed.

Franklin was driving the little carriage around to take Josef and Marie back home. *Ole Andrew did the right thing sometime; Franklin smiled.*

Josef turned back to Andrew and mouthed, "Thank you."

Celestine followed Andrew up to his room.

"Your pirate, Sugar is a damned bad father and you should know that. No matter how you fancy him in your romantic mind, he's an ass and his children suffer because of it. That little girl is going into her life with a broken heart, because she has a son of a bitch for a father. I doubt if she'll ever trust a man enough to marry. Thank God for Josef."

He sat down and began to take off his boots. She walked over to him and began to take them off for him.

"You're a hero, sir. You've done my family a great service and I love you." She put her head on his knee and sat loving him. She knew she was holding back someone's wonderful husband and father and she had no right. He put his hand on her head and caressed her hair.

"Will you marry me, Sugar?" He hadn't meant to say that, but once it was out and on the table, he sure as hell wasn't taking it back.

"Oh, my darling you don't know how much I want to say yes, but I can't and you know I can't." She was beginning to tear up. Why did her life have so damned many missed moments? Why did she have to lose Maurice and why Jean and now, why could she not be young and fertile enough to say yes to this wonderful young man? It wasn't fair damn it. She got up and sat in his lap, and leaned into his chest.

"I'm sorry, my darling. I'm truly sorry." She whispered to him.

He held her and wondered why things didn't go as he wanted anymore. He was supposed to be able to pick any wife he desired and she'd know she was special for being asked and she'd say 'yes' without a moment's question. He lifted her chin and kissed her and wondered if he could live with a woman who couldn't give him children and if he could; would she leave this weird city and her strange family? He sat for awhile with her head on his shoulder and felt the love for her he thought would break his heart. He began to see it had all been a wonderful interlude in the story of his life. He felt her breathing and caressed her hair and looked over at the big mirror and noticed it was sitting crooked on its marble base and the mosquito Baire had a strange tear that hadn't been mended. There was dust on the chandelier and a funny shaped wax sculpture on the mantle under the candleholders. He could smell the mildew in the old house and odors coming from the stable too close. One of the tall French doors was warped and dragged when it was opened, probably from being kicked in by lovers or too many wounded men on stretchers not fitting through the doors. He looked down at the love of his life and wondered what he was doing loving the mistress of a pirate who didn't appreciate his own children.

Suddenly the air in the house was stifling hot and humid, he needed to be in the open and breathe in fresh air and feel the breeze from the big river in his hair and not have to worry about little run away girls who longed for papa's that weren't coming home. He wanted some of his mother's good roast venison and his father's smooth sour mash whiskey in a crystal glass sitting on the big front porch watching the Ohio River flowing to parts known and un-known.

He needed a diversion and he needed to be around normal people for a few hours and see what the world'd been doing while he was living with this bewitching courtesan he so loved. He decided to accept Elliot Dubonnet's invitation to a dance. Young Dubonnet had been asking Andrew to meet his sister and Andrew had turned him down so many times it was beginning to be rude.

"My pet, I need to think and clear my head. Would you mind if I went out for the evening? Maybe we can talk in the morning and make some decisions about what we both want and where our love is taking us?" He wouldn't hurt her, if she turned to him this minute and said, 'let's get married,' he'd say 'yes'. He was not going to hurt this love who'd rescued him from himself.

"I'd like that, my darling. I'd love to see you go and have a good time with your friends. Wake me if it's not too late." She reached up and kissed him and she thought of Pierre and wondered if he'd come to her after Andrew moved out.

Chapter Twenty-Six

Andrew was met at the door by Elliott and he walked over to the big mirrored coat rack in the main hall. He took off his hat, gloves and sword stick and turned to see in the reflection a beautiful young woman. His breath caught in his throat, it could be Celestine ten years earlier except she had auburn curls; the girl had the innocence he'd dreamed Celestine must've had and she was checking him out through the same reflection when she thought he wasn't looking.

"So, Andrew, shall we ask her to join us?"

"Of course, she's pleasant to look upon." He didn't' want to tell this young man that his sister was as beautiful as his mistress and he'd love to know her better. She may be a shrew or even one of the silly eye lash batters he so despised.

He watched as Elliott went out to the gallery and approached his sister. She was listening and then he saw her stomp her dainty foot and say something to her brother that made him run back to Andrew with total disgust.

"Sorry Andrew, Henriette is being her usual spoiled brat self. She said she was not 'pleasant to look upon'; she is 'devastatingly beautiful and much more than the cackling, giggling females that you're used to. And until we admit it, she's not going anywhere." Elliott heard his friend's great laugh and watched as Andrew walked out onto the gallery. He whispered something in Henriette's ear and then he was taking her in his arms and kissing her. Elliott nearly fainted with shock and appreciation for Andrew's skill. Elliott wanted to be like Andrew Down.

Celestine knew Andrew had found someone the morning after the party. He was shy and awkward and didn't want to tell Celestine he had found a younger version of her. She was having breakfast when he finally came down, kissed her and sat at the table. Celestine was thrilled with this bittersweet ending. She'd been so worried about hurting him and now he was worried about hurting her.

"Is she wonderful, my darling?" Her face was kind and expectant and he saw no jealousy in her eyes.

"Sugar, she can't hold a candle to you." He couldn't believe he was about to tell the woman he'd proposed to the night before that he'd found his true love. Was he really that fickle?

"Don't be silly, darling, if she's wonderful, tell me. I don't want you going off with a mouse or someone you think your parents would like. Did she sweep you off your feet?" Her eyes were laughing and she actually felt happy for him. She'd been frightened that her jealousy would get in the way, but that was reserved for Jean.

"Sugar, she's a version of you that will say 'yes' when I ask her." He hoped to God he hadn't offended his dear Celestine.

"Andrew, you flatter me, darling. I know she's wonderful. Did she sweep you off your feet?"

"Yes." He got up and took her in his arms and kissed her and knew he'd always remember her as his savior.

Andrew hired cleaning women to come in and clean the house top to bottom and then hired carpenters to repair every loose board or crooked door in the place. He had the whole house painted and the courtyard tended and brought back to life. He was ashamed that he'd felt it was her fault. Hadn't this house been a hospital for him and his fellow soldiers? The least he could do was put it back the way they found it. He left for Kentucky the next week and would be gone until the wedding three months away.

Celestine was thrilled with her 'new' house. If things turned out this well with her clients, she loved this *l'amour* business of hers.
Pierre was back in her life. Colette was living with Pierre again because her lover kicked her out and she had no place to go. Letty was in school

in Paris and Pierre wanted her as far away from her Mother's reputation as she could get and still be happy.

Colette came to dinner once and they'd laughed about the 'good ole days' and she'd shared stories about her new life and how she wished she hadn't fallen so hard for her latest lover. Pierre and Celestine enjoyed her company and tales of a life that was foreign to them, but neither could ever grasp her need for her own kind. Colette left early and Pierre spent the night.

"We've come a long way, our little foursome." He said as he blew out the lamp and pulled her into his arms.

Elliott Dubonnet came to call the week after his sister's wedding. He was so shy she didn't quite know how to approach him. He was mesmerized. He'd been terrified. *This was Andrew's mistress for God's sake. Why'd she even look at him after having Andrew?* She did all the talking and he didn't say a word, until she began to talk about her life. Suddenly he wanted to hear everything. He wanted to hear about her life before the convent; her life with Maurice and especially rescuing Marguerite. He couldn't hear enough about the affair with Laffite and the more she told, the more she embellished. On the third visit, he was in her bedroom. She was in her nightgown on the bed; he was in his shirt and breeches and he felt like he'd lived there forever. He reached over on his own and kissed her. It was the sweetest kiss she'd ever gotten and she knew this young man was going to be a joy. She needed his quiet ways; his compliments and the soft touches. She loved her new profession. *After Elliott I'll take a more aggressive male.* She said to herself. *He's nice for now, and he'll make a wonderful gentle husband for some lucky girl, but he's not really my cup of tea.*

Epilogue

1858

Celestine was no longer curious about dying. She was looking forward to it; hoping for it. Her worn out body was no use to her anymore. She mourned her decaying body for years and wished for youthful movements. She could feel her breathing getting shallower; it'd soon stop and she could release her soul and go to the next world. She had so many friends and loved ones in that world she'd be going home.

Feeling the sun on her face and a soft River breeze caressing her skin; her breathing stopped.

She was up and walking toward the sun and into that gentle wind and he was there. The love of her life was standing on the deck of le Celestine, the big ship's sails full of the Gulf Wind, but resting on a calm sea. The sun created a million points of light on the still, gray waters of the Gulf. She'd longed for his smile and now it was here and it was hers again. She caught a hint of cloves and rosemary as he gently reached for her young beautiful hand. The silks of her sea blue dress were folding against her legs and her soul was racing with love.

"I've been waiting for you, wife. Come, my little dove, we mustn't lose the wind."

About the Author

F. J. Wilson was raised on the Gulf Coast of Mississippi in the fishing village and artist community of Ocean Springs, ninety miles east New Orleans; the city far from her reach but close to her heart. Much of her time growing up was spent reading under her grandmother's big camellia bushes hiding from housework and the inevitable call to come inside and help start 'supper'. In a time when young girls dreamed of big weddings and picket fences, she dreamed of the dangerous but darkly handsome Heathcliff and the English moors of days long gone. With Hemingway's Paris, Scott Fitzgerald's language and Margaret Mitchell's South keeping her company, why would she ever want to clean her room?

Raised with small town values but dreams of a bigger life, she was more than ready to leave home in 1965 and began her education in the Theatre Department of the University of Southern Mississippi. From there she finally reached New Orleans and began a film career that sent her to New York, where she co-wrote an episode of the Emmy award winning Kate & Allie. Eventually her work in TV and film would take her to Los Angeles and all over the United States, Canada and New Zealand.

Her passion for the South and New Orleans brought her back to Mississippi in 2000. In 2007, her love for writing and her love of films collided, and she wrote humorous articles for the Arts and Entertainment Section of the Hattiesburg American newspaper. She's been writing short stories and novels about Southerners since her retirement in 2008.

F. J. Wilson has one son, Jason, who lives in Monroe, Ct. and she now lives in Hattiesburg with her two Springer Hound Spaniels and is at the time married to her computer and her love of writing.

For more on F.J. Wilson, please visit www.chancespress.com.

www.ingramcontent.com/pod-product-compliance
Lightning Source LLC
Chambersburg PA
CBHW070330260626
47160CB00003B/1005